THE BLACK UMBRELLA

A Novel

JOANNA ILLINGWORTH

ONE

I t was because of the thunder no one heard Amelia banging down the front door. All thunder was loud, sure, but southern thunder cracked like a gunshot echoing off the sky. Like the Fourth of July fireworks my dad bought every year and lit in one giant, booming mess of madness. Southern thunder was loud and forceful and dramatic – a genuine Southern Belle. (Don't let the stereotype fool you – real Southern Belles are anything but genteel.)

Amelia, never one to be silenced, gave up knocking and barged right in.

"Your doorbell's still broken," she shouted from the front entryway.

"Hey," I called out, "we're in the kitchen."

Three years earlier, one of my little brother Cale's friends, desperate for a playmate, rang the doorbell 75 times in a row causing it to give up the ghost. Mom and Dad never did get it fixed since Mom thought doorbells were undignified. She said people should knock politely and wait to be announced, as if we had a tuxedoed butler named Charleston waiting to declare the name of whatever neighborhood kid was at the door asking Cale to go outside and play.

"Brolly, it's time," Amelia said as she walked into the kitchen, singing the last word like she was Oprah in possession of a favorite thing. Amelia's barging in was because we were going to Ben's house to watch a movie. He was the new lifeguard at the rec center pool. Amelia and I had spent the first part of the summer surreptitiously ogling his swooping blonde hair and red swim trunks and Tom Holland smile. Over time he became Pepper's friend and then our friend and then the boy I flirted with at the pool snack bar and then the boy who invited me over to his house to watch a movie. It was one of those things that took forever to happen while happening so fast it made my head spin.

A lightning bolt flashed in the kitchen window as thunder rattled through the house like ten lanes of simultaneous bowling strikes. A second later, the rain started, a loud, hard rain that scraped against the house like sandpaper.

"Where exactly are you two off to on this lovely evening?" Mom joked. I hadn't told her yet because I didn't want to talk about it out loud.

"We're going to Ben's," Amelia said with a conspiratorial grin. The gold bangles on her wrist jingled as she shimmied her excitement.

"Oh, Ben?" Mom grinned. "Isn't that the young man who's trying to court you this summer, Brolly?"

"Mom, no."

I turned movie night at Ben's into me and Amelia and Pepper all going because in no way was I ready for a me and Ben alone situation. For the last few weeks, whenever Ben was on break at the pool, we'd talk and flirt and glance at each other more than necessary. It was breezy. Casual. It happened in the daylight, behind sunglasses, surrounded by toddlers in water wings and moms in giant sun hats. It was just enough to be fun and not enough to be real. Movies at his house was on a completely different level. Every time I thought about it my right eyelid twitched in frightened anticipation.

"Family," Dad cheered, bursting through the back door soaking wet and holding three reusable grocery bags in his hands. His glasses were dotted with rainwater. I took the bags from him and set them on the counter as he shook off his jacket and hung it on the hook by the back door. He rounded the corner of the counter and kissed Mom on the cheek as he pulled a dish towel from a drawer and rubbed it through his hair. "Lovely to see you, Amelia. What are you girls up to?"

"We're going over to Ben's."

"Oh?" Dad said, winking at Mom. "Isn't that the young man courting Brolly?"

"Yeah, right," Cale said, sliding into the kitchen on his sock feet. He never walked into any room, always sliding or spinning or karate-chopping. "Brolly's been drooling over that lifeguard dude all summer. It's super embarrassing."

"I've told y'all one-thousand times," I said. "It's dating, not courting. And I'm not dating Ben."

"Yet," Amelia smirked.

Cale made a gagging noise.

"We're friends," I said, ignoring them.

"Sure, friends," Amelia said, grinning at my parents, "until I get Brolly to see what's right in front of her face. Ben is completely into her."

It had been Amelia's one goal over the summer, getting me and Ben together. From the first moment we saw him, sitting up in his lifeguard stand, twirling his bright silver whistle around his index finger, Amelia decided he was the one for me. I told her it was an impossibility. He wasn't just the new lifeguard, he was an unattainable mirage, all broad shouldered and long limbed. Chiseled abs in mirrored aviators. A Greek god sent to earth to rescue hapless swimmers from drowning. He wasn't out of my league, he was un-league-able.

"Pepper's coming, too," I said, trying to steer the conversation away from relationship talk. "We're all hanging out. As friends." I leaned over the counter when I said friends, looking both my parents in the eye to emphasize my point. Plus, the idea of me and Ben as anything more than flirty friends was laughable. It'd be like when Thor dated Natalie Portman in the second Thor movie. No one believed that and no one would believe me and Ben.

"First day of senior year tomorrow," Dad said, eyebrows raised, "are you sure you should be going out tonight?"

"Why don't you have your dad take you," Mom said, talking over him, "the rain is really coming down. I'd rather you not drive."

Amelia and I exchanged a look.

"His house is just around the corner, so we were going to walk," Amelia said. "Maybe we could borrow an umbrella?"

As if on cue, the rain grew louder, pounding against the kitchen window, demanding to be let inside.

"We don't have any umbrellas," I said, sighing. "My parents don't believe in them."

Amelia threw my mom an incredulous look. "You do know umbrellas exist."

Mom laughed and rolled her eyes. "Yes, but they're also bulky and messy and can carry you away when the wind picks up."

"Mom, you're not Mary Poppins. Anyway, Dad, could you take us?"

He wordlessly pulled his jacket from the hook and we were off, all three of us running to the car and scrambling inside. My hair, which I'd actually spent time on, was done for. Amelia gave Dad the address while I fidgeted in my seat, taking the scrunchie from my wrist and pulling my long brown waves into a ponytail.

My stomach churned as Dad turned onto Ben's street. The idea of spending real, non-pool time with Ben thrilled me, but in a roller coaster sort of way. I was excited but scared and hoped it wouldn't last too long. I'd dated guys in the past. Okay, two guys, neither of which were worth reminiscing about, but this was Belongs On A Billboard Ben. A few weeks before he'd jumped into the pool to rescue a flailing six-year-old. Turned out the kid was faking, but when Ben got out of the pool, every head turned and stared as he rose out of a water like he was a model in a cologne commercial. He didn't fit in amongst us damp, ponytailed mortals.

Dad pulled into the driveway and chuckled, pointing out the windshield. "Ben's house is exactly like our house but with a blue front door."

Amelia poked me in the ribs. "Babe, his house is just like yours. This was meant to be."

"Every fifth house in this neighborhood is just like mine. The odds were pretty favorable we'd live in the same one."

We thanked Dad for driving us and jumped out of the car, running through the rain to the front porch. Amelia held her bag in front of her chest so her white t-shirt wouldn't become translucent. Before either of us had a chance to knock, Ben opened the front door. He was barefoot and wearing a royal blue polo with dark jeans that covered the tops of his feet. My heart thudded into my throat and I realized too late I was staring. It was the first time I'd seen him in actual clothes instead of shirt-less and in his regulation red swim trunks.

His blonde hair swooped across his forehead and he brushed it back with his thumb. "Come in," he said, smiling.

Amelia started up an unending stream of chatter as Ben led us inside and through the kitchen, where he picked up a giant bowl of popcorn, and down to the basement. By the time we got downstairs, Amelia had already covered the thunderstorm, school starting the next day, how Ben's house was just like mine, if he was going out for the swim team and did he put butter on the popcorn and if so what kind. Amelia's talent for squeezing in the maximum amount of words into the least amount of time was unparalleled.

Most of Ben's basement was taken up by an oversized L-shaped sectional and matching loveseat forming an open square in front of a huge flat screen TV. I immediately worried about where I should sit.

"Hello ladies." Pepper stood up to greet us. "Always a pleasure."

"Pepper, we were with you three hours ago," Amelia said.

"Yes, and that time with you was a pleasure as well."

Pepper's name was Jones Pepper but on the first day of 4th grade Mrs. Martorell read all of our names back to front, including the comma. Since that day he'd been Pepper Comma Jones, best friend to Amelia and me. The trouble with having a guy best friend was how many well-meaning people assumed we would eventually hook up, which annoyed me and Amelia to no end. And yeah, we'd both thought about it. Everyone who's friends with anyone thinks about it. We loved Pepper, he was our number one guy, but not like that. He was like a lemon; a necessary and fantastic ingredient, but you didn't want to bite right into him. Pepper was freakishly tall in elementary school but stopped growing in the seventh grade, making us the same height. He was definitely cute. His black, wavy hair curled up around his ears and he wore brown-framed glasses that were a shade darker than his brown skin. Amelia said he had the gaze of a movie star, but Amelia said a lot of boys were movie star somethings.

Ben walked over to a small refrigerator in the corner of the room and pulled out a few sodas and some bottles of water. Amelia rushed to sit next to Pepper, giving me a look that said I should sit on the loveseat, so I did. Ben arranged the drinks on the coffee table and flipped open two giant pizza boxes from Big Mike's.

"Dig in," he said and sat next to me, close enough that I could feel him but not close enough to be touching. Sitting next to Ben was like sitting next to a burning fire, the side of me next to Ben scorching and the other side so cold I was shivering. His elbow accidentally grazed mine when he reached out to fill his plate with pizza, his thigh moved closer to mine when he leaned back and stretched his long legs underneath the coffee table, his bare feet visible underneath the glass. I wished I was wearing more than a tank top and shorts. I needed an additional layer to ease the scorch of every barely-there touch.

"Anyone have a movie preference?" Pepper asked. "Might I suggest the cinematic classic *Back to the Future* starring Crispin Glover?"

Amelia scoffed. "Oh please, Pepper, *Back to the Future* stars Michael J. Fox not Crispin Glover."

"Yes, but Crispin Glover brings so much to his role. He is transformative as George McFly."

"If it's time travel you want, we should watch *Bill and Ted's Excellent Adventure* starring Keanu Reeves, the hottest man Hawaii ever produced."

"Amelia," Pepper said, adjusting his glasses, "Keanu Reeves was born in Beirut, Lebanon, not Hawaii, obviously, and how can you even say that? *Back to the Future* was groundbreaking! It's a pivotal film in the time travel genre! I own the Collector's Edition!"

Pepper was not one to be crossed when it came to the subject of time travel. He knew a lot about a lot of things, but time travel was his specialty.

"Why do you know even where Keanu Reeves was born?" Amelia said, exasperated.

"Everyone knows where Keanu Reeves was born."

Pepper and Amelia continued to argue celebrity birth cities and the merits of what deems a movie "classic" while I bit into a slice of pepperoni and looked around the room at everything but Ben. The walls were covered in a dark wood paneling and a stack of framed movie posters sat on the floor waiting to be hung. I could only see the top one – *Jurassic Park*. I wondered if Ben was a huge fan of the movie or if his mom bought it as a basement-TV-room decoration. If the poster underneath was *The Greatest Showman*, it was definitely his mom.

"You'll need to be the tie-breaker," Ben said to me, softly, failing to interrupt Pepper and Amelia's spirited argument.

"Hmm?" He motioned to the couch across from us where Pepper and Amelia were both waving their hands in the air, like two cats batting at a toy. "Oh, right. Well, *Bill and Ted's* is definitely fun, I mean, who doesn't love the Ziggy Piggy? But you can't go wrong with *Back to the Future*. Pepper's right, it's a classic."

Pepper sniffed. "Thank you, Brolly, that's exactly what I've been saying."

Ben tossed the remote to Pepper, inching even closer to me as he leaned back onto the loveseat. I held my paper plate in my lap with both hands, afraid to seem too eager or too aloof or too anything. Amelia told me I should just be myself, but I didn't know what that meant. Being overly flirty felt wrong and being standoffish felt wrong. My skin prickled with the awkward in-between.

Ben reached up and turned off the lamp next to the loveseat, throwing the basement into darkness except for the light of the TV. All my sweat glands jolted into high gear next to the heat of Ben's body. I wanted to move away, to gulp down some air that didn't smell like him, but my body kept inching closer to his.

Marty McFly had barely gotten the DeLorean up to 88 MPH when Ben set his plate aside and nudged me with his arm. "Hi."

Even in the low light of the TV I could see that he had two tiny freckles right below his left eye. "Hi."

"I'm glad you're here." His hair swooped down almost covering one eye and his arms were crossed over his broad chest. "It's cool I won't be starting senior year at a new school all by myself."

"I seriously doubt you will have any problems making friends." I thought about Pam Byers, self-appointed queen of Central High. She'd get one look at Ben and my little half-lived almost-romance would combust into oblivion.

"Is that what you want to be? Friends?"

His words hung in the tiny space between us. Pepper and Amelia were eating popcorn, completely engrossed in the movie, unaware of the loud record scratch happening on my side of the room. He leaned in further, his left hand falling down between us and brushing against my thigh. My brain pole vaulted into a pit full of one thousand reasons why he would never be interested in me. It wasn't that I thought too little of myself, just that he was too much. I made sense with an average guy, a blend-in, not a guy so hot he scalded your retinas.

My brain shouted at me to jump up from the loveseat and sit next to Amelia in the safe zone. Instead, unbelievably, and so slowly it nearly didn't happen, I moved my hand out of my lap and into the space between us, our hands touching palm to palm.

Ben's entire body relaxed and he sighed into a smile as he laced his fingers through mine.

We didn't say anything else, but our hands stayed together, Ben's thumb occasionally sliding up and down mine. My inner dialogue was a hyper-jumble of *this is awesome* and *this isn't possible* and *what am I doing* and *get a hold of yourself* and *this is happening it is actually happening.*

When the credits rolled, Amelia made a big show of yawning and stretching her arms over her head.

"So tired," she said, yawning again. She closed her eyes and ran her fingers through her straight blonde hair.

"It's not even ten," Pepper said, eyeing her with suspicion.

She glared at him. "Right, so tired. Would you drive me home?" She looked over at me, on the verge of batting her eyelashes. I knew exactly what she was doing but was powerless to stop her. "Brolly, you can totally stay. No need to end the party just because I need my beauty sleep."

"I can take you home," Ben said, squeezing my hand.

Amelia noticed mine and Ben's linked hands and did a little shoulder shimmy. I wondered if Ben had any idea he was the main attraction in Amelia's wicked but well plotted plan to get us together. All summer she'd been promising this would happen, knew it in her bones, she'd said. I told her she was delusional but once again, Amelia knew me better than I even knew myself. I looked over at her and could see she was vibrating with satisfaction.

We all went upstairs to the front door and Amelia and Pepper made a big show of leaving, complete with Amelia winking at me so obviously I was surprised Ben didn't outright make a comment. He played along, pretending like, oh, yes, Amelia is so tired and Pepper must drive her home, leaving us here alone together. After they left, he turned to me and reached out to grab the pinky on my left hand.

"You okay to stay for a bit?"

"Sure," I said, as my whole body zinged with nerves.

He walked up the stairs and I followed him, suddenly curious why I hadn't seen any adults since I arrived.

"Where are your parents?" I asked as we stepped onto the upstairs landing. It really was exactly like my house, same floor-plan at least. Ben's house was neater than ours, less lived in, all the décor professional instead of personal. He went into the first door on the left, which was Cale's room in my house.

"My mom's at my grandparents in North Carolina. My grandmother fell and broke her hip so my mom's there helping her out. My dad's at a conference in Florida."

I stepped into Ben's room and looked around. It wasn't messy, more disheveled, like the room version of a wrinkled t-shirt. Books were haphazardly tossed onto a short bookshelf, some clothes on the floor, a small desk against the wall with papers and pens piled in a heap next to a welcome folder from Central High. No posters on the walls, no pictures. A cluster of swimming medals dangled from his closet doorknob. The walls were a cool grey and his bed, which wasn't made, had the same cool grey sheets and a grey comforter with a black star pattern. It looked like bedding a set designer would choose for a nonde-script teen boy.

"You're here all alone?" I asked.

Ben pressed his lips together in a half-smirk half-smile. "You worried about me?"

I lifted one shoulder in a half-shrug.

He hit a button on a Bluetooth speaker next to his bed, smoothed back the comforter and plopped down. I went hot all over. I was in Ben's house, in his bedroom, and his parents were out of town, out of the entire state. Ben, who was unattainable in every way possible, was sitting on his bed with a look that said he wanted me to join him. The song playing was some pop ballad I'd heard before but couldn't name. It had a slow, seductive beat that made my mouth go dry and my hands shake.

"I'm actually glad we have some time alone," he said. I kept post near the door, itching to run. He twisted his hands together and looked up at me through his swooping blonde hair. "I was hoping, well, it's just that I wanted us to...I was wondering if..." He took a deep breath and quickly blew it back out. "It's been really great this summer, getting to know you and hanging out at the pool. And tomorrow with school starting and everything, we'll probably both be busy, and I don't know if we'll have the time we have now so I was wondering if...not really wondering so much as I wanted to ask you something." His voice trailed off and he looked down at his hands, fidgeting. He was nervous.

Realization smacked into me like one of those unexpected waves that knocks into the back of your knees when you're trying to wade out of the ocean.

"Ben." It came out more sarcastic than I wanted. "I am not going to sleep with you."

"What?" he said, looking surprised. "Wait, no, that's not... I just wanted to hang out with you and talk."

"So that's why you brought me up to your room? And sat on your bed? And turned on this music?"

He looked around the room and his face turned pink. "I didn't really...yeah, I guess this does look like...yeah." He stood up and took a few steps toward me. "I'm an idiot. Please forgive my lack of awareness and general boy brain. I promise, I do not want to have sex with you."

My eyes went wide, cheeks flaming red, betraying me.

"Wait! That's not what I meant either! I'm failing miserably here, Brolly. Can we please, please start over?" He sat down on the floor in front of the bed and looked up at me with pleading eyes. I slid down next to him, leaving some space.

"I like you, Brolly. I think you're so smart and cute and fun and I just want to spend time with you. I didn't think how it would look, bringing you up to my room and my parents aren't home. I didn't mean to make you uncomfortable." He shuffled around to face me, his legs crossed and his elbows on his knees. "Here I was planning to ask you to be my girlfriend and instead I've come across like a teenage predator."

His nervous expression calmed my heart rate down to an appropriate rhythm. "I don't think you're a predator," I said. "I just...I don't know what you expect from me. I don't think I'm what you're used to."

His head dropped to the side. "What I'm used to?"

"You know. You're...you," I said, motioning to his body, his hair, his face. "You have to know the effect you have on people."

He huffed out a tiny laugh. "Do I?"

We both smiled, the tension melting between us. He gave me a tentative look, like a puppy that wanted his ears scratched. I scooted a tiny bit closer.

"Let me make my intentions perfectly clear." He took a breath, steeling himself. "I want to be your boyfriend. I want to watch movies with you and read the same books you're reading and give you my jacket when it's cold. I want to know your favorite flavor of ice cream and if you drink coffee to wake up in the morning and if you're into politics or art or both. I want to figure out your expressions and learn your laughs and kiss you goodnight."

His confession hit me like a thousand tiny pin pricks. If Amelia were there, first she'd squeal and say I told you so, then she'd kick me for continuing to doubt him when he was saying the actual words to my face. Because Ben was good. Ben was nice. Ben was into me.

"Only goodnight?" I said, still scared, still unsure.

"Not only goodnight."

He leaned forward but hesitated, asking permission. I leaned in, saying yes. Then he kissed me, long and slow, his hand lingering on my neck. It was innocent and hopeful. Sweet.

When our lips broke apart, he laid his forehead on my shoulder. I could feel him smiling. "I like you, Brolly Parker."

"I like you, too," I said.

Amelia was going to completely lose it when I told her.

TWO

I was late to pick up Amelia and my favorite plaid button-down was missing. I couldn't be expected to go to school without my favorite plaid button-down. Even though it was August and so humid you could brush the moisture off your skin like hot raindrops, Central High's thermostat was set to a constant and chilly 65 degrees. One needed light layering to survive.

Another summer thunderstorm was rolling through and the power had gone out. Mom walked past my room with a pencil behind her ear and a yellow notepad under her arm. She wrote the first draft of all her novels longhand. Every single time she was interviewed about her books, people marveled that she did this.

"Mom," I shouted, "did you borrow my plaid button-down?"

She backed up and paused in my doorway, squinting into the darkness. "Brolly, shouting is so unbecoming."

"Sorry, it's just that I'm late to pick up Amelia and I can't find my shirt."

Amelia was grounded from driving after she hit a parked car – her mother's parked car. Plus, she wanted me to pick her up so she could screech directly in my face about last night and frankly, she was going to reach all new levels of screeching when she found out Ben kissed me.

"Check my closet. And would you mind taking Cale to school? I've got to get this draft done today. But please be careful, it's really coming down out there," Mom said as she disappeared down the stairs.

Cale came out of his room shining a flashlight in my face. "Have you seen my magic quarter? It's missing." Cale couldn't do his latest trick without his magic quarter. If he couldn't do his trick, he couldn't impress the fifth grade girls, and if he couldn't impress the fifth grade girls, he couldn't be king of Waterson Elementary School's fifth grade class. A king is nothing without his quarters.

"I can't find my shirt. We've all got problems."

"Mom said you have to give me a ride."

"No shirt, no ride," I said, hurrying past him into my parents' room. I couldn't wait to see the look on Amelia's face when I told her Ben kissed me. Her departure from movie night was so carefully orchestrated he'd surely face Amelia's wrath if he hadn't kissed me, a fate no boy at Central High had yet to survive.

I tripped over a pile of books on the floor next to Mom's desk and flipped the light switch in the closet only to remember the power was out. Lightning zig-zagged across the sky, lighting the closet enough that I could see clothes everywhere; on the floor, hanging on hangers, stacked on the top shelf. I dug through the laundry basket – no sign of my shirt. I flipped through Mom's row of hanging clothes. I'd already searched the laundry room, my hamper, my closet, the piles of clothes on my bedroom floor.

I dragged Mom's desk chair into the closet to scan the top shelf but lost my balance on the squishy cushion and fell into a pile of clothes on the floor.

"It's not going to be in there," Cale said. "Help me find my quarter."

"Find your own quarter. And hand me that flashlight."

"I need it."

"Then bring me my phone," I shrieked. "We're gonna be late."

He held the flashlight up in the air and made a sound like a lightsaber. Little traitor. Thunder rumbled through the house, lightning flashing every few minutes, lighting my search in two and three-second increments.

"Cale, seriously," I pleaded, "I need to text Pepper and see if he can pick up Amelia." She would for sure explode into a thousand tiny Amelia's all shouting at me about how I harmed her emotionally for making her wait twenty additional minutes to hear the story about Ben and the kissing, but there was no way I was going to make it in time. I wasn't even dressed.

"I'm not your errand boy," Cale said, shining the flashlight under Mom and Dad's dresser.

I climbed back onto the chair and balanced on one foot while holding onto the top shelf, noting my mother's shoe problem. There were rows and rows of boxes filled with every kind of shoe imaginable buried under sweatshirts and jeans and books and tote bags. I tugged on something plaid and everything toppled down onto the floor. I hopped off the chair and reached all the way into the back of the closet, scooped up everything I could and threw it all into the bedroom where there was a tiny bit more light. A long, rectangular shipping box covered in duct tape landed on top of the heap. "*Old books*" was written across the top in my mom's careful cursive

Our house was one giant library, piles of books around every corner, biographies and novels and gardening books and how-to books spilling from every shelf. Mom wrote a best-selling series of novels set in 19th century England, eight books so far, and had stacks of every translation all around the house. We had *The Arrington Series* in Spanish and German and French and Dutch, all telling the same story of snooty English aristocrats sneering at each other on their lavish English estate. Out of all the books in our house, I couldn't imagine what books could possibly warrant being sealed in an old box. The tape was old and came off in thin, yellowed strips. I pulled open the cardboard flaps but there weren't any books inside, just a dusty, old umbrella. It was black with a heavy, carved wooden handle. A loud clap of thunder shook the house, rattling a spoon in an empty coffee mug on Mom's desk as I lifted it out of the box.

"What's that?" Cale asked, crawling out from under the bed.

"Some old umbrella."

"But we don't have any umbrellas."

"We do now. Get your shoes on. I have one more place to look and then we can go."

"But I haven't eaten breakfast," he whined as I raced downstairs with the umbrella and slipped on Mom's green flip-flops from the basket of shoes by the front door.

"Where are you going?" Mom asked, rounding the corner from the kitchen. "You're not even dressed."

"I'm gonna check my car for my shirt."

"It's pouring out, you'll be soaked through. And you're late as it is."

"I'll be super quick. I found an umbrella in your closet," I said, waving the black umbrella over my head and flinging open the front door.

Lightning flashed through the house like a storm of paparazzi sent to record the moment. A wooden frame holding a family photo from last Christmas shivered on the wall next to Mom's head.

"What did you...wait." Mom's eyes grew wide. She reached for me, but she was too far away. "Hand me the umbrella, Brolly. Now."

Cale ran down the stairs and bumped into Mom on his way into the kitchen.

"It'll just take a second," I said, stepping onto the porch. The rain blew sideways, soaking my bare legs before I could even get down the porch steps.

"Wait," Mom shouted. "Brolly! Wait! DO NOT OPEN THAT UMBRELLA!"

Her voice sent a shock of panic through me as I pushed open the umbrella against the stinging rain. I turned back to look at her, but it was too late.

A crackling, thunderous boom punched through my chest, knocking the wind out of me and throwing my body backwards. I didn't have time to recover when an explosive flash of light sizzled over my skin and through my veins, blinding and burning through me. My entire body spun, end over end and I couldn't react, couldn't think, couldn't do anything but cling to the umbrella handle and scream and scream, my lungs and throat on fire.

I was about to break, my bones creaking under the wild, spinning pressure when, in an instant, it all stopped. My body floated; a feather carried by the wind. Darkness itself swallowed me whole and I traveled, slowly, down-down-down, drifting, circling the blackness until I was thrown onto the ground in a heap.

My ears were ringing. I couldn't catch my breath. Huge drops of rain beat down on me, pounding against my skin. I pushed myself off the ground, my hands and legs covered in mud.

Something was wrong.

It was dark and I wasn't in front of my house anymore.

Thick, black sheets of rain whooshed down around me so loud I couldn't hear my own thoughts. I couldn't see my house. I couldn't see my street.

"Mom?" I shouted. "Mom, where are you?"

No one answered.

Hot, fearful tears stung my eyes, mixing with the cold rain. My breath punched out of me in short staccato beats of panic. I turned in a circle, stumbling and falling in the inky, wet blackness. My legs and arms shook with fear and I couldn't stand back up. A voice shouted through the rain.

"Mademoiselle? Est-ce que ca va?"

It wasn't my mom.

"Mademoiselle, prends ma main."

It was a man.

I pushed my hair out of my face and my fingers streaked mud across my forehead. I peered up to see who was speaking. The man's hand was outstretched toward me, but I couldn't move. Couldn't take his hand. Everything was wrong, cataclysmically wrong.

The man took a step closer. I squinted up at him, but the rain clouded my vision. He approached me with caution, reaching out and then pulling away, like he was afraid I would bite him if he came too close. His wet hair fell over his forehead and his eyes were wide, darting back and forth from my hands to my face.

"Laissez-moi vous aider, s'il vous plait."

I recognized the last word he said – please. My French teacher drilled it into us every single day of freshman year. But I couldn't understand why this man would be speaking French. Or where he came from. Or why it was so dark. Or what was happening to me.

"Mademoiselle, s'il vous plait."

It was ridiculous, the entire situation. Rain seeped into my bones making me wavy and limp and a strange man was shouting at me in French. I needed my mom.

"S'il vous plait," the man said again, his hand outstretched, water running off his fingertips in small streams.

I was unsteady, dizzy, covered in mud and shaking so hard my teeth rattled.

"Mademoiselle?"

He bent down to get closer to me, his tall boots splashed with mud. He was looking me over, checking my arms and legs. I needed to get up, figure out where I was and what happened, find my mom, but I was frozen in place.

"Mademoiselle, avez-vous eté attaqué?" He was speaking so quickly, and the rain was so loud, it was hard for me to catch what he was saying. But three years of French were enough to help me understand the word attack. He was asking me if I was attacked. I looked down at my grey sleep shorts and Central High t-shirt, both covered in mud. I looked fine, just dirty and drenched.

I wrapped my arms around myself and squeezed my eyes shut. Why would he think I was attacked? Where was my house? Where was I? The man took off his jacket and held it out for me.

I didn't take it, didn't move, unable to process a single thing that was happening. I thought maybe I fell off the porch and hit my head. Maybe it was all a hallucination, a fever dream, and in reality I was in the back of an ambulance racing down the interstate while an EMT shouted to the driver that I'd been struck by lightning. Maybe I was severely concussed, my brain conjuring up this whole scenario to keep me calm.

But I wasn't calm. Vein-shredding panic raced through my bloodstream. The rain continued to beat against my body, the wind threatening to carry me away at any moment. I chanced a look at the stranger. Up close, his eyes gave him away. He was more boy than man. And he didn't have a clue what was going on, just like me.

"Comment vous appellez-vous?" he asked.

Tears fell from my eyes mixed with a steady stream of rain drops.

"Are you asking for my name?" I shouted.

He leaned closer to me. "Do you speak English?"

"What? Of course I do." My arms ached from holding myself so tightly.

"What is your name?"

"Br...," I took a breath. "Brolly...my name is Brolly." I croaked out the words.

"Please, Mademoiselle Brolly, allow me to help you."

He was holding his hand out again, asking me to decide. I noticed my mom's green flip-flops were gone. My muddy, bare feet were the final crack in the dam. I choked on a sob that had been building in the back of my throat, a sob that quickly turned into inconsolable weeping.

He bent over and held his arms out. "Let me help you. Please."

I reached out and took his hand to stand up but lost my balance and fell back down into the mud. He reached out again. "It is all right. You are safe."

I barely registered his words, letting the darkness take over.

Coming back around was like swimming up from the deep, a slow, cloudy climb ending in a sharp brightness. I was too scared to open my eyes, too afraid to find out the last few minutes were real. Except, it must have been longer than a few minutes. I was lying in a bed but definitely not my bed; too soft and it smelled wrong. Wet hair clung to my face and neck as I shivered under a heavy blanket. There were voices in the room.

"I discovered her lying in the grass down by the shore. She was not wearing any clothes and was very disoriented. I did not know what else to do, so I delivered her here."

"You did the right thing, m'lord. Does she have any injuries?"

"None that I could see."

It was a man and a woman. They were talking about me.

"Perhaps we should call for the doctor?" the woman asked.

"Yes, of course. I will have Girard go as soon as the storm calms."

The voices moved away from me, their tense whispers stirring up a fresh panic. I couldn't focus, couldn't think through the searing pain in my head. I drifted back to sleep, my mind repeating the same message over and over.

Wake up.

Wake up.

Wake up.

The second time I woke up was faster, a jolt, like being shaken awake by Dad telling me I was late for school. I was afraid to open my eyes, afraid to see I wasn't in my own bedroom, afraid I was still stranded inside a nightmare. Or maybe an elaborate joke. Cale's favorite thing was hiding in random places throughout the house and jumping out to scare me when I walked by. The louder I screamed, the happier he was. But this was too much, even for Cale. Hearing someone stir beside me, I cracked my eyes open the tiniest bit and saw a woman standing next to the bed, pouring something into a delicate teacup. She smiled when she sensed I was awake.

"Good morning, m'lady. I brought you some tea."

I opened my eyes all the way and stared at her, waiting for her to say something more. Something that made sense.

"I am Jane, m'lady. How are you feeling?"

My head was stuffed full of cotton balls and even though I'd been sleeping for far too long, my body sank like dead weight into the bed, like more sleep was the only thing that could cure me. My thoughts blurred together, my heavy eyelids threatening to close. I forced some words out before I drifted off again. "How did I get here?"

"Have some tea, m'lady, and we shall get you sorted."

I didn't want tea.

I wanted to go home.

When I woke up again, the light in the room was different. Duller. Pushing my hair back from my face, I sat up and the same woman from earlier was standing next to the bed. Had she not moved at all?

"Good day, m'lady," she said, picking up a new teacup sitting on a saucer. "My name is Jane if you remember. How are you feeling?"

My vision was clearer than before, although my head still throbbed like I'd been pelted by rocks. The woman, Jane, was wearing a long black dress with a white apron tied around her waist. Her brown hair was pulled back into a tight bun with tiny wisps of grey escaping around her face. She looked familiar.

"How about some tea before I help you dress?"

I looked down and saw I was wearing a long-sleeved ivory nightgown with lace on the cuffs of the sleeves that reached the tips of my fingers.

"Where…" my voice was scratchy and garbled. Clearing my throat, I tried again. "Where are my clothes?"

"You were not wearing clothes when m'lord found you, m'lady."

"What do you mean I wasn't wearing clothes?"

I couldn't remember much, but I was pretty sure I wasn't naked.

"M'lord discovered you in the storm. You were wearing some strange underclothes. Filthy, they were. Mary has set to washing them but I would not care to be hopeful. Let me help you dress, m'lady. There are some lovely dresses I have been instructed to-"

"I want my own clothes," I interrupted. "And I want to go home."

She ran her hands down the front of her apron and looked at me with a smile. There was kindness in her eyes, but wariness too. "To be sure, m'lady, but you cannot go running out in your dressing gown now, can you?"

"Dressing gown? I don't..."

I caught my reflection in a dresser mirror next to the bed. My long brown hair was matted and wild, almost as wild as my red, watery eyes. I took in the strange room; curved walls covered in a dark French toile wallpaper, a fire burning in a huge fireplace across from the bed, above the fireplace a large painting of a woman straight out of one of my mom's 19th century novels. It looked like a bed and breakfast run by a Jane Austen enthusiast.

"What's going on here?"

"How do you mean, m'lady?"

There was a soft knock at the door and a guy walked into the room.

"Jane, has she...oh, do pardon me," he said, averting his eyes and backing out of the room.

"Wait," I shouted. "Come back here!" My legs tangled in the long nightgown as I struggled to get out of the bed. He stepped halfway back into the room with his eyes fixed on the floor.

"I did not realize you were in your bed clothes. I shall return at a more appropriate time."

"Are you the French guy? From the storm?" The memories were still a murky jumble, but I remembered him, how scared he looked and the way he reached out to me.

"Lord Westbourne," he said, bowing at the waist.

"Look, I'm not...I'd like my clothes back and possibly a ride home. I have no idea how I got here...the storm must have...I don't know, blown me here or something? Can I use your phone? I don't have mine and I need to call my parents."

He paused for a moment, a long moment that crawled up the back of my neck like an imaginary spider I couldn't wipe away. He stood directly in front of the door with his arms crossed behind his back, guarding my way out. Jane was standing next to me, her eyes wide. "Jane will help you dress," he said, "and Doctor Valier will be here soon to examine you."

"Doctor? Look, I appreciate you helping me out, but I don't need a doctor. I mean, some ibuprofen would be amazing because my head is killing me, but I'm fine, really. I just need my clothes and a phone. And maybe an Uber." I looked around the room. "What is this, some kind of themed bed and breakfast place?"

His eyes remained focused on the floor. "This is Chateau du Lac, where you have been a guest since the storm."

"Since the storm?" I wrapped my arms around myself and squeezed my ribs. "When...how long have I been here?"

"Mademoiselle Brolly, I believe it would be best if you dressed and-"

"I appreciate your help, really, but I don't even know who you are. I just need to go home." My throat went dry. I couldn't understand why they wouldn't let me use a phone. Or tell me where I was. These were simple questions with simple answers.

"I am Lord Westbourne."

He didn't say anything else, holding his stiff stance in front of the door like the declaration of his name was all I needed to know. I looked at Jane and she hadn't moved, still clutching the teacup and saucer in her hands. I'd never heard of a place called Chateau whatever he said so I couldn't figure out how I'd gotten there. I closed my eyes and tried to remember what happened. It was storming. I opened the front door. An explosion.

I opened my eyes. "What's going on here?" I asked, looking

back and forth between the two of them. "Can't one of you just let me use your phone?"

Jane and the Lord guy exchanged a look. "You seem agitated," he said. "I will give you some time to-"

"Please," I said, not giving him a chance to say whatever inane thing he planned to say next. I didn't want to get dressed in some costume they had planned for me or see a doctor. I didn't care who this Lord person was. I wanted to leave. Immediately. "At least tell me where I am. Maybe I can walk."

He paused again, long enough for my irritation to turn into trembling worry. His voice was softer when he said, "Since the storm you have been a guest of Chateau du Lac and-"

"And what the *hell* is Chateau du Lac?" I shouted, waving both hands in the air. "Nothing you're saying makes any sense whatsoever."

His head jerked up, surprised. He walked fully into the room, hands still behind his back. He was wearing thick, cream-colored pants that looked like leggings with tall, shiny black knee boots, a dark blue double-breasted jacket with long tails in the back and six large gold buttons on the front. His shirt was stark white with a stiff collar standing straight up to his jaw. He looked like a mash-up of every Mr. Darcy character from every film adaptation of *Pride and Prejudice*.

"And why are you wearing a costume?" I asked, knowing he wouldn't answer.

He pulled his eyebrows together in a deep frown and cocked his head to the side, like he was talking to a small child.

"Mademoiselle Brolly, Chateau du Lac is in Lille." He had an accent.

"Lille? Is that anywhere near Waterson Heights? There's so many subdivisions around here, I can't keep track."

I walked over to the window expecting to see a suburban street. Expecting to see cars and sidewalks and mailboxes and grass that needed mowing. All I could see was water. I leaned closer to the window, smashing my face against the glass and in every direction, as far as I could see, water.

"I am terribly sorry, Mademoiselle Brolly," he said. I turned around to look at him and he was glaring at me as if he was the one who should be scared, not me. "I am afraid I do not understand your question. Surely you must know, Chateau du Lac is in Lille, France."

I laughed to keep from screaming.

"France. You're telling me that I'm in France right now. France, the country. We are in France."

He didn't say anything but the look on his face told me everything I needed to know. I was having a mental break with reality while wearing a frilly nightgown in front of an oddly dressed…

Wait.

Wait, wait, wait.

It couldn't be.

No.

The lightning. The storm.

Every time travel conversation I'd ever had with Pepper scrolled through my brain in an instant.

But it was impossible.

There was no way.

I pressed my fingertips to my lips and closed my eyes. Everything around me shifted from a dull haze into terrifying clarity; his clothes, the maid, his accent, the nightgown, the room, the tea…but it couldn't be. There was no possible way even ten percent of what I was imagining was true. Pepper was wrong. Time travel wasn't real.

The Lord guy was still watching me, quietly, waiting.

I swallowed, the thickness of realization swelling my tongue and churning my guts into a knotted, heavy stone, and forced myself to say the impossible.

"What day is it?"

His posture was so straight it looked painful. "Today is Wednesday."

"No, I mean, the date. What is today's date."

"It is the 23rd day of August."

"Tell me the year."

His eyes narrowed the tiniest bit. "The year is 1826, of course."

Of course.

THREE

826. He said the year was 1826. And he didn't smile or say gotcha or reveal a hidden camera. My family didn't jump out from a hiding spot, pointing and laughing at the big hilarious prank. Lord Westbourne said the year was 1826 with one hundred percent sincerity. And I didn't know what to do with that information.

I kept going over and over it in my mind, each thought leading to something harder to imagine. I couldn't be in 1826. I couldn't be in France. I was at home. I was getting ready for school. It was the first day of my senior year. I was looking for my plaid button-down and Cale was looking for his magic quarter. Amelia was waiting for me to pick her up and Ben...oh, God. My almost-boyfriend, Ben. I never gave him an answer last night, never said yes to his question. He'd walked me home and kissed me on my front porch and said he'd see me at school. The memory of it was so fresh I could still feel his lips pressing warmly against mine.

I glanced over at Jane. She looked as scared as I was. Lord Westbourne remained stoic. They were both waiting for me to say something, this stranger in their house, demanding to know what year it was.

"Take me back," I said. "You have to take me back to where you found me. I have to go back."

"Mademoiselle Brolly, please allow me-"

"No." I stood directly in front of him and looked him in the eye. "I don't know what's going on or how I got here but I need to go home. Please take me back. Now."

"Very well. Jane will help you dress and-"

"Now!" My tone was angry, but my bottom lip quivered. Several traitorous tears fell from my eyes.

If only Amelia had been with me. She would have had this Lord guy shaking in his tall, black boots and offering us whatever we needed. Amelia was the nicest person you'd ever meet, but when she needed something to go her way, she usually got it. If she were with me, we'd already be half-way home. With snacks.

"Of course," he said, bowing low and stepping aside from the doorway.

I brushed past him and walked barefoot out the door onto a small landing. The lace edges of the nightgown dragged along the cold stone floor. Lord Westbourne led me down a terrifyingly long, stone spiral staircase followed by an infinite maze of confusing hallways and stairwells. When we reached the front door, I charged ahead of him, eager to get where we were going. Outside it was…weird. The air was softer somehow, cleaner, like smelling a dryer sheet meant to smell like fresh air. There was a cobblestone drive out front and the pebbles were sharp and rough under my feet. It didn't slow me down.

I had to go home.

Because I couldn't be in France.

I couldn't be in the 1800s.

"No," I said out loud. "Just…no."

My hands twisted in the long nightgown as I walked across the rough texture of the driveway as fast as my bare feet would allow. Lord Westbourne's tall boots smacked against the cobblestones in a click-clack rhythm. It reminded me of the metronome on top of Mom's piano.

We reached a narrow path that led down toward the water.

"Are we…is this an island?"

"Yes, Chateau du Lac is on Lac Bleu."

Of course, I thought, *Chateau du Lac. Castle of the Lake.*

"Here we are," he said when we reached the shore at the end of the road, as if here was somewhere to be. All I could see was water. Everywhere I looked, water. "This is where I found you." Lord Westbourne motioned to a patch of thick grass a few yards up from the shore. There was nothing significant there, only grass and mud from the rain. "I had returned from Lille and was securing the boats for the storm. It began to rain. I found you lying just there."

"How long have I been here?" I asked, doing my best to remain calm and not completely break down. I needed answers and Lord Westbourne was the only one who could provide them. I didn't want to scare him away.

"Since yesterday evening."

"But it was morning," I said to myself, searching the small patch of land for something, anything. Lord Westbourne stood on the cobblestone path, watching me.

I flopped down onto the grass. It was damp and soaked my nightgown. I didn't care. "I need a minute."

"Of course," he said, turning his back and taking a few steps away.

A breeze blew over me, ruffling the lace cuffs of the nightgown over my trembling hands. I ran through a list of details from that morning at home. It was storming. The power went out. Amelia texted reminding me to pick her up. Ben texted good morning with a heart emoji. I was looking for my plaid button-down. I found an umbrella.

"The umbrella!" I shouted, smacking the ground and jumping up to my feet. The nightgown stuck to my legs in long, damp drapes.

"Pardon?"

"I had an umbrella with me. It was black with a carved wooden handle. Did you see it?"

"I did not see an umbrella, no, but it was quite dark. Perhaps the rain washed it away?"

I paced back and forth. "I have to find it. It's really important."

Lord Westbourne helped me search the small patch of grass but there was no umbrella. No trace that anything happened apart from rain and wind. We walked beyond the grass to a stony beach that led up to a tree-lined hillside. We searched the shore, walked through the trees, scanned the lake, but there was nothing.

Worry crept up my spine. If all of this were true, if I had actually time traveled to the 19th century, I needed a way to travel back. So far, the umbrella was the only thing that didn't fit. I'd found it taped inside a box, hidden in my mom's closet. It had to be what brought me here. And it would be what would take me home.

At the water's edge, I stood on the smooth stones, the water cool against my feet. A breeze spun through my hair. A flock of birds swirled over the water and landed in a nearby tree, happily chirping to one another. None of it *felt* like a dream but solid and hard, like a fixed point I couldn't wish away.

Lord Westbourne stood next to me with his hands clasped behind his back. He stuck his elbow out, offering me his arm like I was on the Homecoming Court and not some wild-eyed lunatic in a muddy nightgown on the edge of the world. "Shall we go back?"

"Back where?" I mumbled, more to myself than to him. I turned away from him and walked down the shore, my legs struggling inside the yards of fabric from my wet, lacy nightgown.

"Mademoiselle Brolly, I do suggest you come inside."

"Just leave me alone," I said, walking away from him.

I didn't look back.

I paced the jagged shoreline around the entire castle, searching for the umbrella, for anything at all that would hold some clue as to how I arrived or how I could leave. If I couldn't find the umbrella, maybe there was a portal of some kind or a portkey, something linked between this time and mine. I walked through the wooded tree line again, searching through the brush and the undergrowth, half-hoping to find a DeLorean hidden behind some bushes. I searched every part of the island that touched the water. Every few minutes I stopped my mad pacing and stared out across the water, hoping to see the umbrella floating in the gentle ripples pushed by the breeze. But there was nothing.

The sun had dipped into the lake when I finally trudged back up to the castle doors, my feet cut and bloodied from my desperate search. A girl in a maid's uniform found me as I stumbled inside.

"Are you quite all right, m'lady?"

"No," I said, and began to cry again. In my former life, as I now called it, I rarely cried. Amelia cried at puppy videos on YouTube and perfect test scores and Ingrid Michaelson songs. *I like to feel life, not just observe it*, she always said. Not me. I was too much of a realist. Mom said I was irritatingly pragmatic. But time traveling to an alternate reality unleashed my inner weeper. Maybe in this new time I'd become an alternate me. Maybe I'd suddenly like pickles and hip-hop.

"Let me help you to your room, m'lady," the maid said, pulling my arm over her shoulder and ushering me further inside the castle doors. The cuts on my feet left small smudges of blood across the marble floor. I cried the entire way back to the round room at the top of the castle thinking about how alternate me couldn't suddenly like hip-hop since it wouldn't exist for another three hundred years. Then I cried harder when I realized it was actually two hundred years and alternate me was still terrible at math.

We made it to the top of the spiral staircase and Jane was there with a doctor waiting to examine me. He was an old Frenchman with gnarled, arthritic hands and the widest nose I'd ever seen outside of a cartoon.

"Je suis le medicin," he kept repeating as he looked me over. His bony hands held my wrists like they were made of glass and the slightest pressure would shatter me. He stared into my eyes for an uncomfortable amount of time. In broken English he asked me what happened, where my family was, how I ended up on the island in the storm. "How come to this place?"

I remained silent, afraid to say anything, not knowing how to say it even if I could.

He gently washed my sore feet and wrapped them in soft bandages. I climbed into bed and did my best to keep from crying. Again. The doctor left, shaking his head as he went. Jane came back in and sat next to me on the bed.

"Would you like some tea, m'lady?" Her concerned smile reminded me of my mom last winter when I was sick with a terrible flu. Their eyebrows drooped the same way.

"I want to go home," I said as fresh tears slid down my cheeks into my ears and my tangled hair. Jane patted them dry with the back of her hand.

"Rest now and I shall bring up some tea and biscuits a bit later."

I closed my eyes, believing when I opened them, I would be back in my own room, in my own bed. Home.

FOUR

I stayed in the room at the top of the castle, my feet healing from my walk of madness that first day. I itched to escape the tower and search for the umbrella. If I found it, I didn't know for sure that it would take me home, but it was the only option that made any sense. It wasn't like I could run away or swim to safety. I was in a water-locked castle in 19th century France. What could matter beyond that immovable fact?

I wished I could call Pepper. He'd know exactly what to do. I should have listened to him all those times he talked about time travel instead of arguing about how ridiculous it was. *Time travel isn't real*, I always told him. *There's no logical explanation for it. It's a fictional concept used by storytellers to weave fantastic tales.* Pepper would shake his head and smile, his belief stronger than ever, just like his friendship. If I ever did get home, Pepper would kill me for time traveling without him.

"Pepper," I whispered, pacing around the stone floor, as if uttering his name would conjure him out of thin air. "What should I do?"

I was so deep in thought I almost missed the low knock at the door. I jumped into the chair in front of the fireplace and pulled my knees up to my chest underneath the fresh nightgown Jane had laid out for me. I expected her to barge in offering tea I wouldn't drink. But it wasn't Jane, it was him, the one who saved me and pulled the rug out from underneath me.

Lord Westbourne walked in carefully, the way you'd walk next to a sleeping baby, and sat down next to me in the other chair facing the fireplace. We both watched the fire, afraid to be the first to speak.

"Mademoiselle Brolly," he said finally, quietly, like he was afraid I would bolt at any second, "Jane tells me you are not eating." He kept his eyes on the fireplace instead of me. "It appears you are in no condition to inform us how you came to be here. Doctor Valier seems to believe you are in good health, if not a bit stubborn." He waited, giving me time to say something. I didn't. "In light of that, I have come to inform you that you may remain a guest of Chateau du Lac for as long as you need." He paused again, clearing his throat so softly he barely made a sound. "Would that be agreeable?"

Agreeable? I laughed bitterly at the idea of anything about my situation being agreeable. I was facing the very real possibility that I would never see my family again. Never see Amelia or Pepper again. Never see Ben. "I need to go home."

"Yes, I quite agree." He leaned forward in his chair and then leaned back again, his posture so straight it made my spine ache. "Mademoiselle Brolly, I should be delighted to offer any means of aid in order for you to reach your family. As I have previously stated, you do not seem to be in a condition to travel. You do not seem to be able to," he paused again, rubbing his hands in small circles over his knees, "communicate your needs in a manner to which we can understand."

I held my breath and considered blurting out the awful, unbelievable truth. Yes, thank you, Mr. Lord Person, for your weird and generous offer. I'd like to go home to Spring Hill, please, because that's where I live. It's a suburb of Nashville, a city you've probably never heard of considering it's the 1800s and we are in France. It's in Tennessee. In America. My family has a house in a subdivision called Waterson Heights. It's a pre-fab flash community where every fifth house has the same floor plan and there's a clubhouse for moms to host Tuesday Boozeday book club; the kind of moms who use cruise as a verb. You know the type. They own too many decorative throw pillows and think the phrase *Live Laugh Love* is inspirational. Only you don't know the type because you're a stiff shirt Lord who never fully exhales and you live in a giant castle. In France.

I'd say all of this and then the good Lord would promptly throw me from the castle tower for witchcraft or insanity or both. I glanced over at him without turning my head and squeezed my lips together to keep the truth from flying out of my mouth. As much as I didn't want to be there, I didn't want to be kicked out, either. I kept my eyes focused on the fireplace, on the flames licking up the sides of the wood. I listened to the cracks and pops, hoping they would drown out the thoughts in my head. Lord Westbourne couldn't help me get home, didn't know what, or when, home was for me. He was offering me shelter. And kindness. There was only one thing I could say to him that he'd be able to understand.

"Okay."

After several more tension-filled moments, Lord Westbourne stood up and went to the door, paused with his hand on the doorknob and turned to look at me. I could see him out of the corner of my eye as his mouth opened, as if he wanted to say something, but he closed it just as quickly and left.

I unfolded myself from the chair and went to the long window on the far wall where thick, heavy curtains kept the light out. Jane opened them every time she came into the room only for me to shut them as soon as she left. I yanked them open now and let the sunlight stream in. I pressed my nose against the glass. It was a long way down, five or six stories at least. I'd just told the Lord I was willing to stick it out, but then what? Was I supposed to accept this life, this rudimentary existence with no indoor plumbing, no electricity, no phone, no family, no friends?

Was I supposed to stay trapped in a tower like some fairy tale princess with too much hair?

Obviously not.

Because I was going to find the umbrella.

I was going to go home.

I walked to the door and cracked it open a sliver, fully prepared to see Jane on the other side, listening, waiting to pour tea down my throat and shove a fresh nightgown over my head. I cracked the door open further but no one was there, just the dark, winding staircase. My feet were still sore, but I took a few tentative steps down the cold, stone stairs. My hair fell into my eyes so I gathered it up with both hands and twisted it into a messy knot.

At the bottom of the spiral staircase, I went left down a short hall and found another staircase leading to another hallway. A million closed doors. Even more stairs down and another long, empty hallway full of closed doors. Amelia's voice rang in my head telling me at least my butt would look amazing going up and down all these stairs.

The castle clanged with a hollow emptiness and I wondered where all the other people were. Maybe they ran away, scared of the mysterious girl in the tower who appeared out of thin air. I hadn't thought to bring a candle with me since it was the middle of the day, but most of the stairwells and hallways were dark with only the occasional oil lamp lighting my way.

Cale would love it, using every dark corner to jump out and scare me to death. Once, he'd hidden in my room until I got into bed and turned out the light. When I was almost asleep, he'd reached up and grabbed my leg from underneath the covers. I had screamed so loud my parents thought I was being murdered. Dad nearly had to peel me off the ceiling and Cale was grounded from video games for two weeks. He'd said it was totally worth it.

I traced my hand down the walls as I shuffled across thick rugs and stone floors. I was about to give up, sure I'd been swallowed up by a magic castle with no front door, when I found the grand staircase I'd followed Lord Westbourne down that first day. I crept down, holding onto the wood railing, and listened for any signs of life. There was no need for me to sneak around. It wasn't like they were holding me prisoner. Lord Westbourne would let me leave, help me even, if I could just tell him where I needed to go.

I made it down to the large, wooden doors that led outside. Pushing one open, I slipped out, still unnoticed, and hobbled down the rocky path to the shore. The bright sunlight blinded me after being in the dark castle. My feet were sore and I had no idea what I was doing, but I couldn't sit in that tower for one more minute.

Three wooden rowboats were pulled up onto the shoreline. The middle boat appeared to be the closest to the water, so I leaned down and pushed it with all my might. I might as well have been pushing against the side of a building. I moved around to the other end and pulled. And pulled. And pulled. It didn't budge. I walked back around to the top of the boat, sat down on the rocks, and pushed the boat with my back, my heels planted firmly in the jagged surface of the rocks, until the boat slid forward into the water. I dragged it further and fell in, the bottom of my nightgown soaked and my feet throbbing.

The black umbrella was in the lake. I was going to find it.

I'd never rowed a boat before and was clumsy with the oars, scraping the bottom of the lake and barely moving the boat. After several minutes of struggling and pulling and pushing, I was out in the water. The mid-day sun glared overhead turning the surface of the water into a high beam spotlight. I squinted my eyes into tiny slivers and scanned the water as I rowed the boat out further from the castle. I thought about the umbrella and its heavy, wooden handle. Maybe it sank to the bottom of the lake and I'd need to dive down to find it. Peering over the side of the boat, I couldn't see the bottom. The sun's abrasive glare made it impossible to see more than a few inches, the light casting everything in a white-trimmed blur.

I don't know how long I rowed the small boat, but I ended up on the backside of the castle, my arms and my resolve weakening by the second.

"It's gone," I said, out loud, wishing someone could hear me. Wishing someone could help me. Wishing there was a person alive who could understand what was happening to me. I tried again, louder this time. "They're all gone!"

Was it really only a few nights ago Amelia and Pepper and I went over to Ben's? And Ben asked me to be his girlfriend? I thought I had time, time to answer Ben's question, time for more kisses, more movie nights in the basement. Time to figure things out. But time was reversed, flipped inside out. My family wasn't even alive, wouldn't be for hundreds of years. I was completely and utterly alone.

"Mademoiselle Brolly?" It was Lord Westbourne, calling out to me, rowing a second boat across the lake. "Mademoiselle Brolly, are you quite all right?"

"They're gone," I said as he rowed closer. I didn't care if he could hear me or not. "Or I guess they aren't here yet. I'm ahead and they're behind, or something." I was trying to work it out, trying to define the ache in my chest. "Either way, everything is gone. All of it. All of them. They're gone."

Lord Westbourne reached my boat and pulled it up against his boat. "Mademoiselle Brolly, please allow me to escort you back to the castle."

My humorless laugh echoed across the water. "Why not, I've got nowhere else to be. My entire life is gone. Or hasn't started yet? I'm here too early, everyone else too late."

I watched him pull out some rope and tie our two boats together, end to end, so that his back was to me. He rowed us around the lake, faster than I did, from the back of the castle to the shore where the boats were kept. He didn't talk, just rowed, oars pulling through the water in a soothing rhythm. I shrugged down into the bottom of my boat as he pulled it onto the shore.

"Go ahead without me," I said, my voice muffled from my arms crossed over my face. "I'm just going to stay here."

"Mademoiselle Brolly, you cannot stay here forever."

"Exactly," I said. "That's exactly right, you totally get it. That is exactly my problem. Thank you for saying it so succinctly."

"Did you find her, m'lord?" Jane asked, scurrying over and peering inside the boat.

"She went out onto the lake. Alone. And now she insists on staying here." I could hear in his voice how much I perplexed him.

"Oh no she does not," Jane said, pulling my arms and forcing me to sit up. "Let us get you inside, m'lady."

I resisted, but resistance was futile when it came to Jane. She hoisted me up and out of the boat and pulled me up the road to the castle, Lord Westbourne walking a respectable distance behind us.

Back in the tower, I went to the window to look down at the lake, hoping something would catch my eye, something I missed. But there was nothing. I sagged against a small table next to the window and noticed some thick, beige sheets of paper lying on top. Maybe writing down what was happening to me would unlock my brain and I'd be able to remember where the umbrella went. On top of the desk, a long, delicate quill lay next to a small silver jar. I picked up the jar and swirled it around, the inky liquid painting the sides black. I sat down in the desk chair and took the large quill in my left hand, moving it back and forth. The feathered plume brushed against my arm like a whispered breath. I dipped the sharp point into the inky liquid and dragged it across the paper, drawing small circles and learning the feel of the feather. Then I started writing to the one person I wanted to talk to the most.

Amelia,

I miss you. So much so that I'm writing longhand with a giant feathered quill like some sort of Elizabethan heroine writing her memoirs or a character from one of my mom's books. Remember that time we watched *Pride & Prejudice* for Mrs. Reilly's Honors English and then you made me watch that scene where Matthew Macfayden walks toward Keira Knightly in the sunrise like 20 times in a row? Would you believe I'm living that scene? Only I'm not. Not like that anyway. There is a handsome guy in a starched shirt but he's not gliding across a field to tell me that he love, he love, he loves me. Honestly, I don't know how to tell you where I am or how I got here or if I'm ever coming home. The short version is, I found an old umbrella in my mom's closet and when I opened it, I arrived here. So far, no one seems to be upset about what's happening. They keep offering me tea and trying to dress me like a paper-doll while I stand flat and motionless. Worst of all, I'm a terrible time traveler. I lost the umbrella and am totally grouchy to everyone even though they've been nothing but nice to me. You'd be so much better at this. You'd at least love the clothes.

I dipped the quill in the ink jar for the hundredth time, my fingers sore from pressing the pointed tip of the feather into the rough paper. Both of my hands were ink-stained, most of the words I'd written smudged into an indecipherable mess. I let out a heavy sigh, balled up the paper and tossed it into the fire. It wilted and crumpled before turning to ash.

FIVE

"Jane?" She looked up as she was clearing away yet another tray of fruit, bread and cheese I'd barely touched.

"Yes, m'lady?"

I'd been thinking about it for the last few hours. Weighing the pros and cons. After my disastrous boat adventure, I forced myself to make some decisions. I thought about what Amelia would do if she were in my situation – probably squeal and clap and dive right in to all things chateau. I thought about what Pepper would do – write a dissertation about time travel using a quill and ink, interviewing every single castle resident until they banned him for being a nuisance. Mom would probably fact check her novels, see if the details she wrote about were accurate. (From my limited experience, they were.) But what about me? So far, I'd sulked in my room and refused to cooperate, turning myself into a sitcom teenager. I knew it was time to move on, knew it was time to stop being a catatonic, weepy shell of a person who stared at fires and never took a shower. That wasn't who I'd been at home and it wasn't who I wanted to be now. As terrifying as it was, it was time to move the story forward.

"I think I'm ready to get dressed."

Jane clapped her hands and smiled. "Wonderful, m'lady. I shall draw a bath."

"A bath?" I walked over to the mirror and grimaced. Amelia always said second day hair was the best hair, but I was working on four. Or was it five? The strongest dry shampoo in the world wouldn't be able to touch the atrocity my hair had become. Plus, if I was being honest, I smelled like Cale's hamper on laundry day. And it was probably about time for me to start my period. I couldn't be sure because I had no idea what day it was and didn't have the period tracker on my phone. "Actually, a bath sounds pretty great. Where…is it?" I'd become all too (and unhappily) familiar with chamber pots, but I had no idea where a bathtub might be.

"The bath is in the adjoining dressing room, just there." She pointed next to the fireplace. I could make out a faint outline of a door I hadn't yet noticed in all the hours I spent staring at the walls. "I will bring up some water right away, m'lady."

Jane hurried out of the room as I walked over to inspect the hidden door, the outline of it barely visible in the rich, patterned wallpaper. I ran my hand over the surface and pushed in, but nothing happened. I traced my fingers along the chair rail that ran the length of the room and found a small latch, closed my eyes and lay my head against the door. Opening it meant making a decision. If I stepped outside of my room and chose to participate in this life, it meant accepting the dream as reality, believing I was truly in another time and place. Each moment that ticked by made the dream theory less plausible. I even considered I'd somehow fallen into one of my mom's novels, but she never wrote about a castle on a lake. My life was now a complete unknown and I was at the door, a hidden door in the wall of a room at the top of a castle in 19th century France. A door that would open the next part of the mystery.

I pulled the latch.

The dressing room was bright white, a stark contrast to the

dark walls and heavy curtains from the bedroom, with curved bead-board walls and floor-to-ceiling windows covered in long panels of sheer fabric. A deep copper tub sat in the middle of the floor and two massive armoires stood side by side on the wall opposite the windows. A row of low, built-in cabinets ran along the side wall, bending in with the curve of the wall. I was staring dumbly at the tub when Jane came in carrying two large buckets of steaming water.

"Perhaps you would like to look at some dresses while I fetch more water? The dresses from these wardrobes belonged to m'lord's mother. He will not mind if you borrow one." she said, pouring water into the tub.

I watched the steam rise and nodded my head slowly as she scurried out, leaving me alone again. The cream-colored armoires each had large Ws carved into the doors and long silver handles. I opened the first door and found it stuffed full of dress after dress, all folded in neat stacks. Running my hand down the row, I touched the different fabrics and tried to imagine putting one on, playing the part, doing my best to fit in. I pulled out a cornflower blue dress from the middle of one stack and was inspecting the long row of tiny buttons up the back when the girl from the first day, the one who helped me back to my room, came in with more water.

"Oh, hi," I said.

"M'lady." She curtsied while holding two large, and very likely heavy, buckets of water.

"I never thanked you, you know, for helping me the other day."

She smiled and bowed her head as she tipped the buckets into the copper tub, steam rising from the water.

"What's your name?" I asked. She appeared to be about my age.

She looked nervous. "My name is Mary, m'lady."

"Hi, Mary. I'm Brolly."

"Yes, m'lady," she said, quickly curtsying and backing out of the room with her now empty buckets.

Jane came in, pushing past Mary in the doorway and dumping more hot water into the tub.

"I think I scared her."

"Scared, m'lady?"

"Mary. All I did was ask her name and she looked terrified."

"Yes, well, guests of Lord Westbourne do not typically speak so informally to maids like Mary."

"What do you mean?"

"I mean," she said, gathering up bath supplies from around the room, two embroidered towels that looked more like fancy shawls than towels, a bar of soap, a small, clear bottle with some kind of oil in it, "you might be the first person of your...status... to ask her name."

"I don't have any status."

"You are a guest of Lord Westbourne. That, my dear, is status." She laid out the towels, soap and oil on a small stool next to the copper tub.

"That's ridiculous."

"No, m'lady, that is society." She put her hands on her hips, wisps of brown and grey hair curling around her face, her cheeks pink. "Now, have you chosen a dress?"

"You said these are his mother's?" I asked, holding the blue dress above my head so the long skirt twirled out over my bare feet.

"*Were* his mother's. Lady Westbourne has passed on, m'lady. Shall I help you into the tub?"

"What happened to her? And what? No!"

Jane shook her head. "Come now, m'lady, it is not a sight I have not seen before. There is no need-"

"No! Seriously, no."

Jane paused, eyes wide, stunned I didn't want help bathing. "Just alike..." she muttered to herself, as if I wasn't there.

"Jane, I can take a bath by myself. Seriously."

She threw her hands up in resignation. "If that is how it is to be I shall leave you to it."

"Wait," I said, "what's the oil for?"

"Rosemary oil. For your hair, m'lady?"

"Right, I knew that. Thanks."

She eyed me, probably trying to figure out why I was so strange. I sort of hoped she would. "I will be off to change the bedding and shall return to help you dress."

"But..." I paused. Odds were, left to my own devices I wouldn't be able to put on the dress I'd chosen. "Okay."

Jane left the room muttering to herself as I silently counted to 60 to make sure she wasn't going to come back in and try to scrub my armpits for me. Slipping the lacy nightgown over my head, my uniform since arriving to Chateau du Lac, I sank down into the deep tub until the steaming water hit my chin.

SIX

Clean and dressed, it was time to make my way downstairs and find the elusive Lord Westbourne. I promised myself I would attempt to be present, even though nothing about the present made sense. Until I found the umbrella, I would work on finding a new reality rather than wish my life away sitting in front of a fireplace and drinking pots of tea.

I ended up changing my mind on the cornflower blue dress and instead chose a pale pink one with a high waist and cascading pink ribbons down the front, not something I would ever wear in a million years. Amelia would have loved it. Amelia would have also gasped so hard she would have passed out if she saw me wearing it. I managed to get Jane to compromise on my hair, insisting that she leave it down and loose. I wasn't sure how to use the rosemary oil so I rubbed some into my scalp and through my hair, hoping I did it right. At least it smelled nice.

Jane was scandalized at every turn, looking at me like I was an insolent child for suggesting I leave my hair natural and bathe unassisted. She also remained tight-lipped about Lord Westbourne, avoiding every question I asked.

"What's the deal with the Lord guy?"

"I do not understand the manner of your question, m'lady," she said, buttoning up the one thousand tiny buttons on the back of the dress.

"Lord Westbourne…what's he like? He seems, I don't know, uptight?"

"Hmm," she smirked, offering nothing further.

"I should probably go talk to him; don't you think? He is letting me stay in his house, after all."

Jane gave a curt nod and motioned for me to follow her. I left the dressing room in itchy, billowy pants-as-underwear under my layered skirts and thick tights that went up to my mid-thigh, my feet tripping in too big, square-heeled pumps with giant bows on the toe. Amelia always said fashion was about altering clothes to fit who you are, not altering yourself to fit the clothes. I wished she was there with me to alter the clothes to fit who I was. Instead, I was walking around in a costume, unable to see any shred of myself.

Jane led me down the long, spiral staircase and through the same series of hallways and stairways I'd walked before. This time I took it all in, the heavy tapestries hanging on the walls next to large portraits of men and women, formal and stiff-backed. They scowled at me, like they were holding the keys to secrets I desperately needed to uncover, hidden behind gold baroque frames and expressionless expressions. At the end of the third hall, we walked down two sets of stairwells, one narrow and one winding, the final one opening to a wide, wooden stair-case with plush green carpet running down the middle. Staircase wasn't the right word. The steps were wide enough for ten people to link arms and form a kick-line. The staircase ended in what looked like a hotel lobby, an impossibly huge space with a shiny marble floor. It reminded me of the Hilton Hotel lobby in downtown Nashville. When I was seven, Mom and I went to see Disney on Ice and she parked our car in the underground garage of the Hilton next door to the arena. We took the elevator up to the lobby and I was sure we'd arrived in a palace. There were massive lighting fixtures hanging from the ceiling and huge, luxurious seating areas surrounding the widest staircase I'd ever seen spilling down from the second floor. The castle's grand entryway had all the same richness minus the electricity and businessmen in suits.

Before I could take it all in, Jane rushed me across the marble floor and over to two tall, wooden doors on the right side of the foyer. She pushed them open and we walked into another room with an impossibly high ceiling. This one was lined top to bottom with row after row of tall bookshelves filled with books.

"The library, I presume," I said, under my breath.

Lord Westbourne was sitting behind an ornate, wooden desk across the room. He stood up and walked toward us. "Mademoiselle Brolly, how lovely to see you." He bowed a bow that didn't contain any hint of sarcasm. "Are you quite well?"

"I'm...okay. Better." The words stung with betrayal to the life I'd left behind, but as soon as I said it, it was the truth. "I'm sorry about earlier with the boat and everything. I was kind of...thank you for coming to get me."

A hint of a smile crossed his stoic expression but vanished just as quickly. "Would you like some tea? Jane, please have Mary bring up some tea for Mademoiselle Brolly."

"Yes, m'lord," Jane said with a curtsy before shutting the tall library doors.

I crossed the room and sat down on a burgundy velvet couch with a lumpy cushioned seat and a high, curved back. There were so many bookshelves I didn't know where to look first.

"You must love to read," I said, dumbly, the room and the company shrinking me into something small and insignificant

He didn't respond. His eyes searched mine, curious, watching. He looked younger than I imagined a Lord should look, maybe early twenties with long limbs and a strong jawline. His thick, dark hair was swept high off his forehead and his eyes were golden brown. He was handsome in the traditional sense, all starched and properly groomed.

"So, you're a Lord?"

"Yes." He sat on the edge of a chair covered in a dark floral print, back straight, hands clasped in his lap.

"What does that mean exactly? Is it normal for someone so young to be a Lord?"

Color crept up his cheeks. "That is quite forward."

"What, asking your age? I'm sorry, I didn't mean-"

"Mademoiselle Brolly, I-"

We both paused, him out of politeness and me out of awkwardness.

"Just call me Brolly," I said.

"It would not be proper," he said in a hushed tone, like someone might overhear and report him to the manners police.

"Yes, that seems to be a big focus around here."

He raised his eyebrows, two perfectly shaped triangles over his eyes. "Is propriety not valued where you are from?"

"Where I'm from," I said, straining for a way to explain, "I'd say where I'm from its every man for himself."

"You do not speak like someone…it certainly seems as if you are a long way from home."

His expression was impossible to decipher, a mix between amused and wary, like he was afraid of me but also fascinated. The feeling was mutual.

"Yes, I think so. A very, very long way."

Mary came in with a tray full of tea and fancy appetizers. There were roast beef sandwiches on tiny buns and flower-shaped sugar cookies and two small bunches of grapes. I inhaled all of it.

Lord Westbourne sipped his tea and watched me over the edge of the delicate china teacup.

"I am pleased to see you have your appetite back. Doctor Valier said it would be a good sign."

"Sorry," I said, cookie crumbs flying out of my mouth like an impatient toddler. "I just figured out I'm starving."

"Please, eat as much as you like. Perhaps when you are finished you might accompany me for a walk?"

My first instinct was to say yes, great, a walk sounds amazing. But it also meant another step out, another step away from where I should be, another step deeper into this strange place. I thought about my promise to myself to be present, to push forward.

"I don't think I could walk on the rocky shore in these shoes." I pulled up the bottom of my dress to show him the shoes and he immediately averted his eyes.

"The castle," he cleared his throat, "has a lovely garden. I have noticed you prefer to walk in your bare feet, but I think you will find the garden much more suitable for walking in shoes."

I thought he might be trying to make a joke, but there wasn't a hint of a smile on his face.

"I've walked around every square inch of this castle. I didn't see a garden?"

"The garden is in the castle's center courtyard."

That sounded interesting enough. "A walk would be good. Thank you."

His eyes flitted over me as I finished the cookies. Once I swallowed the last bite, Lord Westbourne stood up and swept his hand toward the door. I brushed the crumbs off my dress and walked into the massive entryway. The grand staircase ended in two large, marble columns that stretched up two stories to an intricately painted ceiling.

"So, you're rich," I said, craning my neck to see every detail of the ornate patterns etched into the ceiling. Lord Westbourne stopped and turned on his heel, staring at me.

"I must say," he said, smiling a wry, close-lipped smile, "it is quite forward to discuss such matters, but...yes. Very."

"Hmmm," I said, my gaze still trained on the ceiling.

"One would think you rather enjoy showing off the column of your neck the way you stare at the ceiling."

"Shhh, I'm counting."

"Counting?"

"Your Ws. They're everywhere. And I'm keeping track."

I'd first noticed them in my room, hidden in the wallpaper, etched into the furniture, woven into the carpets. There were Ws everywhere, large and small, intricate and simplistic.

"See?" I said. "There's a W at the top of this pillar, carved into the marble. Haven't you noticed?"

"Men such as myself do not carry on in such a manner, staring at the ceiling with our noses in the air."

I snorted. "Oh, there's no doubt you have your nose in the air."

I didn't know where my sudden playfulness was coming from. It was only a short time ago I was in the castle tower in a near-catatonic state. But Lord Westbourne saved me, sort of, and was letting me stay in his castle on the lake. And there was something about him, something that broke my guard down even as I tried to build it up.

"No one has ever noticed," he said, motioning to the W I had just pointed out, stamped into the top of a small table against the wall.

It was a challenge.

I looked at him then, a smirk creeping across my lips. "I did."

"Yes…well."

He opened a narrow door on the wall next to the library and I walked through. Seeing that I was unsteady in my borrowed shoes, he offered me his arm, the same way he did on the shore. I wanted to resist, wanted to make a joke, but the way he was watching me silenced my cynicism.

I took his arm.

SEVEN

L ord Westbourne led us down a short path between two stone walls and around a corner onto a walkway that opened into a massive garden right in the center of the castle. The walkway was framed on both sides by tall, thin, perfectly sculpted trees. I half expected to see a W carved into each one.

"What kind of trees are those?"

He looked up, as if noticing them for the first time. "Cypress, I believe."

"They're so...perfect."

"Yes, the castle gardener has the gift of precision."

Past the trees were rows of tall hedges with sharp corners and smooth tops, not a twig out of place. Everything in the garden was designed with an absoluteness, perfectly spaced and coordinated. Every flower complemented the next flower. Every tree stood at attention. My mom had a small flower garden on the side of our house that grew wild most of the time. She kept the weeds at bay but everything else grew where it pleased. Nothing about Lord Westbourne's garden was wild. It was a huge, perfect paradise surrounded by the castle's high stone walls with tall round turrets in each corner.

"Oh, now I get it." I said, spinning in a circle to take in the whole thing. "The castle is built in a square. That explains all the staircases."

"Have you always had such a talent for observation, Mademoiselle Brolly?"

"There's a lot here to observe," I said.

We walked for a while in silence, cobblestones crunching under our feet, my mind full of questions. I couldn't think of a single thing to say.

"If you will allow me," Lord Westbourne said, "your dress is quite lovely." His tone was almost a question, like he wasn't sure he should be saying it. I looked down at the borrowed dress.

"Oh, it's not mine."

"Yes," he said.

I knew immediately how ridiculous I sounded, as if he didn't already know I was homeless and dress-less, totally at his mercy. I didn't know what to do, didn't know how to make conversation with a rich Lord who lived in the extreme past on a different continent in another world. Nothing about my life prepared me to stroll a castle garden with a guy like Lord Westbourne. "Your house, castle, I mean, this garden, even all the Ws, it's all so beautiful."

"Thank you. Chateau du Lac has been in my family for many years."

I pulled on the ribbons cascading down the front of my dress, "So, we're in France but you seem…English?"

"Yes, I am English. I am only visiting Chateau du Lac."

"And you're here all by yourself?" Here I was again, asking a boy if he was all alone in his house. I doubted this time it would end with Lord Westbourne asking me to be his girlfriend.

"My mother and father have both passed. I have a sister who traveled with me to France but chose to stay in Paris with our aunt. She does not appreciate the castle's charm as much as I do."

We reached a fountain in the middle of the garden, a large

stone pillar with a marble bowl perched on top. Water was spilling over the sides of the bowl, the stream splitting in the middle of the stone pillar to reveal a large W. I pointed to the W and crossed my arms in satisfaction. Lord Westbourne narrowed his eyes at me. "Yes. Well. Shall we sit?"

He motioned to a wooden bench between two cypress trees across from the fountain. I kept talking as we sat down, afraid to leave room for him to form his own questions.

"I'm sorry to hear about your parents. That must be hard. Were you close to them?"

He looked at me with a piercing glare and I worried I'd said too much. "Mademoiselle Brolly, do forgive me but, why the sudden change in demeanor? Moments ago, you were goading me about my home, my wealth, and now you ask after my family?"

"Look, just because I took a bath and ate some food doesn't mean anything's changed. I'm still way, way, out of my depth here."

His expression shifted to the puzzled, curious gaze I was growing used to seeing since I'd crashed onto his castle shore. "You asked if I was close to my mother and father?"

"You know, like, did you have a good relationship with them?"

He stared into the distance, his face unreadable. "I had great respect for both my father and my mother," he said, offering nothing more. "And you, Mademoiselle Brolly? Do you live with your family?"

His voice was measured. He knew it was a loaded question.

I thought about my cluttered and chaotic house, the couch with the worn, grey cushions you could sink down into, the piles of books on the stairs, the houseplants perched on windowsills in various stages of life and death, the mismatched frames lining the halls filled with beaming smiles from beach trips and Christmas mornings and everything in between. I'd never given much thought to my house, to the structure of it, the contents inside it. But now, I longed for it. I wanted nothing more than to pull out a metal stool from under the bar in the kitchen and talk to Mom and Dad while they cooked dinner. To sit on the front porch swing with Dad and eat ice cream while the sun set.

"Yes," I said. "I live with my parents and my brother."

"Here in Lille?" He was pressing. I couldn't blame him.

My chest tightened. "No."

He waited a beat before he said, "Mademoiselle Brolly, are you in any sort of trouble?"

I didn't answer him. Instead, I looked up through the trees at the summer sky, like an artist's rendition, with perfect, swirling puffs of clouds.

"My offer was sincere. You may remain a guest of Chateau du Lac for as long as you need. However," he paused, "is there anything I should be made aware of? Anything I should be… cautious of…regarding your situation?"

"You're English," I said, dodging his question, "but you have a castle in France. And you keep calling me Mademoiselle. How exactly did you become a sometimes French, sometimes English Lord who lives on an island part-time?"

He paused again. I noticed that every time I said something, he had to take a moment to digest it before he could respond, like he was translating my nonsense into something more suitable. "Chateau du Lac belonged to my mother's family. I spent time here as a child."

He wasn't unkind, but his words lacked emotion, like he was delivering a line. Or he didn't trust me.

"What about all the Ws?"

"My mother's family name was Watford. I believe that begins with a W?"

It was a joke, I suspected, but the delivery was so dry he might as well have called me an idiot.

"You don't get many visitors here, do you?"

He shook his head a fraction of an inch. "None like you, Mademoiselle Brolly."

We were both quiet for a moment, weighing the things said and unsaid between us.

"Mademoiselle Brolly, will you allow me to inquire after a few more particulars?"

I nodded despite my hesitation. "Yeah, okay."

He ran a hand through his hair, nervous. It was the most human thing I'd seen him do.

"Jane mentioned you had some distressing dreams while you were recovering from the storm. She said you called out several names, both your mother and father and two other individuals – an Amelia and a Ben. Might I ask, are you married?"

I closed my eyes and Ben's face came into view, his wide grin and shining eyes. His laugh. Hearing his laugh, even hearing it in my memory, squeezed my heart. It wasn't until Pepper introduced us I learned his name was Ben. Amelia and I were hanging out at the rec center pool when I went over to the snack bar to do a little recon on the hot lifeguard.

"Hey Pepper, what's good today?" I'd said.

"I would be remiss if I didn't warn you that the hot dogs have been roasting for longer than the FDA recommendation would allow."

"And the popcorn?"

"Freshly popped and infused with a light dusting of salt," he'd said with a flourish and a bow.

"So." I had attempted to sound casual as Pepper scooped popcorn into a brown paper bag. "You and the lifeguard seem friendly."

"You mean Ben? He'll be at Central with us this year."

"Oh?" I'd turned to look at the newly christened Ben sitting up in his lifeguard stand, twirling his whistle. Pepper huffed and slid my bag of popcorn across the counter.

"Honestly, aside from his escape plan in the event of a zombie apocalypse, I don't really know the guy."

"Hmm," I'd said, staring but not staring.

"I see the way you and Amelia admire him. I can't say that I blame you. He's attractive if you like that hunky, handsome, mysterious kinda thing."

"Gross, who would want someone like that," I'd laughed.

Pepper had arched his left eyebrow, waiting for me to figure out what he already knew. "Do you want me to introduce you?"

"What? No. Don't be so dramatic I was just, you know, making conversation. Hoping to get a little info to prepare for the zombie apocalypse."

Pepper had straightened up, eyes narrowing at me intently. "The first thing you need to consider is what's in your weapons arsenal."

"Mademoiselle Brolly?"

Lord Westbourne's voice shook the memory free. He was looking at me expectantly, waiting for an answer. "I'm not married, no. Ben is…he's someone I've been hanging out with. He's kind of, I don't know what you'd call it. He's a maybe. An almost." I didn't know how to explain Ben or talk about my life. I didn't have the vocabulary.

Lord Westbourne took in the information, his lips wrinkling at his effort to figure me out. "And Amelia?"

"Amelia Vine is my best friend." It was the truest thing I'd said since arriving to Chateau du Lac. Amelia and I had been friends since the first grade. She was the opposite of me – eternally optimistic and full of life. When we were seven, I'd worried my parents would find out I didn't believe in Santa and Amelia, by choice, continued to believe. When we were eleven, I'd worried I would never grow breasts and Amelia wore a training bra believing it would happen when it would happen. Where I was dark, Amelia was light. When I was stuck, Amelia took my hand and pulled me forward.

I looked up and Lord Westbourne was watching me, waiting.

"Do you know where she is?" he asked, so softly it could have been the shush of the breeze through the Cypress trees. He folded and re-folded his hands in his lap. I knew he couldn't possibly work out where I was from, but he was asking all the right questions. It was almost comforting.

"Yes? It's hard to explain…she isn't the one missing. It's me." I looked up at him, afraid of what he'd say next.

"You are lost."

I breathed out hard through my nose. "Yes. I'm lost."

He thought some more, still folding and unfolding his hands. "Perhaps the question I should ask, Mademoiselle Brolly, is if you are hoping to be found?"

It was weird how right he was, how close to the truth. I knew my predicament had nothing to do with hoping to be found, but the suggestion of it made me sink into myself. If it were as simple as being rescued, I'd climb to the top of the castle tower and wave a white flag until my arms fell off. But no one was coming for me. I had to do it on my own.

I looked out into the garden, not wanting to answer him. I didn't want to explore the terrible possibility that I might be lost forever.

"You never did answer my first question. How old are you?"

He waited another beat, adjusting to the whiplash change in subject. "I am eighteen years old."

It surprised me. "Really? You seem older."

He pulled and straightened the cuffs of his sleeves from underneath his jacket. "You presumed me an old man?"

"No, just older than me. We're practically the same age and you're a Lord and have a castle island getaway. And you're so proper and stiff."

"Stiff?"

"You know," I said, over-exaggerating my posture and attempting to look at him as sternly as he was looking at me.

He leaned back against the bench, the tiniest of curves in his posture, his ill-achieved attempt at relaxing. "Becoming a Lord is an inherited position," he said. "My father was a Lord and when he died, I became Lord. And I am not stiff. I am English."

"Oh, okay, so everyone in England walks around with perfect posture and a constipated expression?"

"Not everyone. There are at least two or three individuals whose backs maintain a constant looseness unbecoming a true citizen of England."

He smiled then, the tiniest close-lipped smile. But it was a smile.

"England sounds awesome."

He sat back up, a hardness returning to his posture and the set of his jaw. "England can be a bit garish, stifling at times and overly rigid. Expectations can twist like a vice, to be sure." A small sliver of emotion pushed through his stoic character.

"And you don't feel the vice here?"

He thought about it, taking his time. "The perplexity of expectations, Mademoiselle Brolly, is that you cannot outrun them by land or by sea."

The moment weighed heavy, too heavy, like he was sharing something he shouldn't.

"I can't imagine. I would freak out."

His face crumpled into a question. "Freak out?"

I smiled and drummed my hands against my thighs. He had no idea who I was or how I came to be in his world. We had absolutely nothing in common on a tangible level, didn't even speak the same language.

"It's an expression. It means...panic. If you're freaked out, you're disillusioned. Incredulous. Frightened."

"Quite the list." He was smiling, almost. "Upon my honor, you are safe here. There is no need to be frightened, or freaked out, as you say." His robotic delivery made me laugh, the first time I'd laughed since opening the black umbrella on my front porch.

"Don't hurt yourself, Lord. You might crack that carefully shellacked exterior."

He stood up and walked over to the fountain. "Is that what you are hoping will happen, for me to crack?"

I hopped off the bench and stood next to him. A few drops of water from the fountain splashed onto my hands and the front of my dress.

"Maybe."

That night, Jane came into my room to help me take off my dress. She was carrying a package wrapped in brown paper.

"I thought you should like to have this, m'lady."

I took the package from her, sure there couldn't be anything in it I wanted. I untied the twine, pulled it open and gasped. Jane reached out for me like I was going to fall.

"These are…where…" I couldn't form a complete thought.

"Yes, well…would you like some tea, m'lady? I could bring it up once we get this dress taken care of." She moved behind me to unbutton the long row of tiny buttons. I hugged the package to my chest, its contents the touchstone I needed. Inside were my clothes, my own clothes, from my own time and my own life. The grey sleep shorts I'd worn since the ninth grade with the frayed hem on the back of the right leg. My soft, navy Central High t-shirt from a 5k fundraiser. It had a hole in the left armpit. They were throw-away clothes, something I threw on after I took a shower the night before I came here. But in that moment, they were the only things that mattered in the world because they meant that it was all real. I was home that morning, on my porch. I time traveled to the 19th century. It was all real.

I unfolded the clothes and remembered I hadn't been

wearing underwear. Of course, on the one night I needed to wear underwear so I'd have a pair when trapped in the past, I hadn't put any on.

Jane finished unbuttoning my dress and picked up the night-gown she'd laid out on the bed.

"I'd like to be alone," I said.

She nodded like she understood and turned to go.

"Wait," I called after her, "thank you for this. So much. Thank you, Jane."

"Of course, m'lady," she said. "And might I say, if you need to talk about anything, anything at all, I have a listening ear."

I didn't know how to respond, but tears stung my eyes. The need to talk to her about what happened to me burned in my throat. But I knew I couldn't tell her. I'd learned on my walk with Lord Westbourne that dancing around the truth was more exhausting than remaining silent. Jane wouldn't understand, couldn't understand.

"I dare say," she said, wiping the tears from my cheeks, "everything shall be as it should. You must be strong and face what is to come, but all will be well."

"How can you know that?"

"I know what I know," she said with a smile. "I have seen some things in my time, things that surprised and terrified me. Those things came to be reconciled as I know you will be."

I grabbed her in a hug, squeezing my arms around her and trying to soak in her assurance. She hugged me back just as tight.

After she left, I pulled off my remaining underclothes and put on my shorts and my t-shirt. They smelled wrong and were stained with mud, but it didn't matter. They were real. I could feel them and touch them and smell them. A fresh pang of sorrow washed over me.

It was real. It was all real.

I crawled into the soft bed and pulled the covers over my head, repeating over and over...

Home.

Home.

Home.

EIGHT

t was mid-afternoon and Jane had me dressed in a pale, yellow dress with delicate panels of lace from the neckline to the floor. I'd started my period in the night which resulted in Jane outfitting me in a cotton belt looking contraption with two metal clips that attached to a massive, diaper-like wad of cloth meant to act as a pad. It was beyond unsettling but what could I do? The nearest Walgreens was two hundred years in the future.

I sat on the window ledge watching the sunlight skip across the bright blue of the water. The ripples of the lake and the curves of the shore were familiar to me by that point, the blue of the lake the same color as the blue rug in my bedroom at home. I'd found it at IKEA and instantly loved it. Amelia called it The Hideous Blue Rug and threatened to throw it away when I wasn't looking. It'd only made me love it more.

After Jane brought me my clothes from home, I'd doubled my time searching for the black umbrella, going out every chance I could to look for it. There was a well-worn path circling the castle, evidence of my relentless searching. I'd been out that morning, circling the island like a vulture circling roadkill. With each day that passed, I knew the odds of finding the umbrella grew smaller and smaller, but I wasn't giving up.

A soft knock at the door. I knew it was Lord Westbourne. Jane never waited for me to invite her in, always barging through the door like an overbearing mother. I liked it.

"Come in," I called, keeping my spot at the window, the sun shining on my face.

Lord Westbourne walked stiffly through the door and waited; his eyes downcast.

"Hey, Lord W. What's up?"

He made a sound in the back of his throat as he peered up at me. I wondered if my little nickname was a bad idea or if he liked it. He'd never tell me either way, that was for sure.

"Good afternoon, Mademoiselle Brolly. I trust that you are well?"

I'd spent the previous night tossing and turning, my mind a constant stream of worry about what my family must be thinking, what Amelia thought happened to me, if Ben thought I was ghosting him. Pepper had probably guessed what happened to me, but even if he told everyone, they'd never believe him. As hard as I was working to adjust to my new timeline, my mind was a constant flood of thoughts of home. But I couldn't tell Lord W about it.

"I'm good, thanks," I said.

"I do not intend to bother you, but I wished to deliver this small gift. My hope is that it will ease some of the pain you have endured in recent days."

From behind his back, he pulled out a delicate white parasol made entirely of lace. It was hyper-feminine and gaudy and nothing at all like the umbrella I lost or anything I would ever use ever. He was beaming.

"Wow, thank you. That's...so thoughtful, really."

"I understand it is not the umbrella you lost in the storm, but perhaps it can serve another purpose? Perhaps another walk in the garden?" He handed it to me, gently, a peace offering. It was feather light. I opened it up and twirled it around. The sunlight cast a lace-patterned design across Lord Westbourne's face.

"I'd like that, thank you."

"Of course," he said, bowing low and slipping out.

A minute later Jane burst through the door. "Did he give it to you? Did m'lord give you the parasol?"

"He did," I said, pulling the parasol closed.

"My, how lovely, m'lady. Such a lovely thought." She was grinning and staring at me like it was my turn to say something.

"It was. He's a nice guy."

"Guy, m'lady?"

I laid the parasol on the desk and looked out the window. "You know what I mean. He's a nice boy, although boy isn't the right descriptor either."

She sniffed and straightened the already straight blankets on the bed. "Lord Westbourne is a generous Lord and a benevolent soul."

I didn't understand her tone. "Yeah, that's basically what I meant when I said he's a nice guy."

Jane muttered something under her breath and left the room. I picked up the parasol and opened it back up, twirling it by the window so the lace pattern danced across the floor. Lord W and Jane were trying to make me comfortable, happy even, which I loved. The parasol was truly a kind gesture. But it wasn't the umbrella I needed.

A thought swept over me like a gust of wind. Maybe it wasn't about what umbrella I used, so long as I opened it outside. Maybe it was about the place I was standing and less about the umbrella itself.

Deciding it was worth a shot, I left my room and made the half-mile trek down to the front doors, shirking away from the hallway paintings and their stone-cold expressions. I went down the cobblestone path to the patch of grass near the shore, where I landed that first night. I closed my eyes and thought back to the morning I traveled through time. I'd been holding the umbrella in my right hand. I had opened the front door with my left hand and stepped onto the porch. I had opened the umbrella with my left hand.

Opening my eyes, I recreated the scene, holding the lacey parasol in my right hand and opening it with my left hand, ready for the explosion. Ready for the wild spin. Ready to go home.

Nothing happened.

I was still in 1826. I was still in France, still lost.

I squinted up at the sun, cursing its brightness. It was a long-shot, thinking the lacey parasol could hurl me through time, but the disappointment still stung. Maybe I needed a storm. I needed thunder and lightning and hard, heavy rain.

The next time it stormed, I'd be ready.

NINE

I went back inside, my yellow dress swishing across the marble floor. I climbed the grand staircase and took a right instead of my usual left. Using the parasol like a walking stick, I walked down the long hallway, taking in more paintings, more oil lamps. All of the doors were closed and I didn't want to assume permission enough to open them. At the end of the hall, I took another right and found myself in a narrow hallway dotted with a few oil lamps and more doors, so many doors. I turned around to go back when a door swung open right as I walked past it.

"Oh! M'lady!" Mary startled when she saw me. "You should not be here!"

"I was just looking around. I think I took a wrong turn."

"Yes, m'lady," she said, motioning for me to follow her down the hall.

"You can call me Brolly."

"Oh, no, m'lady," she said, covering her heart with her hand, "that would not be proper."

"What part of the castle is this, anyway? It looks different than anything else I've seen. Where are all the scowling paintings?"

"These are the servants' quarters, m'lady, and if Phillipe catches you here it will be trouble for both of us." She pointed me back down the stairwell I'd just come up and into another hallway.

"Who's Phillipe?"

Mary looked down the hallway, nervous. "Phillipe is the butler, m'lady, and Head of Staff."

"How many people are on staff? All I ever see are you and Jane."

"There are quite a few more than myself and Jane. We are the only two who speak English, so we are the two who tend to you, m'lady." she said, motioning for me to take a left at the next corner.

I stopped and touched her arm which made her flinch. "Maybe you could give me a tour? Help me learn my way around?"

Her smile was strained. "Of course, m'lady."

We continued down the hall when one of the doors opened and Lord W stepped out.

"M'lord," Mary said, curtsying low and wrenching her arm out of my hand.

"Thank you, Mary," he said, excusing her without saying so. She turned and walked away, my tour suddenly over.

"Good afternoon, Mademoiselle Brolly. What a pleasure to see you again so soon."

"I was just looking around the castle and ran into Mary. She was about to give me a tour."

"Would you permit me to do the honors?" he asked, bowing but keeping his eyes on me.

"Sure, that would be nice."

He led me around the corner to a new hallway. "I know the castle is laid out in a square," I said, "but there are so many levels and side-staircases it's easy to get turned around. Maybe you could draw me a map."

"Perhaps," he said. I couldn't tell if he was serious or not.

I followed Lord W around the castle as he pointed out drawing rooms with small tables and low couches and chairs, bedrooms with massive, curtained beds and ornate seating areas, sitting rooms filled with marble busts of past family members, sitting rooms crowded with floral furniture and sitting rooms crowded with green velvet furniture. Basically, if you needed to sit down, the castle was the perfect place to be. Lord Westbourne's descriptions of each room were museum-employee-level detailed with origins of the artwork and materials used in the woven rugs and the type of wood used for the hand-carved beds, but nothing personal, nothing that told me anything about why he was here all by himself in a huge castle filled with chairs.

I was pretty sure I'd only seen a tiny portion of the numerous rooms when we arrived at the bottom of the spiral staircase that led up to my room. Lord W stopped and turned toward me, looking down at the floor.

"I should like to make a suggestion, if I may," he said, speaking slowly, choosing his words so carefully.

It fascinated me, watching him work out his words in his head before saying them out loud, like he was measuring each word for its weight and significance. No one ever did that. Lord W did that.

"I can sense our way of life at Chateau du Lac is...new to you...and I should like for you to be comfortable here." He looked up at me. His golden hazel eyes searched mine. "You have spent so much time alone."

"I'm fine-"

"I thought you might-"

"I just thought-"

The line of his mouth, always so straight, so unreadable, was turned up into the tiniest hint of a smile.

"What's on your mind?" I asked.

"I should like to invite you to dinner tonight. With me."

His hands fidgeted at his sides.

"Sure, okay."

His eyes widened, like he was surprised I said yes. "Oh. Well. That is wonderful, thank you, Mademoiselle Brolly. Jane will help you dress. Dinner is at seven."

I looked down at my yellow dress with the lace overlay.

"Dress?"

"Yes, dress for dinner." He watched me, waiting for my reaction. "As much as you enjoy defying the rules of propriety-"

"What, because I choose to bathe unassisted and go for walks without a chaperone?"

"A marvel, truly," he said, his posture softening the tiniest bit.

I put my hands on my hips. "And what exactly happens if I don't 'dress' for dinner? The servants run amok? Chaos ensues?" I would have welcomed a little chaos. The constant castle silence was starting to wear on me.

"Chaos aside, Mademoiselle Brolly, would you do me the honor of joining me for dinner? You may wear whatever you like."

It was a date pitch, like he was asking me out, but the sentiment was all wrong, too formal. Too king of the castle. Besides, how could it be a date when all he was doing was asking me to eat dinner at a table instead of in my room. We both lived in the castle. It was only normal we would eat dinner together. That's a thing people would do. Even if one of us had an almost-boyfriend sometime in the far-off future.

"I'll be there," I said.

"Until then." He bowed gracefully and disappeared down the hall.

I climbed up the spiral stairs to my room, tossed the parasol onto the dresser and fell down face first onto the bed. Before I had time to process my conversation with Lord W, Jane came barreling in, arms loaded down with puffy, shiny fabric.

"I knew you would agree to his dinner invitation. I told him there was no need for worry," she said, pushing me aside and laying out several ornate dresses on the bed.

"What do you mean, worry?"

"Never you mind, m'lady. Now, let us pick out a gown for your dinner with Lord Westbourne."

"He said I didn't have to dress up if I didn't want to."

"That," Jane said, pointing to the dress I was wearing, "is a day dress. And these," she fanned her hands out over the dresses lined up on the bed, "are gowns fit for a dinner with a Lord."

I could see how excited she was, her hands clasped together over her breasts, her eyes wide and sparkling at the thought of dressing me up in a proper gown. It made me laugh.

"Okay, okay," I said, holding my hands up in surrender, "how about this. I'll put one of these on but…you have to do my hair, too."

Her mouth popped open in surprise. "May I style it to my own liking?" She was practically jumping up and down.

"You better," I smiled.

"Oh, wonderful," she said, clapping her hands together. "Which gown should you chose to wear, m'lady?"

I jumped up off the bed and took a good look. Each dress was fancier than the first with complicated beading and tiny buttons covered in lace and yards and yards of heavy fabric. I chose the one in the middle, a silk gown of midnight blue with intricate beading across the bodice.

"A lovely choice, m'lady, very lovely."

I sat down at the dressing table next to the bed and shook out the long waves of my hair. Jane smoothed her fingers through it, working out the tangles. "Such beautiful hair. Just like your mother's?"

"Yes…why would you say that?"

"Daughters often favor their mothers, do they not, m'lady?"

"You know, you remind me of her."

Her hands stopped moving and she looked at me in the mirror.

"Do I, m'lady?"

"Sort of, yes. Although you're much louder and much nosier

and invasive." Jane laughed. "But there's something about you that reminds me of her, something in your eyes."

"How lovely," she said, more to herself than to me.

"Jane, how come all of the servants in the castle speak French except for you?"

"And Mary."

"Yes, and Mary. I saw her today. She was helping me and... wait, don't change the subject. Why don't you speak French?"

"Because I am English, of course,"

"Then how did you end up living in France?"

"I am only here while m'lord is here. I travel with him when he goes on his trips. I have been looking after m'lord since he was a baby and I intend to look after him until I am dead and gone."

That was all she had to say on the matter. She worked my long hair into a loose braid down my back and wrapped it into a twist at the nape of my neck. There was a vase of fresh flowers on the dressing table and Jane picked off a few of the blooms, winding them into the braid. She stood behind me with her hands on my shoulders, admiring her work.

"Thank you, Jane, it looks really nice."

"I should not worry, m'lady," she said, leaning down to speak softly into my ear, "he will take care of you. As will I."

I couldn't say why, but I believed her. I knew that as long as I was at the castle, however long that may be, I would be okay.

TEN

"This is your dining room? Seriously?"

Lord W and I were sitting in a room five times the size of my room in the tower. It had an impossibly high ceiling, and the walls were covered in a dark crimson wallpaper featuring an intricate floral design hidden behind dozens of landscape oil paintings of all different sizes. The tall windows were covered in an even darker crimson velvet material that pooled several feet onto the floor. In the middle of the room sat a long, mahogany table with twenty matching high-backed mahogany chairs with crimson seat cushions. Silver candelabras with long, tapered candles lined the center of the table. Against one wall was a matching sideboard as long as the dining room table covered in silver serving dishes. I immediately started looking for Ws.

"You find it too much?"

"I think everything about you is too much," I said, gawking.

"I could…arrange something else?" His voice sounded small, maybe a little wounded.

"Oh, no, this is so nice, really. I'm just not used to this sort of fine dining. If it was up to me, I'd be having pop-tarts at the kitchen counter."

He frowned, thinking. "The family does not go into the kitchens, only the staff. But it is possible Cook prepared tarts for this evening." His eyes were so terribly earnest, so desperate for approval, it threw me. "I thought this room might be more comfortable for you than the main dining room."

"There's a main dining room?" I screeched, blowing any chance I had at acting civilized.

"Yes, Mademoiselle Brolly. This is the breakfast room."

I laughed at the idea, my mouth hanging open. "I guess we're gonna have to continue that castle tour. Sounds like there's a lot more to see."

"That would be lovely," he said.

"Lord W, I mean it, this is incredible. I'm incredibly appreciative. This castle is incredible and you've been so incredibly kind and apparently I've been reduced to a bumbling idiot who can only use the word incredible. I'm a pretty lowkey girl."

"Lowkey?"

God, this guy. I was almost charmed. "Simple, I mean. You don't need to try and impress me, even though, look," I exclaimed, holding up my hands, "I'm wearing gloves!"

"You, Mademoiselle Brolly, are anything but simple. And might I add, you look lovely this evening."

His gaze made me overly aware of my ornate up-do and low-cut gown. Jane had a great time making me presentable, so proud of her work once I had the gown on with the gloves and the hair. I looked awkward and a little bit silly, but Lord Westbourne's approval settled over me like a warm blanket. Not that I was looking for his approval, but it was nice to be admired. "I told Jane I'll never be able to eat wearing these things."

I still had my hands in the air showing Lord Westbourne my gloves when, quiet as a whisper, there was a man in a tuxedo standing at my elbow with a large soup tureen. He looked terrified as he pushed it towards me.

"Should I?" I asked, motioning to the ladle. He nodded yes as

I picked it up, my gloves too slippery on the ladle's polished, ceramic surface.

Lord W served himself from a second tureen and a second tuxedoed man. I took the gloves off, a task which took some time as they were very long and very tight, gripped the ladle to scoop up the soup, and poured it into my bowl.

"Serving dinner in this fashion is called 'a la russe,'" Lord W said, a twinkle in his eyes. "There are those who think it much more proper to serve food in this manner and then away the dishes rather than placing the dishes onto the table."

"Oh, right," I said, laughing, "because it would be far too common to have dishes on the table."

"Yes," he smiled, "and we do strive to be anything but common."

I took a sip of my soup and a low whine climbed up my throat. "Is this," I closed my eyes and moaned, "is this lobster bisque? It is fantastic!"

I'd been eating bread and fruit and cheese in my room since I got there and hadn't realized how much I missed hot food.

One of the tuxedo men came through a door at the far end of the room carrying a silver tray with a glass carafe of wine. It looked just like the one my parents used for special occasions. He poured a glass for Lord W and then moved around to my glass.

"Is that wine?" I asked.

Tuxedo man stopped mid-pour and gawked at me.

"I'm sorry, it's just, is there anything else? Could I have some tea?"

The man straightened up and sneered at me.

Lord W gave him a look. "Phillipe, please accommodate our guest."

So, this was the famous Phillipe, head of staff, the one Mary warned me about. He bowed toward me and then toward Lord Westbourne. "Oui, m'lord."

"Wait, just wait," I said.

Phillipe froze, waiting, judging, while I considered my options. I'd never had wine before. I'd had beer a couple of times – once at Pam Byers' Halloween party and once at Amelia's when we were thirteen and curious. If I was going to try wine, there was no time like the present. I chuckled at my own private joke and smiled at Phillipe.

"Wine would be wonderful, thank you," I said, trying my best to look like I knew what I was talking about.

Phillipe's look of disdain grew worse.

"Phillipe, please pour some wine for Mademoiselle Brolly. Verser le vin, s'il vous plait."

"Oui, m'lord." Phillipe's sneer prickled across my skin.

"Merci," I said, earning a look of surprise from Lord W. "What, I can't speak French?"

I took a sip of the wine. It tasted like thick juice with a bitter aftertaste. I took another sip. my eyes shifting around the room like I was breaking an unwritten rule. Another butler entered the room with a tray holding two large plates covered in shiny, silver domes. He set the tray down onto the sideboard, picked up one of the dishes and set it down in front of me. I looked around for where the soup went as I didn't see anyone take my bowl off the table and I wasn't finished eating it. The butler pulled the silver dome off the plate and a delicious smell wafted into my face. It made my mouth water.

"Duck roast," he said in a heavy French accent, "avec orange glaze."

"Merci. Comment vous appellez-vous??" I asked.

The butler's eyebrows shot up.

"I'm Brolly," I said, holding my hand out. "Je m'appelle Brolly."

The butler looked at Lord W, the silver dome still in his grasp.

Lord W nodded, a slight smile on his lips.

"Oui, m'lady. Je m'appelle Girard, m'lady." He bowed next to me, the top of his head nearly grazing my cheek.

"Nice to meet you, Girard. Merci pour…the soup. And this, too," I said, motioning to my plate.

His face remained shocked as he bowed and backed out of the room.

Lord W took a sip of his wine and smiled a close-lipped smile. "You are quite astonishing, Mademoiselle Brolly. Not only have you bewitched Jane with your charms, you may soon have the entire staff under your spell. I do believe that is the first time Girard has attempted to speak English. Most of the French staff refuse to do so."

I rolled my eyes. "All I did was ask his name and say thank you. Is that so wrong? If I'm going to be here, I might as well make friends, right?"

"Friends," he said, shaking his head and smiling a smile that was growing wider by the minute. It was nice, seeing him smile.

I took a tentative bite of the roast duck, groaning from the exquisite taste.

Lord W eyed me. "Do you like it?"

"It's unreal," I said, taking another bite. "Aren't you going to have some?"

He laughed, an honest to goodness laugh, and picked up his fork.

As I was finishing the duck, Girard and Phillipe came back into the dining room, each carrying a tray holding another plate covered in a shiny, silver dome. Girard served mine, pulling off the silver dome. "L'agneau…lamb…avec les asperges et les pois," he said before bowing and leaving the room.

"Lamb with asparagus and peas," Lord W said. I smiled my thanks. "Next you will tell me there are no peas where you are from?"

He was joking again. I liked it. I liked it a lot. "I hate to disappoint you, but we do have peas."

"Lamb then?"

"No, we have that, too, although I've never eaten it. If you're wondering what I miss, it's music. Well, I miss a lot of things, a million things, but music is a big one."

"Music?"

I never would have described myself as being super into music, but at the castle the silence was magnified. "It's so quiet here. Every step you take echoes off the stone floors and the stone walls. Where I'm from, there's always noise or music or TV…" I paused, my mouth running away from me. Even with his reserved nature, Lord W was so easy to talk to I would forget where I was. Who I was. "Ummm…there's always people talking and shouting and singing. There's always a steady stream of background noise. Here it's just me and my thoughts and the super loud silence."

"I imagine your thoughts should be quite entertaining."

"They can be. But don't you think it's terribly quiet all the time?"

He looked around the room then back at me. "I enjoy the quiet. It's why I came to Chateau du Lac, for the quiet."

"I get that, but don't you need something to fill the empty space? Music is a good space-filler. You should get into music."

Two more courses and a glass and a half of wine later, I was feeling pretty good. "So, seriously, tell me, you've never been in your kitchen?"

"Why should I have occasion to do so?"

"I don't know, you want a snack? It's your house? At my house, the kitchen is the center of everything. It's where everyone hangs out."

"Hangs out," he said, as if repeating the words would make them more sensible.

"It's where we gather. We eat and talk about our day. Although, there's so many rooms in this place you could pick a different hang out spot every day and never run out."

He smiled. "You think me a terrible person."

"No, it's just strange," I said, shrugging my shoulders, "having rooms in your own house you've never been in."

"I must say, Miss Brolly, your forthright way with words is-"

"I'm sorry, sometimes I-"

"I was going to say enchanting." He hesitated again, thinking, looking. It's why he was so easy to talk to, his expression was so open, like he was fascinated by every absurd thing I said. "You, Miss Brolly, are unlike anyone I have ever met."

"Ditto. And what's with calling me Miss Brolly? What happened to Mademoiselle?"

"You are not French. There is no need."

I crossed my arms over my chest and sat a little taller in my chair. "I could be French."

His smile grew wider. "You are, most decidedly and quite maddeningly, not French."

"But I can speak French."

"Yes. Not well, but yes."

"Are you mocking my very educated and expertly practiced pronunciation of the French language? Why, Lord Westbourne, it's like you don't know me at all," I laughed, looking him right in the eyes.

It was difficult to do that, look into his eyes. It made my veins quake and my brain spin, two things I did not need to be doing in 19th century France. It wasn't just his upswept hair and sharp cheekbones and caramel eyes, it was the way he looked back at me with a kind of fascinated reverence, like I was precious. No one had ever looked at me like that, not even Ben.

Phillipe and Girard came back into the room, Phillipe carrying a tray holding a layered chocolate cake. Lord W held his hand up and the two men paused.

"Thank you, Phillipe, but this evening Miss Brolly and I will take dessert...in the kitchen." He held my gaze as he said it. Phillipe gasped and nearly dropped the tray and the cake with it. "Will that be a problem?" Lord W said.

"Non. Non, m'lord," Phillipe said, backing out of the room and pulling Girard with him.

"You're so wild," I whispered, giggling, "defying propriety and going into the kitchen."

"Laugh if you must, but there are certain things a gentleman does not do."

"Oh yeah, what else does a gentleman does not do?"

"Pardon me, Miss Brolly?"

"Whoops," I said, hiding my smile behind my hands. "It's possible I may have had a little too much wine."

"Are you finding it impossible to resist?" His eyes were on me, flirty and dangerous.

"Dessert!" I shouted, avoiding the moment and the feeling. "Even a gentleman can't resist the lure of dessert, right?"

"I suppose even a gentleman can be wooed by cake."

"Well then," I said, standing up, "to the kitchen!"

I wobbled on my feet and Lord W caught me, his hands soft on my un-gloved skin. Maybe it was the wine or maybe it was the human contact, but a warm glow radiated from the center of my body and I couldn't stop smiling.

ELEVEN

"So, listen," I said, on my second cup of tea and feeling more like myself, "It's kind of strange calling you Lord W or Lord Westbourne or whatever it is I'm supposed to call you. What's your first name?"

We were sitting at a small wooden table in the corner of the kitchen drinking tea and eating the most delicious chocolate cake, although kitchen was a generous description. It was a long rectangular room located below the main floor of the castle lined with shelves full of dishes and pans and dry goods and a huge fireplace at the far end with long, iron arms that swung out over the fire to hold pots full of boiling liquids. There was a long, tall table in the middle of the room and a shallow counter behind it with a large water pump pointed into a trough.

"Miss Brolly, referring to a gentleman in such a manner is not-"

"Proper, yes, I know. But look at us! Eating cake! In the kitchen!"

He smiled, a small laugh escaping his throat. "Yes, I do suppose we have broken a few rules this evening."

"That's good, it could be a rule. We only call each other by our improper names in the kitchen."

He pushed his plate to the middle of the table, his left hand covering his mouth and his smile. There was a tiny cursive W etched into the middle of the plate. "Surely you are not suggesting we make a habit of coming to the kitchen?"

"I know, I know, it would mean the end of your life as a gentleman and for that I'm sorry. From here on out it's nothing but lawlessness and debauchery, your rich heritage soiled for all of time." My breath hitched on the last word. "The least you could do is let me call you by your first name."

He sat back, considering my question. "But only in the kitchen?"

"Only in the kitchen."

"I think I could agree to such an arrangement," he whispered, even though we were alone. The staff was gone, nearly scandalized to death when Lord Westbourne entered the kitchen. A short, stout woman eyeballed me while she made us a pot of tea and sliced the cake. She pushed the rest of the kitchen staff out the door, barking orders in rapid French.

"Yes! So, you'll call me Brolly and I'll call you…"

He pursed his lips. "Should I not be allowed to call you by your first name as well? Is Brolly not your family name?"

"Brolly is my first name. My full name is Brolly J. Parker."

Lord Westbourne looked stunned. Then, slowly, a small smile crept across his lips. He placed his hands flat on the table and barked out a great big, hearty laugh. I tried to ignore the fact that his laughter lit up his entire face, that he had a bright, beautiful smile.

"Are you seriously laughing at my name?"

"No, no," he tried to say. His shoulders shook and his eyes teared up as he did his best to maintain composure, failing miserably. It was charming, watching his exterior crack against his will. "These many days you have been scandalized by my calling you Mademoiselle Brolly when," he paused to wipe his eyes, "it has been the wrong name entirely. The proper way to address you would be Mademoiselle Parker, or Miss Parker, as it were."

"Are you kidding?" Now we were both laughing. "What will the staff think when they find out?"

"I will be done for, most certainly," he said, running a hand carelessly through his thick, wavy hair, another crack in his careful veneer. I liked this guy, kitchen guy, all open and bright. I knew I was being let in on a secret.

"Thomas," he said, eyes full of mischief, "my name is Thomas John Westbourne, or Lord Thomas John Westbourne, as it were."

My stomach flipped into a pretzel-twist. "Well, Thomas John Westbourne, Lord of England and France, King of the Lake Castle and Captain of Propriety, in here it's Thomas and Brolly, deal?"

Thomas leaned forward, ran a finger through the icing on the cake and put it in his mouth. I raised my teacup in front of my face to hide my smile. Being in the kitchen with him was disarming, like he'd unlocked a treasure chest and swung wide the lid to reveal all the things he kept carefully hidden away in the light of day.

"Yes, I think I should like that. Perhaps I should be allowed to make a rule as well?"

"You want to make a rule?"

"I would. My rule will be that, here in the kitchen, we have complete honesty."

I quirked an eyebrow, a trait I inherited from my dad. "Have you been lying to me up 'til now?"

"I should hope not. But here, in this most secret of places, we may say the things that shall not be possible otherwise."

I wanted to laugh, the idea sounding like the opening of a fantasy novel, but the look on his face held me. He was trying to say something. I wanted to know what it was.

"Okay," I said.

"Shall we start this evening?"

"Oh, now?"

He blinked slowly, thinking. "I shall propose this. If a topic is presented that causes either of us a level of discomfort, a more suitable topic may be presented."

"A more suitable one."

"Would that be agreeable?"

"Yes, quite, very agreeable, m'lord," I said, mimicking his British-with-a-hint-of-French accent.

He laughed, eyes twinkling. "Are you ready?"

"Oh, like right now? You're going to ask me a total honesty question right now? Hold on."

I began disassembling the intricate braid in my hair. Flower petals landed on my shoulders and the back of my chair as I slowly untangled the braid, shaking out my hair and letting it fall past my shoulders. My intention was to stall, to be more myself and less like a dress-up doll, but half-way through I could sense it looked like an attempt at seduction. The proper English gentleman's mouth was slightly open, lips forming a small round Oh!

"Don't be so scandalized," I giggled. "I just want to feel more like myself before hearing your big, maybe-suitable topic."

Thomas coughed into his hand and looked everywhere but at me.

"There," I said, shaking my hair loose. "I'm ready. Hit me."

"Miss Parker! I could not possibly!" His hand actually raised to his heart in shock. It was so cute, so him, it made my cheeks ache from smiling so wide.

"Sorry, so sorry," I said, raising my own hands in surrender, "it's just an expression. I meant I'm ready for your question. I don't actually want you to hit me."

"No, I should hope not." He gathered himself, straightening his already straight posture and folded his hands together on top of the table. "Tell me about your favorite birthday."

It surprised me. I was expecting him to ask me how I got there or where I lived or why I was so different or why I hadn't gone home already. And what could I say to him, this impossible person from the past? That I got a car for my 16th birthday and someone rear-ended me a day later? That every year on our birthdays Amelia and I made strawberry cupcakes with cream cheese frosting and watched *Mean Girls*? That my mom had one of those tacky birthday plates that said *Birthdays Rock! Celebrate You!* around the rim of the plate and the birthday guy or girl had to eat off the plate for every meal on their special day?

"My favorite birthday," I said, more to myself than to him. "Maybe my 8th birthday? My mom was away at a conference and had to miss my party. Then the day of the party I got terribly sick with a cold and we had to cancel. My dad called all my friends and told them not to come. That night I was lying in bed feeling sorry for myself when my mom walked into my room with a cupcake and a single lit candle. She'd made arrangements to come home early because I was sick."

I didn't hold back, didn't skirt around modern words that wouldn't make any sense to him. It was a sort of test, to see his reaction.

"That sounds lovely," he said. I could tell he meant it.

"That's the kind of mom she was. Is. She's…" I was overcome with memories and the ache of missing her. I didn't know how to talk about Mom in the present but talking about her in the past was also wrong. She wasn't dead, at least not to me, but she wasn't alive either. I couldn't call her or go visit her. She didn't exist in the same time I was existing. The more I thought about it, the more my thoughts spiraled with the impossibility of my situation. My family was alive, but they weren't. I didn't know how to grieve in the right way.

Thomas watched me but I avoided his gaze. Instead, I focused on the grains of wood in the table, the tick-tock of a clock hanging on the wall counting down the moments.

"You must miss your mother." His voice was soft, tender, like he could see my struggle.

"Yes," I said, "very much." I didn't know how to think about her. Was she searching for me? Did she think I was kidnapped or…worse? Thinking about her reaction to me vanishing hollowed me out, like someone had removed a huge chunk of my heart out with an ice cream scoop. I tried remembering the little things, like her goofy smiles and her obsession with every single Bravo show and how she chewed on pencils when she was working on a new story. There were chewed up pencils on every table in the house, in between couch cushions, in coat pockets, kitchen drawers and bathroom cabinets. If she ever committed a crime, the police could collect her DNA from the hundreds of abandoned, chewed-up pencils lying around our house. I thought about telling this to Thomas, telling him about my mother and how she was a brilliant, if not eccentric, writer and how much I looked up to her in every way. But I didn't. I couldn't.

"I must say," Thomas said, interrupting my thoughts, "you do not speak like someone British. And we have established that you are not French. Where did you…what is your ancestry?"

It was a welcome distraction but a terrifying question. I didn't know how to explain anything close to the truth, but we promised to be honest in the kitchen. To be Thomas and Brolly and let our guards down. I took a deep breath. "I'm American."

"I knew it!" he half-shouted, his fist hitting the table in triumph, knocking his fork from his plate. "Jane and I were positive you were American. You must know, she is quite fond of you."

I was grateful he didn't ask anything further about America. I wasn't even close to being knowledgeable enough about America in 1826 to fake my way through. "I'm fond of her, too. You don't mind that I've been monopolizing her time?"

He grinned and looked down at his hands. "Time with you, Brolly, is time well spent."

He'd said my name a hundred times before, but always behind the veil of propriety, always according to the set of rules he insisted on following. But this time, he was talking to me, about me, using my name the way a friend would. He glanced back up and met my eyes, sending a buzzing current through me. I blinked it away and gathered up the dishes and took them to the counter. I wouldn't let myself get carried away. Couldn't.

Thomas took my cue and stood up from the table and picked up his oil lamp. The crackling energy from the kitchen faded as we made our way up to the main level of the castle. He bowed when he said goodnight at the top of the grand staircase, proper Lord Westbourne firmly back in place. But now that I knew him as Thomas, I only wanted to know more.

That night, a storm woke me up from a dead sleep. The heavy curtains were drawn in my room but the lightning flashes still peeked through. I jumped out of bed and threw the curtains open. Heavy rain was pouring down and lightning struck in the distance every few seconds. The lake was in an uproar, the wind whipping it onto the shore in angry splashes.

I grabbed the lacey parasol from the desk next to the window and ran, taking the spiral stairs two at a time and flying through each hallway and stairwell and down the grand staircase to the front door. I didn't take time to think, didn't consider what might happen, what could happen. I didn't think about Thomas or Jane or what they would think when the strange girl who appeared on their shore suddenly disappeared just as quickly. My thoughts were only faces: Mom, Dad, Cale, Amelia, Pepper...Ben.

I threw open the front door and leapt outside. My long nightgown was immediately soaked, but I didn't care. I was going home.

"I'm coming," I shouted as I opened the parasol against the wind, bracing myself for wild spinning, the feeling of being ripped apart.

But nothing happened.

I was still standing in front of the castle, fat rain drops pelting my face, the lacey parasol drooping under the weight of the wind and the water.

TWELVE

The next morning was sunny and beautiful, as if the previous night's storm never happened, but Jane had to know, or at least suspect that I'd been up to something. My wet nightgown was in a heap on the floor when she came in with the breakfast tray. I didn't mention it and neither did she.

For the next few days, I doubled my search, rowing one of the boats out into the lake and scanning the water, taking a fallen, thick branch and smacking into the trees along the shoreline, hoping my umbrella would fall out.

It had been days and days, and I still hadn't found it. I decided to take a temporary break from umbrella hunting, a break from wishing for something that every day seemed less and less likely to happen, and find something else to occupy my time. Without school or a social life, every day bled into the next with no discernible difference. Weekends weren't any different than weekdays. There were no schedules, no demands on my time, no deadlines or events to attend or homework to complete. No college applications to worry over. No social feed to catch up on. No Netflix to marathon. But there were books. Shelves and shelves of books. Lord W's library was Beast-level, one that would make Belle's knees quake. I was pretty sure it had more books in it than Central High's library, which had a write-up on the county-wide website for being the best-stocked library in the state.

I hadn't really spent any time there since that first conversation with Lord W, so I didn't know what kinds of books he had. I pushed open the tall double doors and looked around. The room was shaped sort of like a broken octagon, so there were more than four walls. Each wall held a floor to ceiling bookshelf with a break in the middle, so the room was split into two levels. There was a narrow staircase right next to the double doors that went up to the second level. I climbed the stairs and was scanning one of the shelves when Lord W walked in.

"Hi," I said, holding on to the iron railing and peering down at him. Since our first night in the kitchen, we'd made a habit of meeting there after dinner, after everyone else had gone to bed, talking until we couldn't keep our eyes open any longer. It was fascinating, talking to him, because there were so many things we couldn't talk about. I had no idea what his favorite TV show was or his favorite sport to play as a kid. But I knew he hated going to balls, spring was his favorite season, he hated hard boiled eggs and loved to eat toast as a late-night snack. I'd begged Jane to teach me how to make toast and brew tea by myself, something that totally blew Lord W's mind the first time I did it. I burned my hand on the wire toasting basket and spilled the tea, but I did it.

"Good afternoon, Miss Parker." He was smirking up at me, his arms crossed over his grey waistcoat.

"Is it okay that I'm up here? I was looking for something to read."

"You should know, Miss Parker, that it is considered improper for a lady to climb up to the second level of the library, particularly when there is a gentleman in the room." I shrugged and made no move to get down, which made him chuckle to himself. "But, I believe I am growing accustomed to your aversion to propriety."

"I can come down," I said, and took a step toward the stairs, "if it really bothers you."

"Of course not," he said, picking up a book from his desk and then sitting down on the lumpy couch. "I should be delighted, Miss Parker, for you to do as you like."

I continued my search, stepping carefully across the narrow platform, searching down the rows and rows of books, when something caught my eye I almost couldn't believe.

"Thomas!" I cried. He cleared his throat and looked anxiously around the room. "Lord Westbourne, I mean." I half expected to see Phillipe lurking in a corner, making notes on my inappropriateness. "Anyway, look at this. You have, like, every Jane Austen. First editions!"

It made sense. Austen died in 1817 and I was in 1826, a fact that still sounded ludicrous anytime I thought about it. Mom was a huge Jane Austen fan and spouted facts about her since I was little. I knew everything about Austen, or at least enough about her to know that first editions were incredibly valuable. I pulled *Pride and Prejudice* off the shelf and climbed down the stairs.

"This is one of my mom's favorite books!"

I carefully opened the cloth binding and read the title page. It thrilled me to see something so familiar, something that fit. It was strange, holding such an old book that wasn't old yet.

Thomas eyed the spine. "Have you read Austen's work before?"

"I've seen all the mov...I mean, my mom's read all of them countless times. When I was little, she would read me her favorite passages" I sat down next to Thomas on the couch and turned to the first page. "You've never read them?"

"Miss Parker," he said, gesturing around the room, "there are quite a few volumes in this library I have not yet had the opportunity to read."

"But this," I said, shaking the book in his face, "is amazing. It's about this girl who's really smart and she meets this guy and he's all stiff and untouchable and..." I paused, realizing I was about to describe Lord W himself. "It's a love story. And it's filled with propriety. Properness oozes out of this book. You would love it."

He set his book aside and folded his hands in his lap. "I would be so honored if you would read me a passage."

"Oh, umm. Okay?" I don't know what made me suddenly so nervous, but my heart jumped into my throat. I turned to the first page and read out loud - *It is a truth universally acknowledged, that a single man in possession of a good fortune, must be in want of a wife.*

I shut the book immediately, my cheeks flaming red. In my excitement over the book, I didn't consider how the first line might sound to him.

"Please continue, Miss Parker."

"You know what? I don't think this book...it's not...you'll hate it."

"But only moments ago you were certain I would be captivated."

I climbed back up the stairs. "I was wrong. Besides, how do I know what kind of books you like?"

"Please, Miss Parker, choose another book. I would very much enjoy hearing you read a passage."

I put *Pride and Prejudice* back on the shelf and pulled down a copy of *Emma*. I opened it to read the first few lines and made sure I was in the clear before climbing back down the ladder. I sat next to Thomas, pulled off my shoes and folded my legs up under my skirts.

I read to him the entire afternoon, doing voices for the various characters, and making him laugh. I loved the sound of his laugh - raspy and a tiny bit shy. When he laughed, he didn't seem like a castle Lord, but a guy I might know from my own time. It was weird, reading words from a 19th century classic to a 19th century person. I imagined it was a relief for him to listen to me speak like him, how exasperated I probably made him with my American-ness.

I read until Girard came in to light the candlesticks and stoke the fire as the sun began to sink into the horizon.

"Oh, wow," I said, blinking my tired eyes, "I didn't realize I'd been reading so long. I hope I wasn't keeping you from something?"

"On the contrary, Miss Parker, listening to you read has been an immense pleasure."

A blush crept up my neck. "Thanks, it was fun. And this book is better than watching the...better than I remember."

"Is it very much like your life in America?"

"What? This?" I said, holding up *Emma* and laughing. "No, not at all. Although...maybe? Human nature is the same anywhere you go, I guess. But we aren't so maniacally driven to find a spouse if that's what you're getting at."

He had that look again, like I was a puzzle and he was missing the last, key piece. "Is that not what your family expects of you? To be matched into a proper marriage?"

"It's different. It's not so mandated. Or at least for me it isn't. In my world there's all this pressure on parents for their children to be a particular thing. Like, as a parent, your son or daughter needs to be the most intelligent of all the other kids or the most athletic or the funniest or most talented. Parents need something to brag about, so they push their kids to be something the parent has chosen for them, not necessarily something the kid wants to be."

Thomas laid his head on the back of the couch, a wry smile on his lips. "A very familiar concept, to be sure. Perhaps our families are not so different."

"That's the one thing I love about my parents, they never pushed. They never forced their own agenda onto me or my brother, never expected us to be anything other than who we are. They let us have space to figure ourselves out."

He closed his eyes for so long I thought he'd fallen asleep.

His eyes were still closed when he said, "And have you done so?"

"What, figured myself out?"

He nodded his head and opened his eyes to look at me. There was sorrow in them, but curiosity too.

"Pepper and I always talked about backpacking through Europe after graduation. I said I was going to find myself, whatever that means. But I'm starting to think maybe figuring myself out isn't the point. Maybe life is just a long, slow unravel with tiny revelations along the way." I pulled my hair off my neck and twisted it into a knot. "I guess what I'm saying is, no, I don't have it figured it out. I don't have anything at all figured out. But I'm working on it. What about you?"

"Me?"

"Yes, Lord Westbourne," I said, emphasizing his title and hoping to make him smile, "have you solved the mystery of being alive?"

He stared at me for a long time, long enough for the sun to completely set and the room to grow dark except for the few lit candles. It was indulgent, the way he looked at me. It wasn't creepy or invasive or strange, more like a silent conversation occurring in the space between us. When he finally did speak, his voice was low, just above a whisper.

"I believe, Miss Parker, I am getting closer every day."

THIRTEEN

t was midnight and Thomas and I were in the kitchen. He was sitting at the worn table in the corner while I brewed tea and made toast. If Cook knew I was meddling in her kitchen her head would spin off her body, although there really wasn't any way she didn't know as we always left our dirty dishes behind.

"Phillipe came to speak to me earlier today on behalf of the staff," Thomas said, his voice full of mischief. "They have some...concerns."

I wrapped a towel around the handle of the hot tea kettle and poured the boiling water into the teapot to steep the tea leaves. I used a sharp knife to slice four pieces of bread from a loaf on the counter and placed the slices into the wire toasting cage Jane taught me to use. It looked like the grill basket my dad used to cook fish on camping trips. I latched the wire lid shut. "What concerns?"

I held the toasting cage over the fire, watching it closely so the sides closest to the fire wouldn't burn. The process was imperfect, and I definitely burned more slices than not, but I had to admit it was pretty fun, like I was really making something, not just pushing a button on an appliance and letting it do all the work.

"It appears you have been, how shall I put this, helping too much?"

I turned to look at him over my shoulder. Since that first dinner and scandalous invasion of the kitchen, he'd been much looser around me. Fun. But he immediately assumed Lord status as soon as anyone came into the room, like a steel rod had been activated in the back of his shirt.

"I've been helping too much?"

"Yes," he grinned. I flipped the handle of the toasting cage over to toast the other side of the bread. "You clean things up. You make your own food," he said, gesturing to the wire basket in my hand. "They do not quite know how to handle you."

"What, making toast? Don't make me give up the toast, Thomas."

"The toast is wonderful."

I plopped the hot slices onto a plate, brought them over to the table and together we slathered butter and jam onto each piece. "Let me guess, Cook is the one complaining?" Cook didn't like anyone meddling. I knew this because anytime I went into the kitchen she muttered "facheux" under her breath and wagged her finger in my face. I had to ask Mary what facheux meant. "Or maybe Phillipe? I know he thinks I talk too much at dinner and judges me for not wearing gloves."

Thomas laughed, his hair falling into his eyes. He was wearing a loose, untucked white shirt, not the typical starched stiff-as-a-board shirt he usually wore.

"I like you like this, by the way," I said, "all loose and relaxed, wild hair and wrinkled shirt. It's nice."

He ran a hand through his hair, nervous. "You flatter me."

"And I'm sorry about the trouble with the staff. I'll try to be messier and more demanding. I'll lie about on a chaise and ring a bell when I need my nose wiped. I'm sure Phillipe would love that."

Thomas chuckled under his breath and peered up at me. "That would be most helpful." His expression shifted as he took a bite of toast. "Did you do those things...before you were here?"

We'd been slowly broaching the subject in our moments alone. He asked careful questions and I answered as much as I could without sounding like a girl who traveled from the future.

"We don't have servants if that's what you mean."

"Did you work for another family? I only intend to say, it seems you are accustomed to doing things for yourself. I do not know how it is in America, but I assure you, my sister Elizabeth would never make her own food."

I sat back in my chair with my hand on my chin. It was always a challenge, both for me to explain and for him to understand.

"The idea of servants isn't...we don't have them. No one does. Everyone takes care of their own home, does their own thing."

"If there are no servants, what does the working class do for money?"

His face was so sincere, so confused, it made me want to hug him. "The class system isn't the same. There are people who have more money than other people, but the idea is you're supposed to work hard and strive for greatness on your own, earn your own money, do your own thing."

He was quiet for a moment, his eyes tracing the lines of my face. Thomas's gaze, especially when we were alone in the kitchen, splashed over my skin like warm water, both an intrusion and a comfort. I wanted to hide from it as much as I wanted to dive right in.

"What about your family? Do they earn their own money?"

"My dad runs a Farmer's Market. It's kind of like...a community garden that everyone contributes to and you can go and buy fresh produce and meat, things like that."

"And is that an admirable profession?"

"Yeah, I think so. He's a great guy. And a great cook!"

Thomas's eyebrows shot up. "Your father...cooks?"

"Yes," I said, laughing at the perplexed expression on his face. "The gender lines are all a bit gray."

"I do not understand."

"Professions aren't divided up between men and women, meaning there aren't professions only a man can do. Anyone, man or woman, can do any profession they qualify for. I mean, it's not perfect. There's still huge disparities in places and women and minorities are still fighting for equal pay, but it's definitely better than what you're used to. Some men even opt to stay home with their kids while their wife goes to work."

Thomas took a huge bite of toast, stalling. "What about the nurse?"

"You mean to take care of the kids?" He nodded. "We call them nannies, and no, most people don't have one, at least no one I know. The parents do everything themselves."

He rested his chin in his hand, casual and effortless. It sent a shiver across my shoulders.

"Your community sounds very independent."

"It's a different way of life than here at the castle, that's for sure."

He ate another bite of toast. I could tell he wanted to say something, but the words were stuck in his throat. He drank a sip of tea. Ate another bite of toast. "Is that what you want to do? Work a profession while your husband tends to the children?"

"I've never really thought about it. I guess it would depend on what he wanted and what I wanted and what made the most sense for our family."

He narrowed his eyes. "You would choose for yourself? Your family would not choose for you?"

"I take it you don't get the same choice?"

Thomas frowned, the arches of his eyebrows flattening down into straight lines. "My family name, my position, is of utmost importance. Before he passed my father did his best to instill in me a sense of pride in the Westbourne legacy. It is intended for me to marry well, acquire land, build wealth, all in the Westbourne name. That is my station and my purpose."

He said it so resolutely, so finally, I felt suffocated for him. His whole life was laid out for him before he was even born.

"What if you want something different?" I asked.

"Different?"

"What if you don't want to acquire land or any of those other things? What if you want to do something else?"

He huffed out a sarcastic laugh. "Brolly, I am a Westbourne."

I still wasn't used to hearing him say it. When Thomas said my name, there was a reverence to it, like he was giving me a gift.

"My mother is a writer," I said, bouncing to another topic, forcing myself to stay in the moment.

"And what sort of things does she write?"

"Novels. She's written a series that's done really well. You'd like them, they're all about an English estate and the drama that happens to everyone who lives there."

"Is she not American, like you?"

"Yes, but I think she wishes she was English. When she's really tired, she speaks in an English accent, which always cracked me up as a little kid."

He took a drink of his tea, carefully setting the delicate cup back onto the saucer. "What about you? Do you also work a profession?"

I looked down at my hands and ran my thumbs over each individual fingernail.

"I'm…" I didn't want to tell the truth, that I was still a child in many ways. Even though we were only months apart in age, things for him were different, more grown-up. "I'm still studying."

"What do you study?" His questions were genuine, but they made my skin itch. Every question from Thomas only raised twenty more of my own. Was school happening without me? Had I missed every college application deadline? Had my parents given up searching for me? Was Cale okay? Had I missed Amelia's birthday? Had Ben found a new girlfriend?

"Brolly?"

I shook my head free of heavy thoughts. "Sorry. Sometimes thinking about it all, about everything I used to do and be...it's easy to forget, when I'm here, with you." My stomach dropped at my own confession. "Does that make me a terrible person?"

It did. It made me a terrible person.

"Quite the opposite, I imagine. I believe it shows how much you love your family. Painful memories are sometimes the hardest to remember."

"I feel guilty when I'm happy here. When I'm happy with you." The words tumbled out of my mouth before I could help myself. It was something I'd been thinking about, how easy it was to be with Thomas. I didn't want it to be easy. I wanted it to be awful. When it was easy, when I liked it, I didn't work as hard to get home.

Thomas was quiet, his expression kind. It was disarming and strange and exactly perfect. Most people rushed to offer advice after you spilled your guts, would hurry to patch up the wound and send you on your way. There I was, a broken soul lost in a foreign land, but he never tried to fix me. Somehow, he knew it wasn't what I needed. Instead, he sat with me, eating toast, enjoying the silence and allowing me to just be.

"What about you?" I asked after several minutes. "You still haven't told me what you're doing here, all by yourself, so far from home." He could say the same thing about me. I hoped he wouldn't.

His expression changed, became hard, carefree kitchen Thomas flickering out like an extinguished candle. "After my father died, I needed time away. I came here to...think. Although it is a bit harder now that I have a guest who chatters incessantly and forces midnight toast upon me."

His smile was back, the dark moment gone.

"Why Lord Westbourne," I said with a strong southern drawl while dramatically slinging my forearm across my eyes, "you do know how to make a lady feel special."

"Part of being a gentleman, I suppose."

"Did you have to read a manual for that or does it just come naturally?" I joked, making him blush.

"All due to my meticulous upbringing, I fear. Now, tell me a favorite memory from your childhood," he said, shifting the mood. It was one of his favorite topics, my childhood, and an easy answer.

"Blanket forts."

"Blanket forts?"

"My dad, he would build the most amazing blanket forts for me and my brother when we were little."

"I am afraid I require a bit more explanation."

"On cold or rainy days, when my brother and I couldn't go outside to play, my dad would take all of the bedsheets and blankets in the house into the living room. Then he'd move the furniture around so he could drape the sheets and blankets over chairs and couches, making a fort. He'd lay heavy books on the corners to secure the sheets and blankets to the furniture. When he finished, we'd crawl inside and read books or play games. It was the best."

"A fort, made of sheets and blankets and furniture," he said, his chin resting in the palm of his hand again, his fingers curled around his sharp jawline. Candlelight flickered across his face making him look relaxed and a little bit sexy.

"Yes," I said, heat rising in my cheeks. "It was the best. We could make our own little world inside our fort. It was a fun escape."

Thomas shifted in his chair, his smile sliding from his face.

"Brolly, there is something I have wanted to speak with you about."

"Okay."

"I do not wish to upset you, but, you rarely mention your family or your home unless I inquire after it."

I promised Thomas total honesty in the kitchen, but I didn't know what total honesty meant anymore. "It's hard to talk about."

Thomas's penetrating stare melted away my flimsy façade, threatening to expose everything I was trying so carefully to hide. I wanted to tell him everything, every harsh truth. I wanted to tell him how I walked out my front door and landed on his rocky shore. I wanted to tell him how much I loved my family and my friends but now they were so far away I couldn't even imagine reaching them. The words were pushing against my lips, desperate to be set free.

"I...I don't know how I got here," I said, "and I don't know how to get home. It's difficult to explain. I guess lately I've been choosing not to think about it and just be here. With you."

His expression stayed neutral. "You have mentioned a gentleman named Ben."

The way he said Ben's name was like dynamite going off in the middle of the kitchen, blowing my hair back and charring my face. I liked talking about childhood memories and modern customs but talking about Ben made me want to slide from my chair and curl into a ball under the table. Ben had slipped into stories from home, stories about my friends and my life, but I was still wrestling with how to feel about Ben. I was wild about him over the summer, sure. I thought I would die if he ever spoke to me and then, not only did he speak to me, he kissed me, asked me to be his girlfriend. Now he was a million miles away, lifetimes away, as if I never knew him at all. And Thomas. Thomas was sitting right in front of me but sometimes was the person farthest away. We were so different, from completely different worlds, and yet he made me feel so safe. I didn't understand my feelings for him, but I knew I felt something.

"Ben is...a friend."

I watched him, his chest rising and falling with each breath.

The air in the kitchen was charged with something new and unidentifiable.

"Are you betrothed to him?"

"Betrothed?"

His mouth twisted into a crooked line, like he couldn't express what he wanted to say.

"Have you made a promise to him? Are you to be his wife?"

"No," I blurted. How could I talk about Ben? How could I explain? I didn't even know if I'd ever see him again.

"Do you love him?"

"It's not like that," I said, hyper aware of Thomas and me and everything in the room. My slumped posture across from his gracefulness. The candle flame flickering strange shadows onto the wall. Our tea going cold. "We hung out and he was nice. We had fun together. It was new and unknown. It was a beginning."

I had no idea what I was saying. I had no idea why I was saying it.

"And when you go home? You will be with him?" he asked, his voice cracking under his effort to remain neutral.

I looked everywhere but at him. "Would that bother you?"

He breathed out through his nose, a rush of air that sounded like a door whooshing shut. "I have no reason to be bothered."

"You don't?"

"You are a guest in my home. I am merely curious about your life, nothing more."

I looked down at my hands, afraid my face would give me away. There shouldn't have been a reason for his words to bother me. It was a simple question, one of dozens we'd exchanged. But my rapid heartbeat said otherwise. I asked the question I'd been avoiding since our first walk in the garden.

"You mentioned that you have to marry well. I suppose I get to ask you if you're promised to someone?"

He waited an agonizing amount of time before answering. "I am not."

A strained silence passed between us. It was clear midnight

toast and tea was over. Thomas dropped the subject and gave his polite goodnight at the top of the grand staircase. I wandered back to my room in the tower, changed into my t-shirt and shorts and crawled into bed. It shouldn't have mattered whether Thomas was promised to someone or not. It shouldn't have mattered if I was dating someone in my time or if I would be whenever I got home. It shouldn't have mattered at all.

FOURTEEN

The next morning, I pushed a boat out onto the lake and rowed away from the castle. I needed some distance from Thomas and our conversation. I needed clarity, even though clarity was the last thing available in my time traveling scenario. Since I'd arrived at the castle, every day was filled with strangeness, but last night's conversation was the strangest of all.

I'd been stupid. I'd gotten too comfortable. Too complacent. I fooled myself into thinking I could carve out some version of a 19th century life, like I could freeze time and stay inside this magical land of walks in the garden and late-night conversations with a handsome Lord. But I needed to wake up. I didn't even know him, didn't know anything about him that mattered. Most of our talks revolved around me and my life which either meant I was incredibly self-absorbed or he was unwilling to reveal himself to me. Maybe it was both. Whichever it was, it wasn't worth leaving my entire life behind. I couldn't be this girl, couldn't live this life. I had to find a way home.

I rowed the boat out further and further from the castle, further than I'd been before. It was a warm morning and the sun glistened off the lake. I rowed until my arms burned with exhaustion and then just let the boat float for a while. The castle miniaturized in the distance, a tiny version of itself, the four peaked towers tiny dots on the horizon. A bird looped in lazy circles overhead and I scooted down into the bottom of the boat to rest my chin on the side. I was splashing my hand through the shimmering blue water when I bumped into something and jumped, worried it was a fish or worse, a snake.

I peered over the side of the boat and, unbelievably, saw one of my mom's green flip-flops, floating on top of the water.

I grabbed it and held it up, sure my eyes were playing tricks on me. I'd been out in the boat for a while. Perhaps I had sun poisoning and my hallucination was manifesting as an Old Navy flip-flop. I bent the green foam in my hands and it sprang back into shape. Kicking off my castle shoes and pulling off my thick tights, I slid the flip-flop onto my foot. There was a nick in the plastic from when Mom dropped a steak knife while unloading the dishwasher. We'd all marveled the knife hadn't cut her foot, only the hard plastic between her toes. I scrambled back up onto the bench inside the boat and positioned the oars on either side. If the flip-flop was in the lake, the black umbrella must be too, and I would row every inch of the lake until I found it.

Without a phone or a watch, I had no idea how long I rowed around the lake. The sun was high in the sky when I started and had fallen steadily back down to earth by the time I gave up. My arms were limp noodles and my nose, cheeks and forehead were sunburnt when I pulled the boat up onto the shore. I hadn't found the umbrella or any so-called clarity.

"My goodness, m'lady, where have you been?" Jane said when she found me walking into the castle. She hurried over, assessing my face and the wet ring around the bottom of my dress.

"I went out on the lake. It's a nice day." I had the flip-flop hidden against my thigh inside my tights.

"You look truly done in, m'lady. Let us get you to your room and I shall draw a bath."

I followed her to the top of the tower, hesitating around every corner in case Thomas was standing there. He wasn't.

In the dressing room, I hid Mom's flip-flop underneath a stack of dresses as far back into the wardrobe as I could reach. Jane came in carrying her steaming buckets of water. "M'lord will not be dining this evening, m'lady. Would you prefer to have dinner in your room?"

"He's not having dinner?"

"No, m'lady. Shall I bring a tray?"

So that was it. He wasn't going to hang out with me anymore because he thought I was with Ben. I told myself it was for the best. Told myself it would give me more time to look for the umbrella. Told myself home was what I needed, not some guy in a castle who totally didn't get me. Still, it stung like rejection. I couldn't verbalize what I wanted from Thomas, but it wasn't silence.

At midnight, I snuck down to the kitchen, hoping he'd be there waiting for me, but he never showed.

FIFTEEN

"Wake up, m'lady, quickly, quickly!" Jane pulled off my blankets and tugged on my arms. "You must wake up!"

"Why," I said, yawning and plopping back down on my pillow.

Mary scurried in from the dressing room holding a soft grey dress and am armful of underclothes.

"Lift your arms, m'lady," Jane said, trying to take off my t-shirt.

"Hold on just a minute." I tugged my t-shirt back down and glared at Jane. "What's going on?"

Jane was breathless. "Lady Elizabeth has just arrived. We must make you presentable and quickly. Now up!"

It took a second for my sleep-fogged brain to catch up. "Wait, Lady Elizabeth like the sister Lady Elizabeth?" The look in Jane's eyes said it might as well have been the Wicked Witch of the West. "I didn't know she was coming."

"No one did, m'lady. The kitchen staff is in quite a state." Mary brought over a basin of water and a clean towel. "Lady Elizabeth will be quite displeased if we do not serve her favorites." Jane fussed over the tangles in my hair while Mary wiped down my hands and face.

"So, you're a big fan of Lady Elizabeth?"

Jane and Mary both stopped and looked at each other and then back at me. Mary looked more petrified than usual.

"She will be waiting for you in the drawing room. And she does not like to be kept waiting." Jane meant business. It made the hairs on the back of my neck stand up.

"Which drawing room? There's a zillion just on the east side second floor."

Jane emitted such a huff of exasperation I thought she would faint. "I shall take you there."

I let them finish dressing me. Mary styled my hair into a loose up-do and when they were done, Jane sent Mary away and grabbed me by the shoulders.

"Listen to me, m'lady. Lady Elizabeth is not like Lord West-bourne. You must be extra vigilant. Do not tell her too much about yourself. But be kind."

"What do you mean by don't tell her too much?"

"You do not want to make an enemy of Elizabeth Westbourne."

The desperate look on her face crawled under my skin. I'd never seen her so out of sorts.

"We must go," Jane commanded. I followed her down the long, spiral staircase and through a new maze of hallways. She was walking so fast I could barely keep up, holding up my skirts, my shoes clomping across the thick rugs. We arrived at a drawing room I hadn't been in before. It was sunlight bright and the main wall was covered in a mural of a country picnic scene. Before I could walk in, Jane jumped in front of me and announced my name.

"Good morning, m'lord, m'lady. May I present Miss Parker."

Lady Elizabeth was standing by a window. Her long wavy hair was as dark as Thomas's, but she had a penetrating scowl I'd never seen on his face. Thomas stood to greet me, bowing low at the waist, all our previous familiarity vanished. I wanted to confront him, to ask him where he'd been, why he was avoiding me, but Jane's warning rang in my ears.

"Thank you, Jane," Elizabeth said with a pinched tone. "At last, our fair guest has arrived. I have been so eager to uncover the mystery. Tell me, Miss Parker, do you always sleep the day away when your hosts are waiting?"

"Elizabeth," Thomas said, his voice quiet but his tone sharp.

"Sorry, I was up late," I said, noticing two other women in the room.

Elizabeth looked me up and down, appraising my hair and clothes, probably noticing her own mother's dress.

"Do tell us what would require your attention at so late an hour, locked away in a dusty old castle with my very eligible brother? And you would be well reminded to address me as Lady Westbourne."

"I'm...sorry?" My head ached. I wasn't fully awake and hadn't eaten breakfast and an overgrown mean girl was scolding me for addressing her incorrectly.

"Miss Parker," Thomas said, stiffly offering me his arm and leading me to a small couch covered in a floral pattern, "please excuse my sister. I fear she may be weary from traveling."

"I am not weary, Thomas, I am irritated. It is enough that you are burrowed away in this horrible castle abandoning your responsibilities. Upon receiving a letter from Phillipe about the strange woman you have been entertaining, I left Paris straight away so I could see this mystery person with precise clarity." She walked across the room and sat down next to me on the couch. "Who exactly are you, Miss Parker? Besides an unknown prowler in my mother's dress?"

My cheeks burned at the insult, but Elizabeth wasn't finished with me. She stood up and walked over to the two women seated at a small table across the room.

"What do you suppose, ladies? Have you ever heard of a Miss Parker?"

"I'm American," I interjected, regretting it the instant I said it.

"Oh, American," one of the girls squealed, "I have always wanted to meet an American!"

"I think Americans are vile," the other girl said, her eyes boring into me.

"Tell me Miss Parker," Elizabeth said, her hands folded in front of her, her lips smiling but her eyes calculating, "how did you, an American no one has ever heard of, find yourself here at Chateau du Lac entertaining my brother as he misses a very important ball in London?"

"I do not believe that is any business of yours, Elizabeth," Thomas said. He glanced at me, a quick look of solidarity. I was grateful he was sticking up for me, even though I wasn't sure where we stood.

"It is my house," Elizabeth huffed. "It is my business when I am being taken advantage."

"It is *my* house," he said, standing up and towering over her, "and accordingly I will be the judge of who may or may not," he looked over at her friends, "enter it."

Elizabeth sauntered back over to the window, completely unfazed by Thomas's words. "Honestly, Thomas, you cannot choose to be Lord of the Manor only when it suits you."

"Do not test me, Elizabeth."

"Test you? Is it not you who is testing me and the whole of London society?"

I could see his hands balling up into fists at his sides. "I care nothing for your silly ball or your equally silly friends."

Thomas and Elizabeth glared at each other, neither willing to give in to the other.

"Ladies," Elizabeth said, breaking the silence, "let us see to our rooms. We must do a search to make sure none of my family's belongings are missing." Her eyes cut in my direction as she walked toward the door.

As soon as she left, I collapsed back onto the couch in a heap.

Thomas closed the drawing room doors and walked over and sat next to me.

"Miss Parker, I sincerely apologize. I received a letter only this morning that Elizabeth would be arriving just as she, indeed, arrived."

"I didn't know how to answer her questions. I didn't know what to say."

"It is quite all right, Miss Parker. I will see to Lady Elizabeth. You must not worry."

But that was the thing, I *was* worried. I wanted to ask him if we were okay, where he went yesterday, what this weirdness was between us. I wanted him to tell me what I should do about him. About my being there. About everything. I needed someone to tell me what to do. Instead, I changed the subject.

"I found my shoe."

His forehead scrunched together. "Your shoe?"

"Yesterday when you were...gone," I said, and his eyes shifted from me to the floor, "I went out in one of the boats to look for my umbrella. I didn't find it, but I did find one of the shoes I was wearing when I arrived here. It was floating out in the lake, pretty far from the castle."

He chanced a small glance at me and focused back on the floor. "Was this discovery...helpful for you?"

The tension shifted and buzzed a circle around us, like being tased but politely.

"It's great to have something from home," I said.

He met my eyes and smiled, a real, full smile. "I am happy for you."

It didn't settle things, didn't tell me whether we were okay or not. I needed him to be frank with me, but I knew he never would be. For the moment, I'd have to settle for what he was willing to give.

I couldn't take the tension one more second, so I excused myself and went down to the kitchen to find Jane. The entire kitchen staff was in a frenzy, throwing pots and sloshing sauces and panic. Lots of panic.

"Elle a prevu un diner! Pour ce soir!" Cook screamed. "Je ne peaux pas travailler dans ces conditions!"

"The Lady wants chicken," Jane shouted, barreling through the kitchen carrying five dead chickens by their feet. "Can you believe that? Chicken?"

"Did you meet her, m'lady?" Mary asked, furiously stirring a mixture in a large, ceramic bowl.

"Yeah. It went about as well as Jane predicted. Is she always like that?" I asked, reaching for a freshly iced pastry. Cook walked by and smacked my hand away. "Non. For party."

"Party?"

"Lady Elizabeth requested a dinner party for tonight," Mary said, leaning in close, "and she did not tell m'lord. She has been ordering the staff around all morning."

"Does Thomas...I mean, Lord Westbourne...does he know?"

Mary gave me a disapproving look at my informal use of his name. "M'lord has been informed, yes."

"What's different about a dinner party than a regular dinner?"

"About three courses," Jane barked, rushing past me in a blur. "And yes," she shouted from the cupboard, "you *will* be dressed accordingly. And that means gloves!"

SIXTEEN

I walked down the grand staircase as slowly as possible. Jane wasn't joking when she said I would be dressed appropriately for dinner. She'd trussed me up in a black, silk gown covered in vertical rows of black beading. Black beads draped down from the lace shoulders over the tops of my arms and my hair was twisted into an elaborate up-do. And white gloves, of course, up to my biceps.

"Miss Parker," Lord Westbourne said, staring at me from the bottom of the stairs, "pardon me for saying so but, you are a vision."

My stomach somersaulted like a gymnast at regionals. The glowing smile on his face righted everything that had begun to tilt. "Thank you," I said, reaching the bottom stair and taking his arm. "Can you tell I'm really nervous?"

He looked down at the floor and smiled. "Traditionally, dinner begins with conversation in the drawing room."

"Oh no."

His eyes met mine. "But, I have informed Phillipe to begin dinner precisely at eight."

He led me through the main hall to the opposite side of the

library and into a new set of doors. My mouth fell open when we walked into the room.

Thomas wasn't kidding when he said the dining room was grander than the breakfast room. This room was downright palatial. Instead of reds, the room was draped in stunning dark greens. The walls were covered in a striped wallpaper, every other wide stripe a luminous sheen next to a rich, velvety matte finish. I didn't, couldn't, understand how this room fit inside the castle. Everything was more; the table was longer and there were more windows and more dishes and flowers, hundreds of flowers, many of which I recognized from the garden. I worried I'd go out the next day and the entire garden would be gutted just so Elizabeth could have her dinner party.

I was counting chairs and had only made it to thirty-six when Elizabeth and her friends, whose names I still didn't know, walked in behind us. Elizabeth looked around the breathtaking room and scoffed.

"These flowers are vulgar, and this green is completely out of fashion. Honestly, Thomas, if you are going to hide away out here, at least update the rooms."

"Good evening, Lady Westbourne," I said, extending my hand.

"What," she scowled at Thomas, "am I to do...with that?" She motioned toward my extended hand like it was covered in scales.

"Miss Parker has a different-"

Elizabeth didn't let Thomas finish. "I do not wish to hear about Miss Parker's perverse American mannerisms or be subjected to her endless streams of our mother's old gowns. I wish to eat."

She and her friends pushed past me and went to their places at the far end of the long table. Elizabeth snapped her fingers at Phillipe to pull out her chair.

"You only have three men for dinner," she said, noting the three men seating her and her friends. "There are five guests.

How are three men supposed to handle five guests?" Elizabeth glared at Thomas.

"You arrived this morning, Elizabeth. Chateau du Lac has two butlers and one footman."

"I once attended a dinner party for forty and there were forty men," one of the friends said. "It was exquisite."

Elizabeth had obviously arranged the seating. Thomas was seated at the head of the table and she was to his right with her two friends seated to his left. My seat was placed next to the friends, as far away from everyone as possible and right in front of one of the two fireplaces.

"Phillipe," Thomas said, once he noticed my position, "please move Miss Parker to sit next to Lady Elizabeth."

"Oui, m'lord." Phillipe's smugness was turned up to eleven.

"Phillipe," Elizabeth said, challenging Thomas, "please leave Miss Parker exactly where she is."

Phillipe stood in the middle, a statue in coattails. "Oui, m'lady."

"Elizabeth, it is unacceptable for Miss Parker to sit so far down the table when there is an empty seat next to you."

"What is unacceptable," Elizabeth snarled, "is for someone with no status, no proper name, to be eating at this table at all."

Thomas banged his fist on the table causing everyone, including Elizabeth, to jump. "That will be quite enough."

"I'm fine," I said, trying to soothe the situation. "I can sit here." Sweat beads popped up across my forehead from the crackling fire at my back and the tension in the room.

Phillipe bowed low at the waist and left in a rush. Almost immediately, the three men came back in with three soup tureens. Phillipe served Thomas and Girard, trembling, served Elizabeth. The footman I didn't know served Elizabeth's friends and finally, me. My hand slipped as I attempted to ladle the soup out of the tureen while wearing the shiny, satin gloves. Elizabeth sighed.

"My soup will be cold by the time she is finished."

We sipped our soup in silence, myself and Elizabeth's friends not brave enough to offer small talk and Elizabeth and Thomas engaged in a silent war with their eyes. The second course wasn't any easier. The chicken and peas were easy enough, but it was Elizabeth's questions that made my stomach churn.

"Tell me, Miss Parker, does your family come from money?"

"We have enough, Lady Elizabeth," I said, stabbing some peas onto my fork.

Elizabeth turned her nose up and motioned to one of her friends. "Have you ever seen someone eat peas so barbarically?"

I looked down at my plate to see what I was doing wrong. Was there another way to eat peas?

"Elizabeth," Thomas said, "you will kindly temper your comments toward my guest."

"Can you not see, Thomas, this *girl* is not a guest in your home. She is after your fortune! We do not know who she is, and so far, she has not been able to tell us one honest thing about her life or her family. She is obviously a thief and a liar."

"I believe it is you, dear sister, who is focused on my fortune," he said, taking a bite of his chicken.

"How dare you speak to me in such a manner," she barked, her knife and fork clanging down onto the delicate china. "If only our father were alive to see what has become of you."

"Yes, he would be quite ashamed of the fright his daughter has become."

"That is quite enough," she hissed, standing up so fast her chair fell back with a loud smack onto the stone floor. "Phillipe!"

Phillipe burst through the door, like he was listening from the other side.

"Oui, m'lady."

"The ladies and I will be taking the rest of our dinner in our rooms."

"Oui, m'lady," he said, bowing and backing out of the room.

Elizabeth turned to Thomas, her face pinched with anger. "I will not rest until I discover," she looked over to me and pointed her finger, "who *you* are." She looked back at Thomas. "I will not allow you to be made a fool."

"There is only one fool in this room," Thomas replied, "and she will be taking dinner in her room."

Elizabeth stormed out of the dining room, her friends trailing behind her.

Neither one of us spoke for several moments, the only sound in the room the crackling fire at my back. I stood up and gathered my plate, utensils and wine glass and carried them down to a seat next to Thomas.

"I'm so sorry. I hate that my being here is causing you so much trouble."

His entire countenance softened. "It is not you who is causing the trouble."

"She obviously hates me."

"It is of no consequence to me what my sister deems valuable. Her sights are set on the exact thing she is afraid you will carry away in the dead of night."

"What, your money?"

He nodded, a smile on his lips. And then I was smiling. All the money in the world wouldn't be able to do the one thing I needed to do – go home. We finished our meal and as Girard and Phillipe were clearing the plates, Thomas grinned.

"I was away yesterday, planning something for you. I believe it may ease the pain of Elizabeth's unexpected presence."

My heart banged against my ribs in double-time.

"What is it?" I couldn't imagine what in the world he would plan for me.

Thomas pushed his chair back from the table. "Pardon me for a moment, Miss Parker."

I watched him leave. It took a while for him to cross the vast expanse of the room and I never took my eyes off him. He walked with purpose, almost like a soldier, with precise footsteps and a straight back. He went through the double doors at the far end of the room and returned a few moments later with three men following him. He motioned for them to assemble at the end of the room and it was then I noticed they were holding instruments. A fourth man walked into the room carrying a cello and a lump formed in my throat. Thomas walked back down to his seat next to me and the string quartet arranged themselves into a semi-circle of dining room chairs. And then they began to play.

"Music, Miss Parker."

I tore my eyes away from the musicians and looked at him. He was beaming at me. I'd said I missed music in passing days ago, maybe weeks ago. And he remembered. Not only did he remember, he went out and found musicians and brought them to the castle to play for me. I couldn't stop looking at him, couldn't believe he'd gone to such great lengths. For me.

"Does it please you?" he said.

I looked back over to the players, their arms and hands moving over their instruments in a synchronized rhythm, the haunting music filling the room and the cracks of my heart.

"Yes," I said, tears spilling from my eyes, "yes, it does."

SEVENTEEN

I was sitting by myself in the kitchen when Thomas came in. He'd taken off his dinner jacket and his starched white shirt was wrinkled and open at the collar. Jane had helped me out of my formal gown and into a dressing gown and robe, so eager to know what I thought about the musicians. I couldn't really talk about it, had just smiled so hard my cheeks ached.

"Hi," I said.

"Good evening, Brolly." He set his oil lamp down and slumped into the chair across from me, scrubbing his hands over his face.

"Can I just say one more time how sorry I am that dinner was sort of a disaster?"

He locked eyes with me. "Elizabeth has always believed the world should bow at her feet simply because she is a Westbourne. I supposed I must not judge her too harshly. Pride in being a Westbourne is how we were raised to engage with the world." I smiled at his disheveled hair and resisted the urge to run my fingers through it. "Perhaps my reason for seclusion at Chateau du Lac is no longer a mystery?"

"I totally get it. I would travel through time to get away from her." My hand shook as I poured some tea for us both. What compelled me to say that? Was my subconscious so eager to lay it all out for him, break the magic spell we'd been hiding under since I'd arrived? Thomas didn't seem to notice so I kept talking. "I'm sorry if I made things with Elizabeth even harder than they already were."

"I must apologize for her behavior," he said. "Those terrible things she said…"

"It's okay." I sat down and propped my elbows on the table. "Dinner ended pretty great, though. Tell me, how'd you get the string quartet to the castle?"

"By boat, Miss Parker. You see, a boat is a wooden vessel that floats upon the water and is able to carry things from shore to shore."

"Haha, you're hilarious."

He leaned forward, a mischievous grin on his face. "I shall not reveal all of my secrets."

We sipped tea, stealing glances at each other.

"Elizabeth mentioned a ball. Were you supposed to be there?"

"Yes, Thomas, do tell us what is keeping you from the event of the season?"

Thomas and I jerked our heads up to see Elizabeth standing in the doorway. She was wearing an elaborate dressing gown and robe, much fancier than one I was wearing, carrying an oil lamp, and glaring at us both so hard I swore I could see steam rising from the top of her head.

"Elizabeth," Thomas said, moving to get out of his chair.

"Look at you," she said, walking further into the kitchen, "sitting in the dark, in the *kitchen*. I did not, of course, know where this room was, but I knew there was something amiss and followed the sounds of my beloved brother being taken in. I had guessed things were falling into ruin but had not allowed myself to believe it was this dire."

I sat mutely at the table as Thomas approached her.

"Go back to your room, Elizabeth."

"Why, so you may continue your illicit tryst? Open your eyes, Thomas. Can you not see what this girl is doing to you? Do not forget you are the Lord of Arrington."

I choked on a breath and coughed loudly, earning me a glare from Elizabeth. I didn't care, my mind exploding into a million simultaneous thoughts. Because Elizabeth said Arrington, that Thomas was the Lord of Arrington. As in Arrington Estate, the very same estate my mother wrote an entire series of novels about. The connection wasn't possible. It couldn't be possible.

"I know exactly who I am," Thomas said, his tone menacing.

An evil smile spread across Elizabeth's face. "It has become obvious you do not. The Lord of Arrington would never stoop to," she looked over at me, "this."

Thomas took a step closer to her, standing at his full height. "I will ask you once more to leave this room. In fact, please gather your ladies and leave the castle. It is time for you to go home."

"I will leave when I am ready to leave."

They glared at each other, anger radiating from them both, neither willing to make the first move. My body was covered in goosebumps, the word Arrington spinning in wild loops inside my head. She said he was the Lord of Arrington. It was too much of a coincidence.

Finally, Elizabeth left the kitchen. She took her time, turning slowly and walking out with careful, measured steps. Thomas's shoulders drooped as he walked back over to the table.

"It is quite unbelievable she came down to the kitchen," he said. "She must truly be suspicious of you."

"Thomas, she said you're the Lord of Arrington."

He inhaled deeply and let his breath out slowly. "Yes. In England, I am the Lord of Arrington, a rather large estate, much larger than Chateau du Lac and with many more servants and tenants. It is expected I will continue to grow the estate. Land ownership is valued above all, but societal rank follows closely behind. The formalities can be," he paused, watching me, "enforced in a greater manor. At times those formalities can feel like hands closing around one's throat."

"But, Arrington...that can't be." Even as I sat in a castle kitchen in 1826, it wasn't possible.

"Brolly, what is it that is troubling you?"

I sucked in a breath, unsteady and unsure. "My mother, I told you she's a writer? She writes novels?"

Thomas nodded. "Yes, I remember."

I didn't see a way around it, I was going to have to say it. "The name of her book series...it's Arrington." He didn't say anything, so I kept going. "It's about an estate in England and all of the people who live there, both the servants and the upper class. I've never thought much about it but...that can't be a coincidence can it?"

He traced a line on the table with his index finger, back and forth, back and forth. "It would not be unheard of for an American to be aware of Arrington. It is a fairly known estate."

"But...she's not...she couldn't have known. Unless she read about it in an old history book or maybe it was an old story that was passed down through... maybe she was doing research and found an old record of your estate and..." I was talking to myself, but I could see Thomas's eyes widen. I was splintering, leaking all the secrets I wasn't supposed to share. "Thomas, don't make me say it. I don't want to say it."

Ice scratched through my veins, making my entire body quake. It couldn't be. I couldn't have time traveled to the vacation home of the Lord of the exact same estate my mother made up.

"Brolly, I-"

"Don't say anything, please. I just, I need to think. It doesn't...I can't. I need to...umm...I'm gonna go to bed." As I stood up, I held onto the table to steady my trembling legs. Thomas watched me go without saying another word.

That night, I walked back to my room alone.

The next morning, after breakfast in my room, I went down to the library to find Thomas, prepared for another verbal assault from Elizabeth and her skirted sycophants. I was up most of the night thinking about Arrington and how it might be related to my life in the future, but no answers surfaced. I tried to remember the character's names, but none were Thomas or Jane or Elizabeth. It had to be a coincidence. Any other explanation was too terrifying to entertain.

"Good morning, Lord Westbourne," I said, walking into the library, proud of myself for remembering to address him properly. "Where's Lady Elizabeth?"

He was sitting at his desk re-folding a letter he'd just been reading. "Lady Elizabeth has left the island."

I plopped down onto the velvet couch. "That's a relief."

"She has been visiting relatives in Paris and has chosen to return to them before going back to Arrington to prepare for the ball. After last evening's altercation, we can be sure she will be discussing the matter with every noble family in Paris, probably the whole of France and England."

"How much trouble will that cause for you?"

"It is nothing I cannot manage, Miss Parker." He walked over and sat next to me on the couch. "Did you sleep well? Our parting last night...you did not seem yourself."

"I'm…okay." There was no way to explain it. I needed a redirect. "Actually, I was hoping you would go for a walk with me in the garden."

He smiled, happy that I had moved on from last night's episode. "That would be lovely."

We walked out of the library and over to the slim door that led out to the garden. The morning sun cast a grey shadow from the towers, a charcoal sketch across the stone walls. Thomas walked beside me with his hands folded behind his back.

"Can I ask you something?"

"You may ask me anything, Miss Parker."

"We aren't in the kitchen. Do the same honesty rules apply in the garden?"

His boots crunched on the cobblestones, emphasizing his pause. "I believe they can, certainly."

I worked to keep my tone light. "How is it you're related to the devil incarnate?"

Thomas laughed so hard he stumbled a bit on the stony path. "Straight to the point I see."

"Okay, I'll rephrase. Why is your sister so mean?"

He pulled his bottom lip into his mouth, considering his words before he said them. "For Elizabeth, Arrington is not merely an estate, it is a way of life. Your sudden presence is a threat to her carefully constructed empire. Or at least, that is her perception."

I kicked at some loose pebbles. "Trust me, I got that message loud and clear. But…you don't seem to feel the same way?"

He offered me his arm and we continued walking.

"No, I do not," he said.

"You're not worried I'm just here for your money?"

He looked amused. "Miss Parker, there are a host of things I wish to know about you, some of which I have resigned to never know, but I am certain you are not a thief."

I shook my fist in the air. "Perfect. I've got you right where I want you!"

He paused. "Do you?"

I avoided his question and kept digging. "How did you escape the family snobbery?"

"Snobbery?" He was laughing again. "I suppose it never interested me, impressing a group of people with my wealth or family name."

"But, you're a Lord."

We stopped in front of the fountain. A tiny brown bird was perched on the rim, taking a drink. When it noticed us, it chirped and flew away.

Thomas turned to face me. "Not by choice."

"Okay, so what if you had a choice? What would you do if you could do anything?"

It's something I'd been thinking about, if he weren't a Lord, if he lived in my time and we met, would we be friends? Would we be more?

"I do not understand."

"If you weren't a Lord, if you could make your own choice to do whatever you wanted to do with your life, what would that be?"

"I would never be allowed to make such a choice." He said it quickly, like there wasn't any room for debate.

"But if you were."

He thought about it for several minutes but didn't respond. We started walking again, walked all the way around the garden and back to the slim door leading back into the castle and he still hadn't said anything. We walked through the door and over to the foot of the grand staircase before he finally spoke.

"I shall leave you here, Miss Parker. I look forward to seeing you at dinner this evening."

I watched him walk away, watched him walk to the front door and go outside. I watched him through the window as he walked all the way down to the shore.

I met Thomas in the breakfast room for dinner. He was polite, offering all the appropriate cordialness that dinner required. When Phillipe and Girard left the room after delivering the second course, he set his wine glass down on the table and fixed his eyes on me. His expression was different. Determined.

"I should like to apologize to you, Miss Parker, for the way I behaved on our walk today."

"You don't need to-"

He held his hand up. "No, I do. The reason for my behavior is that your question so thoroughly vexed me I had great difficulty devising an answer."

I didn't say anything, waited for him to go on.

"For the whole of my life I have been expected to perform my duties as they have been laid out before me. It was never a question of want, but duty. The truth is, Miss Parker, no one has ever asked me what I want. Who…I want."

He paused and looked away. His concentrated expression pushed his eyebrows together creating a crease above his nose.

"So, what, and who, do you want?"

His jaw tightened and the muscles in his face twitched. "If I could…that is to say, if I should be allowed…I should like to make my own choice. For my future."

"What's stopping you? If that's something you want to do, you should do it."

His head swiveled from side to side. "Miss Parker, it is not that simple."

He was looking down at his hands, his plate, the table, anywhere but at me. I gave him some time to think before I said anything. "Maybe it is."

His eyes searched mine, a new question in them. We didn't say a word for the rest of the dinner.

EIGHTEEN

R ain streamed down the windows, a curtain of grey
draped over the castle walls. It wasn't the same rain as
the day I traveled. This rain was soft, nap-inducing,
without any of the fire needed to push me through time.

I went down to the library expecting to see Thomas, but he
wasn't there. I walked to his desk and sat down, smiling at the
haphazardness. There were two oil lamps lit, his jar of ink was
left open and there were several quills on top of open letters and
various documents. The letter on top caught my eye and I read it
before I could help myself.

Thomas,

It is with measured pleasure that I write to you regarding my
recent meeting with the Lord Chancellor. I have informed him of
your deviant behavior and harboring of an unknown. This girl,
an American for God's sake, you seem intent on keeping has no
proper family, no title, and no right to your fortune. The fact that
you cannot see this has forced my hand.

I looked around the library to make sure I was alone. My

cheeks burned at the accusations written in Elizabeth's swoopy handwriting.

> I have also divulged your utter lack of will to perform the duties you have inherited. It is astonishing to me that I have been put in this position by my own brother, but I am willing to bear this burden. The Lord Chancellor agrees with me that your current wanderings are not those of a noble Lord, nor of a member of the Westbourne family. You would do well to remember our father's good standing with the Lord Chancellor.
>
> I do not yet know what actions will be warranted in this dire situation, but I assure you, they will be swift.
>
> Your sister,
>
> Lady Elizabeth of Arrington

The letter shook in my hands. I'd never considered Thomas could lose his title, his fortune, because of me. I left the letter on the desk and ran out of the library to find him. I crossed the great hall and looked in the main dining room, the first-floor drawing room, the sitting room, but he wasn't there. I rounded the corner to run up the grand staircase and hurried to the servant's quarters where I ran smack into Jane carrying an armful of bedding.

"My goodness, m'lady. You startled me out of my wits."

"I need to find Thomas. Do you know where he is?"

Jane shifted her eyes left and right, making sure we were alone, and gave me a stern look before pulling me close. "What is the matter, m'lady. Has something happened?"

"Please, I need to find him right now."

"I have not seen him this morning."

I ran back downstairs and across the marble entry to the library before Jane had time to say anything else or ask me any more questions. Something caught my eye in the long, narrow window behind the desk. It was Thomas, out on the lake, rowing a boat in the pouring rain. He rowed past so fast I barely caught a glimpse of him before he was hidden by the trees.

I slumped down into his desk chair and waited, raindrops streaking down the tall window. I picked up Elizabeth's letter and read through it again, absorbing each attack. I had to fix this. I had to repair the rift I'd caused in Thomas's relationship with his sister. A few minutes after Thomas rowed past the window, I watched him go by again. He was rowing with all his might, head down, the tiny boat flying through the water. He was probably thinking about how he was going to kick me out. Send me packing. I wouldn't have blamed him for doing so, but I had no idea what I would do. Where I would go.

Worrying over these questions, I watched him row by again, head down, arms flexed, chest heaving. He made it around one more time before turning the boat back toward the castle. I ran to the front doors and threw them open, waiting for him to walk up the path.

He was ten yards from the castle when he saw me. His harsh posture immediately softened, like a whole-body exhale. My nerves remained frayed. He tromped up the drive and through the open doors, his white shirt, maroon jacket and navy pants completely soaked through. His wet, dripping hair had fallen into his eyes and his boots trailed water and mud across the marble floor.

"Good afternoon, Miss Parker."

My hands twisted into my skirts. "Nice day for a boat ride?"

He held his hands at his sides, narrow streams of water running off the tips of his fingers. "I...yes, I needed to...think."

Trying to find the right way to say it, I went with blurting it out. "Thomas, I saw the letter from Elizabeth. I read it. I'm sorry, I know I shouldn't have read your stuff but-"

He raised his hand, motioning for me to stop. "I wish you had not seen that dreadful letter."

"I was looking for you. I didn't mean to read it, but I was sitting at your desk and it was open and I couldn't help-"

"It is of no consequence to me that you read the letter. I only wish to keep your worries free from such trivial refuse."

"But the things she said. You could lose your title? Because of me?"

He shook his head. "Of course not, my title is an inherited position. Elizabeth is making an attempt, a failure of an attempt, to control my actions. She believes she can frighten me into behaving as she sees fit."

"What about her conversation with the Lord Chancellor?"

"Very likely a lie. The Lord Chancellor would never take a private meeting with Elizabeth regarding such gossip."

I sagged with relief. "I was worried you'd have to kick me out for starting a war with your sister."

Thomas put his hands on his hips. "Kick you out?"

Phillipe appeared with a towel, cut his eyes at me, and retreated to another part of the castle. Thomas dabbed his face dry, waiting for my response.

"I thought maybe you'd ask me to leave the castle. It's obvious my being here isn't great for you."

He moved the towel away from his face. "Miss Parker, did I not make it clear that you may remain a guest here as long as you need?"

"You did but I-"

"I am not interested in going back on my word. I am also not interested in the vulgarities my sister insists on hurling in my direction. You are my guest. You have nothing to fear."

"Okay, but-"

"Miss Parker, if you do not mind, I should like to address my current lack of dry clothing."

"Oh, right. Okay. Good. You should do that." Words spilled out of me like an overturned tea kettle. "I'll see you later? For dinner?"

He bowed low at the waist and left me alone in the entryway, rain pooling on the marble floor inside the open front doors.

NINETEEN

arly that evening, before dinner, I was in the library looking for a book to read and wondering where Thomas was when Jane delivered a note written in Thomas's elegant, slanted handwriting.

Miss Parker,
    Do pardon my sudden absence. I have been called away on an urgent business matter. Jane will see to it that you are properly cared for. I shall hope to return soon.
    Lord Westbourne of Arrington

"Probably cleaning up whatever mess Lady Elizabeth created here in France, m'lady," Jane said, reading over my shoulder.

"He didn't say goodbye," I said, reading the letter again.

"Men like Lord Westbourne do not linger over sentimentalities."

I turned around and looked at her, the letter clutched between my hands. "I think I made things hard for him, with his sister."

She pursed her lips. "If Lord Westbourne has business to reconcile with his sister, that is none of our concern."

But she didn't know the Lord Westbourne I knew. She didn't see him in the kitchen late at night when he let his guard down and laughed without reservation. She didn't see him shed his Lord status and become Thomas, my friend. The guy who listened to my childhood stories and ate my burned toast and made me laugh with his adorable, shy properness.

Without him, I filled my days following Jane and Mary around the castle, pacing the shoreline and scanning the lake for my lost umbrella, reading books from the library, meddling in the kitchen and driving Cook up the wall. She shouted at me in French, her full cheeks flaming bright red. I could only pick up a few words here and there and the ones I did pick up were not exactly complimentary. I kept asking her to teach me new things to cook and she kept refusing.

"I think she likes you, m'lady," Jane said, offering me a plate of warm cookies. "Cook never makes these cookies in the middle of the day."

"My best friend, Amelia, would love her, would totally convince her to divulge all her culinary knowledge. Amelia can be very persuasive. And she makes strawberry cupcakes from scratch even Cook would admit are perfect."

"Pardon me, m'lady, but how do you mean 'from scratch?'"

Her question made me giggle. "Basically, it's the way you guys cook."

"Are there many things that are similar between the castle and your home?"

I took a bite of a cookie and smiled to myself. "No. Not one single thing."

Jane poured me a cup of tea and set the cup and saucer in front of me on the table. "Your friend sounds lovely. I should like to meet her."

"I wish. Castle life would be exponentially more fun if Amelia were here. And my friend Pepper. And my family. You would love all of them."

"What a lovely thought, m'lady. I do believe I would, most certainly."

I followed her out of the kitchen and up to a drawing room where she checked the fire and straightened cushions that didn't need straightening.

"It's so quiet around here," I said, running my hand along the back of an upholstered wingback chair.

Jane turned to face me, a knowing smile on her lips. "He shall return. You must not worry."

"Oh, I didn't mean him," I said.

"Either way, he will be back before you know it."

She wasn't wrong. I did miss Thomas. I missed our walks in the garden and reading in the library. I missed his ridiculous posture and his kindness with Jane. I missed our talks in the kitchen. I missed his careful way with me, his gentleness. I missed his laugh. It wasn't until he was gone that I realized how much time we'd been spending together and how empty the castle was without him.

I was asleep when Jane burst into my room carrying a candlestick, her hair out of its bun and falling around her face in wild strands.

"M'lord is back, m'lady."

"He's back?" I said, trying to wake up.

"Yes, he is back." She was staring at me, grinning.

"Okay?"

"Perhaps," she said, raising her eyebrows at me, "you might be needed in the kitchen?"

"Oh. OH! Thank you, Jane." I pulled on my robe and grabbed an oil lamp. I could hear Jane snickering as I hurried down the spiral stairs.

Thomas was already sitting at the small wooden table when I got to the kitchen. He looked tired, but he smiled as I sat down.

"Good evening, Brolly. I do hope I did not wake you."

"No, no, I was awake. It's so good to see you. Where've you been?"

"I have been about my Lordly business."

I laughed in spite of myself. "What does that even mean?"

He scratched through the stubble on his cheeks, something I hadn't seen on him before. Normally he was so carefully pressed and clean-shaven, put together in a way I never was. "I fear the details may bore you back to sleep." When he took his hand away, there were black streaks on his face.

"You have some...ink...just there." I pointed to his cheek and blushed.

"Where?" He brushed his cheek again, smearing the black ink further.

"That made it worse," I laughed. He scrubbed his cheek with the back of his hand, wiping away the black ink but not the color in his cheeks or the shy glance in my direction.

"There," I said, "you got it. Should I make us some tea? You can tell me all about what's been keeping you so busy." I moved to stand up.

"Brolly," he said, clearing his throat and sitting up straighter, "my time here at Chateau du Lac has come to a close. I must return to England."

I sat back down, the finality of his words clanging through the room like a rung bell. He was leaving? *Leaving?* The stone walls of the kitchen crumpled and sagged, our sacred space closing in on me.

"When?"

"Tomorrow."

I scanned his face, but it was unreadable, almost as if he was looking through me. No hint of an emotion, good or bad. "Tomorrow? But you just got back and I...why do you have to leave?"

"There is some urgent business I must attend to. I have been putting it off and I am afraid I must not tarry any longer."

"Tomorrow," I said, closing my eyes so I didn't have to see the non-look on his face, the cold disinterest.

"I will ask Jane to stay. She will stay with you, Brolly, until..."

I opened my mouth to speak, but what could I say? I couldn't ask him to stay, couldn't tell him thanks for the good times, I'll see myself out. I had nowhere to go. Nowhere to be. I was no one.

"Is this about Elizabeth?"

I chanced a look at him, watched him work out his thought before he said it. "No, it is not."

"Are you...will you come back?"

He looked at me for a long time. There was a second of recognition in his eyes, a hint of the Thomas I'd come to know, but it vanished just as quickly. The flame from the oil lamp flickered and danced. The clock tick-tock'd on the wall, keeping time with my heartbeat pulsing in my ears.

"No. I will not be returning."

TWENTY

The reality of Thomas leaving more than refocused my efforts. I had to leave the island. I was out of time.

The umbrella was lost, that much was certain. And if I couldn't find the umbrella, I needed to come up with a suitable alternative that could take me home. I scrounged through the castle to find what I needed, visiting empty rooms when no one was looking, pawing through the kitchen after hours, raiding the gardener's supply shed. It took a few days, but eventually I gathered everything I would need: a broom handle, a pair of scissors, needle and thread from Jane's room, a black dress from the armoire, some wire from the gardener, a corkscrew and a sharp knife from the kitchen. If I couldn't find my umbrella, I was going to make one. The only missing ingredient was a YouTube video to explain how to put all the pieces together.

I spent the entire night working on the umbrella. I shaved the broom handle down to a thin pole with the knife and pushed it through the corkscrew to create the mechanism to push it open. I cut triangular pieces of fabric from the dress and sewed them together with long pieces of wire in between. I used more wire to connect to the corkscrew so that, when pushed up and down, it would open like a real umbrella. The end result was disastrous. The wiring wouldn't hold the fabric up and out and the corkscrew kept getting snagged on the makeshift pole. It looked nothing like my umbrella, more like a kindergartner's drawing of an umbrella that had gone through a meat grinder. The third time I tried to open it, the entire thing fell apart in my hands.

Jane came into my room the next morning and found me on the floor, crying, surrounded by the broken pieces.

"What is this, m'lady? What has happened?"

I couldn't tell her, the tears coming too hot and too fast. She helped me into bed where I fell instantly asleep. When I woke up, my broken, homemade umbrella was gone.

"The time has come, m'lady, to move you to a proper room."

I was sitting by the window in my room at the top of the castle, staring out at the lake. With no wind, the water was flat as glass.

"I like this room."

"I am aware, m'lady, but it is quite a bit out of the way. We put you in this tower when you first arrived because, well, we did not know who you were at the time and this room kept you away from prying eyes. Would you not enjoy moving to a more proper room? There is a lovely room on the second floor that overlooks the garden."

My eyes itched and burned like they were filled with tiny, sharp pebbles. I hadn't been sleeping.

"No, I want to stay here."

"It is a lovely day. Perhaps a walk?" Jane suggested, clearing the untouched afternoon tea tray.

"No, thank you."

"Fresh air might cheer your spirits, m'lady."

I buried my nose in the book I'd been holding, actual reading requiring too much effort.

She set the tray down and leaned in close, smoothing her hand over my hair. "You should not worry so much, m'lady. If I know m'lord, and I have known him since he was a tiny babe crying in my arms, he will be back."

I didn't want to talk about it, didn't want to listen to any of Jane's excuses for him. He'd left the castle, left me.

"He said he wasn't coming back," I mumbled from behind my book.

"Men say many things they believe to be true when they say them."

I wasn't even sure I wanted him to come back. Yes, we'd become close. I loved hanging out with him and yes, if I was honest, I was highly attracted to him. He was Disney-prince-hot. But it could never be more than that. He was a Lord. He was from the 19ᵗʰ century. He was...him. And I was me. I closed the book and stood up, stretching my arms over my head.

"You're right. I should walk. But only if you'll come with me." Aside from Thomas, Jane was the closest thing I had to a friend at the castle.

"Oh no, m'lady, I could not possibly."

"Please, walk with me."

She eyed my sad face, my bloodshot eyes and gave in. "All right, m'lady, but do not tell Phillipe. He already has no use for the English."

We made our way down to the grand staircase and out the front door. I inhaled deeply, breathing in the fresh air. It was just one of the differences between this time and mine, the air. At home, the air smelled like wet pavement and chemical fertilizer and garbage cans full of leftovers and sour milk. Castle air was fresh and open, untainted. I could smell the lake and the trees and flowers from the castle garden.

"Do you come to the island a lot," I asked Jane as we walked toward the water's edge, "with Lord Westbourne?"

"I do not care for it much, m'lady. I would prefer to stay in England."

"Are you kidding? I know people who would kill to visit a place like this."

She smiled a close-lipped smile. "Yes, well, I prefer the estate in England."

"But...you stayed here. With me."

"I did, yes."

"What about Lord Westbourne?"

"I have a job to do here, taking care of you."

I stopped walking and turned to look at her, a pang of guilt washing over me. All this time, after everything she'd done for me, I'd completely taken her for granted.

"I've never asked, are you married? Do you have any children?"

"No, m'lady, I never married, never had any children." A sadness passed over her face. "Although I imagine if I had a daughter, she would be much like you."

"Like me?" We reached the shore and a small breeze was blowing, pushing the water up onto the stones.

"Yes, very much. I imagine she would have your eyes and your spirit."

I sat down and stripped off my heavy shoes and tights to dip my feet in the cool water.

"Jane, you should put your feet in."

"No, thank you, m'lady," she said, perched on a large piece of driftwood, "sitting here and enjoying your company is exactly what my soul needs."

I splashed my feet in the water, stepping carefully on the slippery stones.

"Tell me more about England. Is it so different than being here?"

"Oh, yes, it is very different. He is different, too, if that is the question you intend to ask."

It wasn't, but once she said it, I needed to know the answer. "Different how?"

She looked out across the water, a faraway look in her eye. "Things are quiet here."

"He said that, too."

She smiled a knowing smile. "Yes, I imagine he would, m'lady."

I needed to know what Jane was getting at but was afraid to push for more. She liked to share information, but never enough, never more than an idea.

"You said you think he'll come back. But if that's true, why did he say he wouldn't?"

"I know what he said and I know what I know. He will be back."

I walked further into the lake, pulling my dress up to keep it out of the water. "I know he doesn't owe me anything. I'm a stranger, but...why do you think he left? I thought...I don't know what I thought."

I thought he cared, at least as much as I did.

"Sometimes," Jane said, "to see something clearly you need to back away until you cannot see it at all." I knew she was talking about Thomas, but she could have easily been talking about me, too. "Now, I must get back to work before Phillipe notices I am gone." I stepped onto the dry stones, out of the water, to go with her. "No, no, m'lady. You stay here and gather up the sunshine."

"Jane," I said, stopping her as she began to walk up the path. "Thank you. For everything. You've been so kind to me and I've been so," I gestured over myself, like it was obvious to anyone who could see me what a mess I was.

"To me you are a treasure, m'lady. It is a joy for me to serve you."

I could hear her humming as she walked away, her words ringing in my ears.

I stepped back into the lake, the cool water reminding me of summer and the rec center pool. The first time Amelia and I saw Ben in his red swim shorts, sauntering across the concrete and climbing into the lifeguard stand. We'd been lying on patio chairs and Amelia had kicked me hard in the shin.

"Look. At. That," she'd said, lowering her sunglasses and staring without a hint of subtlety.

It was all so uncomplicated, so carefree. We'd giggled about the cute lifeguard and shared sandwich bags of goldfish crackers and planned what to wear on the first day of senior year. I knew who I was and where I was going. Life made sense. None of it mattered now because it was all so very long ago. I'd been at the castle for weeks and weeks with no sign of going home. I hadn't found the umbrella. Thomas was gone. I was adrift in a foreign land, a foreign time, with no idea what was going to happen to me. I needed to escape, not just physically, but mentally. I needed to empty my head of all its questions and worries. I needed to float.

Looking back toward the castle, I made a quick decision. I threw my arms over my head and unbuttoned all the buttons I could reach on my dress, twisting and shimmying until I was able to pull it over my head. I looked around and no one was in sight, just the swaying trees and endless water. Pulling off my multi-layered underclothes, I waded into the cool water. It was cold, too cold, but I wanted it. I wanted to be numb.

I swam out from the shore and turned to look up at the castle. It looked like something from my French Lit textbook. Maybe it was.

I closed my eyes and lay back in the water, swishing my arms back and forth at a lazy pace. It was the most in-my-skin I'd been since arriving at the castle, the water cradling my body as I floated further and further out. I wanted to shut out the world and let the water seep into my skin, wash me clean of my new reality. I wanted to open my eyes and be home, shaking off the dream of another time and place.

I tried to focus on Ben, on the short time we had together, the kisses we'd shared, the look on his face when he'd asked me to be his girlfriend. Ben was good, pure, easy. Uncomplicated in a way Thomas would never be. But no matter how hard I tried to focus on Ben, my thoughts kept drifting back to Thomas.

Thomas was the opposite of Ben. Thomas was closed off and uber-complicated and impossible. He was formal and tight. A held breath. He'd never kiss me goodnight on my front porch or hold my hand while watching Marty and Doc talk about gigawatts. Thomas wasn't real, at least not in a way that mattered.

I moved my arm back to pull myself through the water, to continue my drift away, but instead of water my hand smacked into something solid. I flung my body around as the large object crashed into me and pushed me under. I shoved myself away from it and came up for air to see a small boat, now overturned, and someone flailing in the water. I screamed, my arms thrashing, choking on the splashing of the water and the surprise of being crashed into when I heard a voice. His voice. I spun around to see Thomas, red-faced, eyes as wide as the teacup saucers we used to drink our endless cups of tea. Water droplets clung to his clavicle, dripped from his chin and earlobes, the tip of his nose.

"I…what are you…" I tried to speak but couldn't.

"Miss Parker," he squeaked out, "forgive me…I am… humiliated…I did not know you were here."

"Obviously," I sputtered.

We stared at each other, treading water to keep ourselves afloat. Thomas specifically stared right above my head, hard staring, like any sudden glance below my eyebrows would cause an impropriety so outrageous he would burst into flames.

I was staring everywhere. His soaked white shirt, now transparent. The slope of his shoulders. The definition of his biceps. His chest. All I could do was look.

"I must confess, I do not know what to do," he said, the movement of the water tossing us both back and forth.

"I thought you left."

I had one arm wrapped around my breasts while weakly treading water with my other arm. I shivered, but not from the cool temperature of the lake.

"Miss Parker, I am profoundly embarrassed. If you will give me a moment, I shall right the boat and allow you some privacy."

"Okay," I said, cheeks flaming so hot I was surprised there wasn't steam rising from the water.

He struggled to flip the small boat, the muscles in his back stretching and pulling. Once right, he pulled himself up and into the boat. His tan pants were just as wet and revealing as his shirt. I tried my best not to stare, failing spectacularly.

He was back.

He came back and suddenly I knew exactly how much I cared that he did.

TWENTY-ONE

I ate dinner in my room, making an excuse to Jane that I was tired. After Thomas rowed away, I swam back to the shore, pulled on my dress and sat on the rocks until it was safe to return to my room. I was terrified to face Thomas. My entire time at the castle he'd been Thomas John Westbourne, super stiff Lord of the manor. A friend. A helper. Someone to talk to. Any other feelings I'd pushed aside, buried deep within my heart, unable to give them permission to exist. But in the lake, when Thomas was floating in front of me with that wide-eyed look of terror, he was…something else. I could no longer ignore what my heart already knew. Couldn't act on it, clearly, but at least I was being truthful with myself.

After the scurrying of the house quieted down and I was sure everyone was asleep, I made my way down to the kitchen half-hoping he wouldn't be there and half-hoping he'd sweep me into his arms and declare his undying love for me. I'd gotten used to walking through the castle in the dark, a well-worn path from my room in the tower down to the kitchen using only a small oil lamp to light my way, but this time the air was charged with something new. Every step I took was one step closer to him. I'd never been nervous to see him before, but the entire way to the kitchen I worried about my hair, my face, my dressing gown.

When I got to the kitchen, he was already there, sitting in shadow, one candle lit in the middle of the table.

"Hi," I said, setting my oil lamp down. The light from the flame brought his face into view and my breath caught in my throat. His golden eyes sparkled in the lamp light and the collar of his shirt hung open making the column of his neck visible and...tempting. He had the beginnings of stubble on his cheeks and chin.

"Good evening, Brolly," he said, not looking at me.

I tried to steady my breathing so I wouldn't give myself away. "Toast and tea?"

"That would be lovely."

I was glad to have something to do with my hands. I set about slicing the bread and loading the wire basket, setting the kettle on to boil, moving around the kitchen in a practiced rhythm. We didn't talk, both of us unsure what to say. I set two small plates down onto the table, gathered the butter and jam, found a butter knife. When the tea was ready, I poured us both a cup in the delicate china teacups with a W etched on the side.

"So," I said, unable to hide the tremor in my voice, "you came back."

"Brolly, I deeply regret what happened today. Had I known you were there I would never have...it was not my intention to..."

This was what he was worried about? "Thomas, it's okay. It was an accident. Nothing happened."

His eyes were on the table, mouth set in a straight line. I wondered if he knew, could see it on my face, hear it in my voice. The newfound realization of my feelings for him was radiating from every pore, screaming that I cared for him, deeply. Perhaps that's why he was being so quiet. Because he knew.

"Where I'm from it wouldn't even be considered an incident. Really, it's okay."

He looked up at me then. "Please. Tell me."

I covered my mouth with the tips of my fingers, searching for the words. "Propriety, at least the kind that you ascribe to, is basically nonexistent. People swim together all the time, although usually wearing bathing suits."

His forehead crinkled up in confusion. "A suit for bathing?"

"More like...clothes for swimming, I guess. And most bathing suits leave very little to the imagination." I picked up a piece of toast and buttered it before taking a huge bite. "It's really not a big deal," I said around a mouthful of toasty bread and creamy butter. I'd finally gotten it just right, lightly browned with a good crunch.

"Brolly," he said, wrapping his hands around his teacup, "I understand it is different where you are from, but it is...it is shameful for me to have seen you in such a state of undress. Upon my word, for me to have done anything to harm you or your reputation..."

"You didn't. I was just surprised. Besides, what reputation can I possibly have? I only know you and your staff," I joked. "Well, and Elizabeth, but she's already firmly in the camp of hating me. No one saw us, no one knows. It's okay."

He inhaled a loud breath through his nose and blew it out through rounded lips. "Thank you, Brolly." His voice was thick, like he might burst into tears. If he did, I would, too.

"So...you came back."

"Yes," he said, his eyes burning a hole right through me, "I did."

"I'm glad you...I'm happy you're back."

"Yes," he said, as if that answered any of the questions galloping through my mind. I wanted to know why he left and why he said he was never coming back and why he came back and what this thing was between us. He had to see it, feel it, now so real it was almost tangible, like I could reach out and shake its hand.

But if he could see it, he didn't acknowledge it. Instead, he drank his tea. He ate some toast. He watched the flicker of the candlestick flame. He folded, unfolded, and re-folded his hands. He opened his mouth as if to say something. He closed it again.

I spent the entire time working up the nerve to say something. Anything. Conversation had always been so easy between us, so fluid. The awkward silence was new.

"You know-"

"I believe we-"

He smiled a small, close-lipped smile. I smiled back.

"Shall we retire?"

"Oh." *That's it?* "Okay." *Nothing else?* "Sure."

He walked me all the way to the door of my room, following close behind me as we climbed up the last spiral staircase. Normally, we said goodnight at the top of the grand staircase and parted ways, but tonight he was with me all the way up. At the door I turned around and looked up at him, our shadows on the wall behind him standing closer together than we ever had. My body urged me forward, wanting to reach out to him, my wildly beating heart a drum circle turned to eleven. We stood there, looking at each other. Watching. Waiting.

I drank him in, his slow blink and the way his eyelashes gathered in the outer corners of his eyes. The tiny white scar on his left cheek close to his ear. The way his throat moved when he swallowed.

"Brolly, I..." His voice trailed off. I waited. "I shall look forward to seeing you tomorrow."

"Yes. Tomorrow."

He bowed, although not as low as usual because we were standing so close. And then he was gone.

TWENTY-TWO

J ane burst into my room carrying a breakfast tray and talking so fast I didn't catch most of what she said. The last time she'd burst in like that, it definitely wasn't good news.

"Jane, slow down, I can't understand what you're saying."

She set the tray down and put her hands on her hips. "M'lord has asked if you would accompany him on a boat ride around the lake. So up, up! We must dress you!"

It had taken me forever to fall asleep. I kept going over and over those last few moments together the night before, the way he looked at me, how close we were. I'd wished Amelia were there so we could dissect every possible hidden meaning. Things like that were easier with a best friend.

"What exactly did he say?"

"Did you not hear me, child? M'lord requested you take a trip around the lake! Now up!"

Jane rushed me through a bath and shoved a dress over my head. It was the cornflower blue one from that first time in the dressing room. My hair was still damp by the time I made it down the grand staircase where Thomas was waiting for me.

"Good morning, Miss Parker. I trust you slept well?"

He showed no hint of recognition, no sign that anything had changed between us. My high from the night before drained out of my body and I cursed myself for falling for a guy so impossible to read. We walked in companionable silence down to the shore. I struggled to get into the boat, the long blue dress with its multiple underskirts draping around my legs in long, heavy folds.

"Hang on," I said. I walked over to the driftwood to sit down. I pulled my dress up to my knees and Thomas immediately turned away.

"This will just be easier if I'm barefoot." I stripped off my shoes and itchy tights and stood back up. "Okay, now I'm ready," I said, holding my knotted skirts in my hand.

I climbed into the boat and sat down on the plank bench. Thomas pushed the boat out into the water and climbed in, barely shaking the tiny vessel. He rowed us away from the shore, the gentle slap of the oars against the water the only break in the silence.

The need for conversation overtook my inhibition. "What are you thinking about so hard over there?" I asked.

He stayed quiet, head down as he rowed, the muscles in his arms straining with each pull of the oars. His strong jaw was set in a non-expression. He hadn't looked at me once since we got into the boat.

"Hey," I said, waiting for him to look at me.

Thomas stopped rowing. "I must leave. I must go back to England."

The sun reflected off the water and onto the side of his face like a spinning disco ball. His words were a punch, my mind a toppled seesaw from the here-not-here pendulum he was swinging.

"I don't understand this, Thomas. You never explained why you came back yesterday. Or why you left in the first place. And now you're leaving again?"

A breeze blew my hair across my face. Water sloshed against the side of the boat.

"Have you considered what you will...what your plans would be to return home?"

Oh.

"Oh."

"I have made the-"

"No, no, I understand. You don't know what to do with me."

"No, please, that is not-"

"It's fine, Thomas." We weren't looking at each other, not listening, just tossing words across the tiny boat. "I've over-stayed my welcome."

"No, Brolly..."

"You've been very patient with me, and I haven't given you any indication about my plans to go home. But the truth is..."

Thomas's hands were on the oars in mid-row, waiting. "The truth?" His voice cracked. He looked surprised. He looked scared. I *was* scared.

"Thomas, the truth is that...the truth..." I couldn't do it. Didn't know what to say even if I could do it. I was caught between wanting to belong, wanting him, and going home. None of the options were easy. All of them right. And wrong. Everything was so very wrong. "Thomas, please take me back to the castle."

"Brolly, I should like to-"

"Take me back. Please."

Without a word, he turned the boat back toward the castle, the oars smacking the water with increasing speed. He was angry, his breath coming too quick and too fast. He wanted answers, but I didn't know how to give them.

We reached the shore and I leapt out of the boat, dragging my dress through the water.

TWENTY-THREE

I stomped barefoot through the castle doors and up the grand staircase and down the hall and up the narrow staircase and on and on and over and over, navigating the intricate maze like I'd lived there forever. But I hadn't. And I wouldn't. Because Lord Westbourne wanted me to leave.

Once in my room, I stripped everything off, put on my shorts and t-shirt and curled up in the chair next to the fireplace. Every moment of the boat ride swam through my head, each word stinging sharper than the first. It's what everything had been about, all of it, every conversation and long stroll in the garden, every detailed look into my history. He was trying to figure out how to get rid of me.

Jane came in at some point and I sent her away, telling her I wanted to be alone, which I hoped was true since I was about to be more alone than ever before. Thomas was leaving and I would never see him again. We would never have another late-night talk in the kitchen. We'd never read together in the library. Thomas was leaving and his last order of business was what to do with me. With no way home, I'd be stuck in the castle forever. Alone.

Shadows from the light of the moon had crept across the floor when there was a soft knock at the door.

"Jane, I just want to be alone," I said.

"Br...Miss Parker. May I please speak with you?"

It was Thomas. At my door. I waited and he knocked again.

"Please...Brolly..."

I pulled myself out of the chair and slowly walked to the door, pulled it open a tiny crack and peeked through. He had that look, the one from the night before when we stood where he was standing now.

"Would you accompany me downstairs? There is something I should like to show you."

"What is it?" I said, an edge in my voice I didn't fully mean.

"Please, Brolly." He looked down at the floor and shifted his weight from one foot to the other. His hair was disheveled and he was wearing navy pants with a loose white shirt open at the collar and, unbelievably, sock feet.

"Wait just a second." I closed the door and pulled on a long dressing gown and robe over my t-shirt and shorts. I ran a hand through my hair before opening the door.

We walked down through the dark, silent castle. Every framed portrait we passed held sneers and disdainful looks from Thomas's ancestors, the same expressions I'd seen on Elizabeth's face, like they knew I didn't belong and couldn't wait to be rid of me. Thomas led me down to the library where both doors were shut. I guessed he was bringing me there to read me his version of a breakup letter or make me sign a document absolving him of anything to do with me. Then I'd be neatly cast out. I was ready for it even though my hands shook. I understood why he was doing it even though it was breaking my heart.

He handed me his oil lamp and gripped the library door-knobs, looking back at me as he pulled them open. I stepped inside and gasped.

The entire library was covered in fabric. There were white sheets and heavy blankets draped over every surface, across the tops of the tall shelves and over the chairs and couches, hanging from the second-floor balconies.

"You built me a blanket fort." I could barely say the words. I thought he was kicking me out and instead, he was building this.

Thomas walked over to an opening next to the nearest book-shelf and bowed. "After you, Miss Parker."

I ducked my head and crawled inside. There were cushions scattered across the floor and several oil lamps illuminated the enclosed space into a soft glow. I sat on one of the cushions and Thomas crawled in after me, so un-Lord-like, so undignified, the magnitude of his casualness almost too much to bear. I couldn't believe he did it, couldn't imagine how he did it. And I said so.

"Does it please you?" he asked, sitting down cross-legged in front of me, cheeks flushed.

"Thomas, this isn't a blanket fort, it's a blanket castle. I…I'm overwhelmed. I can't even begin to think how you did this? It's so-"

Thomas reached across the small space between us and lightly, so gently, touched the back of my left hand. It was the first time he'd ever touched me without a glove or a sleeve or propriety standing in the way. It was barely a touch, nearly nothing at all, but every nerve ending in my body began to simmer.

"Brolly, there is something I have been attempting to say to you, something I must say to you, and I built this fort, our own little world, in order to do so." He carefully, so slowly, took my hands into his, his touch warm and tentative. "Brolly, this morning in the boat," he squeezed my hands, running his thumbs across my knuckles. My chest was so tight I thought my lungs had collapsed. "I cannot…I do not know how to manage this situation. I feel as if it my duty to help you return home to your family. But you never speak of them unless I inquire. You never share your intentions to go home." A shiver ran across my shoulders and down my arms. "Please tell me how I should help you. I desire…it is my sincere…Brolly, you asked me why I returned to the castle."

"Yes." I could barely get the word out, looking from his face to our linked hands.

"Chateau du Lac has been sold."

The words echoed through me like a metal door slamming shut. "Sold? I don't understand."

"I have been plagued by your question, when you asked me how I would conduct my life if the choice were mine. The Collins' of Kensington have sought to acquire the castle since Napoleon's defeat in 1815. Apparently owning property in France is now very in fashion."

"But you love it here."

"I do, but the castle is part of the family obligation. The obligation that, if I were allowed to choose, I would rid myself of entirely. That was my purpose for traveling into Lille, to draw up the papers with my financial man."

"Okay. I mean, if that's what makes you happy then I'm glad you're doing it," I said. But Thomas wasn't smiling.

"My intention was to leave, Brolly. I instructed Jane to help you find your way home and I…I was traveling back to Arrington. I thought it would be easier if I left but…I could not do it. I could not leave you."

The floor shifted beneath me. My voice came out in a tiny squeak. "Why did you want to?"

His fingers rubbed across mine. "It is an unfair complexity, to be sure."

"Thomas, I need…I don't understand."

"You did not let me finish."

"What?" I was breathless. My bones liquefied, like any moment I would dissolve into the floor and disappear. Thomas built me a blanket fort, was holding my hands in his, but he sold the castle, wanted to leave.

"Today, in the boat, you did not let me finish."

"Okay," I said as tears burned my eyes. I willed myself to

stay present. To hear him. "Finish."

He closed his eyes and steadied himself. "Come to England with me. I want you to come with me."

"What? I can't...what are you saying?"

The room spun. I couldn't keep up. Did he care about me or was I truly just a final detail to deal with before he left? I looked at him, at the desperation in his face. I didn't know how to read it. I didn't know what he was thinking.

With his eyes still closed, he shrugged his shoulders. "I do not understand how to do this, how to confess my affections to someone like you." He opened his eyes and there was something new in them, something concrete. "You, Brolly Parker, are like a wildflower, springing up in the most unexpected of places, forcing your beauty onto whomever happens to find you. And as you know, my life is quite the orderly affair. There is no room for wildness. No room for the unexpected. But I cannot seem to stay away from you. And today, in the boat, I wanted to tell you."

My heart exploded. I wanted to lunge for him, throw myself at him, but I was frozen in place. "What did you want to tell me?"

"I wanted to tell you that...Brolly, you have taken me over." He let go of one of my hands and reached out to touch my face but pulled away. "I wanted to tell you that...you are beautiful and captivating and strong. I wanted to tell you that you are strange and interesting and a majority of the time I am not entirely certain you are real. And I know. I know you do not belong here. And I do not mean here at Chateau du Lac but, here," he said, waving his arm around as if I didn't belong in the same space as him. He was right. "I cannot fathom where you came from, or how. I have considered so many different possibilities I have nearly gone mad with the mystery. But where you are from is of no consequence to me. My only concern is that you are here. Now. With me."

I took a breath, suddenly lightheaded. A tear rolled down my cheek.

"And the singular consideration I have, the one thing I value in this world, is time with you. I do not know how long you may happen to be here, but it is my fervent wish that as long as you are here, that you understand..." He leaned in close, close enough that I could feel the heat from his body. "Brolly, I care for you a great deal. I..."

"Thomas."

"I know your heart is not free. I see the way you drift. I see the pain in your eyes." He exhaled and bit his lower lip. It was so unrefined, so uncharacteristic, it was like we were the same. Like he wasn't a Lord and I wasn't a high school senior. Like we were Brolly and Thomas, two people able to confess our feelings and find our way to each other.

"Brolly, I think about touching you, touching your hair and circling your waist and I cannot. I should not."

His wet eyes searched mine as he reached up and cradled my cheek. His thumb traced away the tears now freely flowing from my eyes.

"I think about putting my lips to yours and...I should not." The simmer in my veins reached a boiling point. I needed him. I wanted him. "I think about so many things that cannot be but... is it possible...just for now..."

I closed my eyes and leaned into his touch as he reached out to hold my face with both of his hands. A wave crashed into me, spinning me upside-down and around and back again. Here he was, confessing his feelings in the most vulnerable way, and even though it didn't make any sense at all, I believed him.

I had to tell him the truth.

I pushed his hands away and sat up on my knees. I unlaced the satin cream ribbons of my robe and pulled it off. Then I pulled the nightgown over my head to reveal my t-shirt and shorts. My clothes, from my time. Thomas's eyes grew wide and his lips parted. I could hear him breathing. I set the gown and robe aside and sat back down, my legs exposed, my arms exposed, my naked heart so very exposed.

"Thomas, these are my clothes, my real clothes from my real life. This is a t-shirt from Central High School, where I was just about to start my senior year but instead arrived here, on your shore, with no idea how I got here. These are shorts I wear to sleep in. Sometimes I wear them to run errands in, in a car, that I drive. I got this t-shirt from a 5k fundraiser run I did with Amelia our sophomore year. We were doing really well, too, until a guy in a chicken suit passed us and we started laughing so hard we came in dead last. I love cookie dough ice cream and texting. Texting! And electricity! And hot water that comes out of the tap! And take-out! And I love my family so much and I miss them so much it's painful to talk about. Because I don't know how to get back to them. I don't know how to get back to my life that isn't here. I don't belong here."

His expression didn't change, still gazing at me like I was his favorite thing in the world.

"Come to England with me."

I didn't know how to respond. I'd just said everything short of Hi, I'm a time traveler from the future. "Are you listening to me?"

"I am."

"Then why aren't you freaking out?"

He smiled. *Smiled.* Beamed like I'd just read out the winning lottery numbers and he matched all five numbers plus the power ball. "Come to England with me."

"You want me to come with you. Even though...even though you know I don't belong here."

He reached for me again. "You belong with me."

A sob-laugh burst out of me, that weird sound you make when you're crying and then suddenly laughing. And I couldn't help myself. I leapt and threw my arms around him, burying my face in his neck. He was surprised but returned the embrace.

"You belong with me," he said, his lips against my ear.

"Yes," I replied. "Yes."

TWENTY-FOUR

"You seem tired this morning, m'lady." Jane was helping me dress as I fought off another series of yawns.

"Yeah, I was…up late."

"I see," she said, buttoning up the back of my dress and smirking at me in the mirror. "And what could have held your attention at so late an hour?"

I caught her eye in the mirror, a sly smile on my face. Her face was the picture of innocence, but I knew she knew. There was no way Thomas built that blanket fort all by himself and no way anyone but Jane helped him. A knock at the door startled us both and we turned to look at each other. Jane went to answer it and I could tell from the change in her posture it was him.

"Good morning, m'lord." She was grinning so hard I could hear it, like her face would split in two from pure joy.

"Good morning, Jane. Good morning, Miss Parker." Thomas bowed, but not before catching my eye, a glance that reaffirmed everything I thought maybe I'd imagined. He was mine. I was his.

"To what do we owe the pleasure of your company this

morning, Lord Westbourne?" I asked. I was trying to look unaffected, but it was no use. Sunbeams radiated from my face.

"It is a beautiful day. Perhaps you should like to accompany me on a walk in the garden?"

"Yes, I'd like that very much."

Jane inhaled and looked like she might sprout fairy wings and a fairy godmother wand and fly down the staircase.

"Wonderful. I shall wait for you in the front hall. Until then, Miss Parker."

He bowed again and left the room. Jane glared at me and did her level best not to ask, her lips pressed together in a thin line desperately trying to hold back the avalanche of questions I knew she wanted to ask.

"If you let me have this one moment," I said, grinning at her and grabbing her hands, "I promise I'll tell you everything this afternoon."

She nodded her head once, squeezing my hands and then shooing me away. I kissed her on the cheek and took the stairs two at a time, catching up to Thomas at the bottom of the spiral staircase. I reached out to hug him and he startled, reminding me it was daytime, Lord time, and he had a reputation to uphold. I noticed Phillipe standing down the hallway, watching, judging, probably cooking up another letter to Elizabeth reporting on all my indiscretions.

"Miss Parker," Thomas said, bowing, ever the gentleman.

"Lord Westbourne," I said, dropping into a curtsey. It made Thomas laugh. Not a small, polite laugh, but a great big hearty laugh at the bottom of the spiral staircase in broad daylight in front of Phillipe. My toes curled inside my blocky heels.

"Shall we," he said and offered me his arm.

We walked down through the castle and out the garden door. I kept my hands on his arm, pressing myself into his side. He walked slowly, straight-backed but pressing just as closely to me. When we walked outside, nature appeared to have gotten the memo about what happened between me and Thomas. Everything was alive, like the garden was smiling at us. The trees stood taller and the birds sang louder, flowers bloomed in rich, coordinated hues. Thomas guided me over to the wooden bench next to the fountain, the same bench where we sat on our very first walk. He looked up at the wall of windows facing the bench and stood back up.

"Shall we walk a bit further?" His eyes shifted from window to window, scanning for signs of life.

"Are you okay?" I asked.

"Yes, quite. Shall we?"

I wrapped my hands around his arm. He was wearing a scratchy wool jacket over his white shirt, but I could still feel the definition of his arm. We walked further down the stone path and around a corner toward the back of the garden where it hit a dead end against the castle wall. Thomas paced back and forth beside the stone wall, opening and closing his hands against his thighs.

"Something on your mind?" I asked.

He stopped pacing and stood right in front of me. Close. He looked at my lips.

"Brolly."

I loved the way he said my name, his English accent adding a drawn-out W so that it came out more like Brawl-ly.

"Yes?"

"Brolly, last night there were many things said between us. Would it be presumptuous of me to say that we have an understanding?"

"An understanding?"

"Yes, an understanding." He was still looking at my lips. "You see I...I want...I should like to..." He took a step closer. "I am quite aware of the insurmountable improprieties we have already committed. The mere fact that I am with you unaccompanied on this walk would send the entirety of London society into fits of hysteria." He moved closer. "And I understand your customs to be a bit…unencumbered. And you know I would never wish to…I should never…"

He was so close to me I could feel him, the rise and fall of his chest, his fingers ghosting over mine at our sides. I thought he wanted to kiss me. I knew I wanted him to kiss me.

He waited, his eyes sweeping over my face in the sunlight. After three breaths, he raised his hand and touched my shoulder, traced his fingers up to my neck so slowly I was afraid he'd change his mind. His touch was warm, and my body instinctively leaned into it. Our eyes met, his gaze burning the crooks of my elbows and the backs of my knees. His hand traveled up to my jaw, his thumb reaching the corner of my mouth and pulling me to him. I grabbed the lapels of his jacket and guided his lips the last few inches to reach mine. He was timid, his mouth barely touching mine, so I pressed in more until he gave in, until he let go and kissed me like he wanted to, like he meant it.

It was more than a first kiss; it was The Kiss. I was free falling, my hands gripping his jacket like a ripcord, the beat of my heart replaced by a great, swirling whoosh that traveled through all four chambers and up into my ears canceling out everything but Thomas…Thomas…Thomas.

TWENTY-FIVE

"Will I be allowed to make my own tea in England?" I asked. We were in the kitchen, waiting for the water to boil for tea.

It was one of our last nights in the castle. In three days, we'd be traveling to England, to a new life together. Thomas kissed the tip of my nose and laughed.

"I had not considered you will have an entirely new staff to torment."

"Except for Jane."

"Yes, except for Jane."

After we kissed in the garden, Thomas kissed me again in the library and again at dinner when Phillipe and Girard left the room to retrieve more dishes. And he was always close, subtly touching my hand or my arm or my waist. I was surprised we hadn't been caught yet. The staff had to know. Thomas's constant smile was a dead giveaway.

I walked over to the shelf against the wall and got two teacups and saucers and set them on the tall worktable in the middle of the kitchen. "I'm excited about going to Arrington and seeing you in your element."

Saying the word Arrington still sent a shiver down my spine.

It was too much of a coincidence not to somehow be related to my mom's books. I hoped once I was at Arrington, some of the missing pieces would fall into place.

"You may be disappointed. It will be constant balls and luncheons and tea with my sister."

"What, you don't think Elizabeth will welcome me with open arms?" As much as I looked forward to figuring out Arrington, the thought of living on the same estate as Elizabeth sent a shiver through me. Thomas had assured me she couldn't do anything but make empty threats, but her threats, even empty, cut like a knife.

He smiled. "And if she did?"

I wrapped a towel around the hot handle of the tea kettle and poured the boiling water into the teapot. "I think you and I both would fall over dead if that ever happened."

He walked up behind me and wrapped his arms around me.

"A happy death with you by my side."

I set the kettle down and snuggled into him. "Are you afraid I'll embarrass you with my lack of propriety? My borrowed dresses and bad habit of making my own food?"

"In England you may have as many new dresses as you like." He held me tighter and whispered into my ear. "I am not afraid. If you are to be my wife, I am not afraid to face anything."

My body went still, his breath warm against my ear. "If I'm to be…your wife?"

"Of course."

I couldn't move, couldn't say anything. My jaw clenched shut, forcing me to think before I spoke. I pushed the words out. "Thomas, I don't…isn't that a little…presumptuous?"

"Presumptuous?" He moved his arms away, the tips of his fingers grazing my waist. Even with multiple layers between us, I could feel him on my skin. His touch rolled through me, enveloping me. There was no doubt I wanted to be with him. But wife?

"We've only known each other a short time and there's been

more than enough evidence I don't fit into your world. How can you say you want to marry me?"

He dropped his hands, the touch gone, a chasm splitting open between us. "I believe I made my intentions clear."

I turned around to look at him. Our bodies were still close, too close.

"You hardly know me. How can you be so sure you want to *marry* me?"

"Brolly, I believe I-"

"Maybe what you're feeling is just…maybe you're trying to rescue me from my traumatic displacement." The words spilled out before I even recognized them as my own, but I kept going. "Maybe I'm just a distraction from the obligations you seem so hell-bent on running away from. Maybe you only asked me to go to England because you sold the castle and you know I have nowhere to go." My breath came fast, all my hidden doubts rushing out like a faucet turned to full blast. "Maybe none of this has anything to do with me."

I immediately regretted most of what I said, but it was too late. It was out there. Now we had to deal with it.

"Is that how you feel?" He spoke slowly, quietly.

"Is that how you feel?" I shouted it, even though I didn't want to. Even though it wasn't truly how I felt. Even though I could see I was hurting him. It was written all over his face.

"Brolly, how can you say these things to me."

Once I'd started, there was no stopping me.

"I'm just being honest. I know I haven't been able to figure out how to get back to my family but that doesn't mean I want some pity proposal. Is that what this is for you? Did you ask me to go to England because you feel sorry for me? Is any of this even real?"

He took a step back to get further away from me. "My heart is firmly rooted in my intentions for you." It sounded like a line. It made me nervous I might be right.

"Firmly rooted? God, why can't you ever just say what

you're trying to say instead of talking around it? I'm so tired of having to decode every word to figure what exactly it is you mean."

A long silence passed between us, a silence that squeezed around my throat with bony fingers of regret. I couldn't look at him, too afraid of what I would see.

"I *mean*," he said, his voice grave, quiet, "that regardless of your traumatic displacement, I am firm in my convictions toward you. I *mean* that I would never portray a disingenuous affection based on your need for purchase. I *mean* that I invited you to join me, to join my life and be beside me always, because that is how I wish for this union to proceed. I have never spoken an untrue word to you."

I looked him right in the eye then, angry that it couldn't be easy, that he couldn't say the one thing I wanted to hear.

"You never said you loved me."

The expression on his face split me in two.

He took another step back, another step away from me, his eyes burning into mine. "Miss Parker, that is all I have been saying."

He kept his eyes on me for one long moment and then turned and left the kitchen.

TWENTY-SIX

I waited all morning for Thomas to show up, to come to my room and hold me and tell me it was all a misunderstanding. But he didn't come.

Jane was bustling around my room, setting down a tray of tea and pastries and picking up the dress I left on the floor. "We must get your trunks packed for the journey to England, m'lady." Her behavior was cryptic. I couldn't tell if she knew about my fight with Thomas and I was afraid to ask. If she knew, she'd have an opinion about it for sure. And if she wasn't already sharing it, it meant she thought I screwed things up.

I stared out the window at the glistening surface of the lake. Was I still going to England? I'd said so many hurtful things to Thomas last night. Things I thought I meant but now, in the light of day, sounded like nothing but my own insecurities. My inability to believe any of it was real. All Thomas ever did was care for me and I threw it back in his face. I needed to fix it, but I didn't know how.

I followed Jane into the dressing room where she'd already begun packing two giant trunks full of dresses.

"You're sure it's okay if I take these?"

"Of course, m'lady. They shall not get much use here what

with m'lord selling the castle and all." Jane picked up the pink dress I wore on my first day at Chateau du Lac and the long, satin ribbons slid through her fingers.

"Do you think it's right? That I go with him?" I whispered the words, afraid to say them out loud but needing to know the answer. "Last night we...we had a fight. I'm not sure he wants me to go anymore."

Jane pulled another dress from the large wardrobe and shook it out, stirring dust through the air that rained down in the late-morning sunbeams shooting across the room. "What does your heart tell you, m'lady?"

I sat down on the floor, surrounded by dresses that weren't mine in a castle that wasn't mine that belonged to someone who shouldn't be mine. "I don't know."

"Then listen harder. The heart always knows what the head sometimes forgets."

"But what if it means..." I took a deep breath, then one more, "what it if means I can never go home?"

Jane placed the dress in the trunk, sat down on the floor next to me and took my hands into hers. "Perhaps what you should consider, m'lady, is if you *are* home." Her words made my bottom lip quiver. "Whatever happened that brought you here, you are here now. I know that does not erase what was. It does not remove the bond of family," her eyes welled up with tears, "but you can make a new life. You can make a family here."

"But if I leave it's like I'm giving up on them, like I didn't do enough to try and get back to them. I'm afraid if I leave the island, it will mean...I'm afraid I'll never get back home again."

Jane's tears spilled over. Her expression grew serious. "I shall tell you something, something I have never spoken of and never wish to speak of again." She let go of my hands and gripped my shoulders. "Many years ago, I lost someone. Someone very, very dear to me. And the one thing that kept me from falling into total despair was the idea that she found a new life, that she found a new family."

"This is different, I didn't just wander off, I-"

"Listen to me, child, listen. I know. What you are going through, I have an understanding. I know what I say when I tell you to start a new life. Do not look back on what you left behind...or *when* you left it."

Small tears trailed down my cheeks. She couldn't understand, couldn't possibly know the truth. But her eyes were so desperate, so sincere, like she believed she knew what happened to me.

"But you can't know...how..."

"Sometimes the impossible is not so impossible, is it?" She pulled her hands off my shoulders and folded them together.

"And your someone, you never saw her again?

She reached up and traced one finger down my cheek. "I have seen evidence, m'lady, evidence that she is all right. And that is enough."

"But don't you wish she would come back? Don't you miss her?"

"With all my heart, I miss her. But prayers can be answered in ways we do not expect."

I wrapped my arms around her neck and held on, trying to make sense of her riddles. "I told him, Jane. I told him the truth about my life and where I came from."

She pulled back and looked into my watery eyes. "And what did he say?"

"I don't think he heard me. Or maybe he just didn't understand."

"Do you, m'lady? Do you understand?"

My tears flowed faster as my breath stuttered. "No."

"Therein lies your answer. Do not worry so much about understanding. Life is full of things we cannot understand."

"Jane, I wish you really knew what happened to me. Even if you couldn't help me, I wish you knew."

She patted my back and smoothed her hand over my hair. "I know enough, m'lady. I know enough."

TWENTY-SEVEN

After my conversation with Jane, I roamed the castle thinking about everything she said and everything Thomas said. They wanted me to stay, to make a life with them in England. And I wanted that, too. But I couldn't shake the feeling I was letting my life go too soon. The truth was, if I could go home, I would. But the black umbrella was gone. I'd searched every stone and blade of grass around the castle, rowed around the lake a hundred times. Since I'd arrived, there hadn't been one single sign I'd be able to figure out how to go home. Maybe home was gone. Maybe time had shifted in such a way that home didn't exist anymore. A small voice in my head kept telling me I couldn't wait for a maybe, couldn't hold out for an impossible chance.

And I cared about Thomas. I loved him. Our fight still stung, but my feelings hadn't changed. Being with Thomas focused all the blurry lines. But he was looking for forever and I didn't know what forever meant anymore. Jane told me to trust my heart and that's what I wanted to do. Maybe it's what I had to do.

No, it's what I was going to do.

My head was down on the table in the kitchen when

Thomas's boots scraped across the kitchen's stone floor. I sat up and my heart clenched. He'd been away from the castle making arrangements for the trip back to England and we hadn't seen each other since the fight.

"Thomas."

His name whispered out of me like a prayer for forgiveness. He set his oil lamp down and leaned against the corner of the table, right next to me. He didn't touch me, but I could feel him all over my body, could feel his strong arms and his broad chest, the faint stubble on his chin.

A lock of hair fell over his eye and he pushed it away. I wanted to say something, wanted to reach out, wanted to shout my apology and fold myself into him, but I stayed still, silent.

He put his fingertips on my cheek, the feather-light touch the connection I needed.

"I love you, Brolly Parker."

"You don't have to-"

"I love you, Brolly. Do forgive me that the words are difficult to say." With the softest touch, he leaned in and moved his hand to my neck. "I believed I was saying it to you in my own way. I now understand how important it is for me to tell you I love you in a way that is meaningful for you. Please believe me when I say that I love you. It is you who has captured my heart. It is you who I want beside me always. It is you that I love."

"Thomas," I said, standing up and fitting my body between his knees. "I'm sorry about what I said. It's just...I know what a big step this is, and I got scared. I'm still scared. Nothing about my time here makes any sense. The only thing, the one thing, that makes sense to me is you. I want you to know that I'm ready, Thomas, to be here with you or in England with you or anywhere in the world as long as we're together."

We moved closer to each other, pressing in.

"You are confident?"

"You're the only thing I'm confident about." His lips were a breath away. "You can kiss me. I want you to kiss me."

He reached down, achingly slow, and wrapped his hands around my waist. His eyes never left mine as he pulled me flush against him. His lips pressed against mine and his hands gripped my waist. Every kiss we'd shared had been electric, a sizzling fire traveling over and through me. This kiss was different. This kiss was forgiveness. A promise. Love.

I broke the kiss, needing to look into his eyes. "I love you, Thomas. I am so in love with you."

His face broke into a wide open, joyous smile and I knew I hadn't been the right kind of alive until that moment.

TWENTY-EIGHT

I t was beautiful the day we left, a blue-skied, sunny welcome to our new life together. I took a final walk through the castle, the place where I met Thomas, my shelter in the storm. I passed through the breakfast room and the dining room and the library and thought back to the moment I arrived, so scared and alone, so utterly displaced. Now I was in love, embarking on a new life in a new world.

I found Jane waiting down by the shore. "I'm glad you'll be traveling with us, Jane. I'm a little nervous about the trip."

"It is a long journey, but we will be there before you know it. You will love Arrington, m'lady, I am certain of it."

Thomas, Jane, Mary and I were waiting at the water's edge while the last of the luggage was loaded in two boats. Thomas arranged for a few more boats to be brought to the island to carry the luggage across the lake. Mary and Jane got into a boat with Girard and Thomas and I got into the last boat. He was beaming as he pushed us away from the shore.

"It just occurred to me," I said, "shouldn't someone be rowing the boat for you? You are a Lord, after all."

"The Chateau has afforded me several luxuries I will miss. I would have a much harder time doing this at Arrington."

"Such a rebel, rowing your own boat. I bet you don't even let Phillipe bathe you."

He laughed. "No, Phillipe does not bathe me."

"Thank God for that."

"I know this will be difficult for you, but Phillipe will not be joining us at Arrington. He is to stay behind at Chateau du Lac to welcome the new owners. Although I am sure you will be able to find someone new to confound once we reach Arrington."

"Can't wait," I said, distracted by the sight of his arms pushing the oars through the water.

The wind shifted, a cool breeze blowing my hair into my face. "I can't imagine what you thought of me that first night," I said. "If you had acted like a Lord and let someone else secure the boats, you might never have found me." It was something we'd never talked about, that first night in the rain. I must have looked like an alien from another planet.

"It was a strange experience, yes. You looked like a frightened little fawn." He paused. "A naked fawn."

He blushed and grinned, so proud of himself for being the tiniest bit salacious.

"Settle down, hot shot. I definitely wasn't naked. When you crashed into me with your boat while I was swimming, that's when I was naked."

"Yes...well." He was still grinning.

I looked over to the other boat and Jane smiled and waved.

"Is Girard coming with us to Arrington?"

"No, he will come back to the castle once he has transported Jane and Mary safely across."

"What will happen to the staff at the Chateau?"

"That will be up to the new owners, but I have seen to it they each have high recommendations. I do not think it will be a problem."

The conversation reminded me of Thomas's status as Lord of Arrington. I'd never run an estate or managed a staff of people. The closest I'd come was last summer when I worked at the

Catholic school summer program, but all that involved was entertaining elementary school kids and making sure none of them wandered off or got hurt. Overseeing an entire estate, I imagined, was a bit more involved than passing out juice boxes and playing horse on the basketball court.

"Does Elizabeth know I'm coming back with you?"

An expression I couldn't interpret passed over his face. "No, she does not."

"Well," I sighed, "that should be a fun revelation."

"She also does not know the castle has been sold."

"Will that matter? I thought she hated the castle."

"Yes, but remember, having property abroad, particularly in France, is very in fashion. Elizabeth's purpose in life is to be in fashion."

I laughed. "Please let me be there when you tell her."

Thomas pulled the oars through the water and a slow smile spread across his face. "There is one part of the sale I did not mention. I am keeping our table."

"Our table?"

"From the kitchen. I'm having it brought to Arrington, for you."

I knew he was a romantic, the blanket fort proved that, but I had no idea he was so sentimental. I liked it. My mouth opened to say I didn't think it was possible to be this happy, but something in the water caught my eye.

"What is that?" I leaned over the side of the boat. "Do you see that? Thomas, can you get closer?" I pointed out into the water and Thomas turned the boat. It couldn't be. After all this time, there was no way. "Do you see it?"

"What is it, Miss Parker?"

He rowed closer and I scrunched down into the bottom of the boat so I could lean over even further into the water. I stretched out my hand and grabbed the black umbrella, my black umbrella, and pulled it out of the water.

Thomas pulled the oars up. "Can it be? Is that the very umbrella you have been searching for all this time?"

"Yes, I...I can't believe it." I quickly set the umbrella in the bottom of the boat and pulled my hands away. I was afraid to touch it, afraid of what would happen. My hands shook and my skin went hot all over.

"How fortuitous," Thomas said, smiling, completely unaware of the decision I'd just been presented with – home.

Would it really be so easy? If I reached down and opened the umbrella, would I find myself on the front porch of my house in Tennessee? And if I did, would I ever see Thomas again? Or Jane? Every time I searched the island for the umbrella, especially in those first few days, I never considered I wouldn't want to leave. But now, in this moment, I was torn. I missed my family, my friends, my life. I wanted to return to them. How could it even be a choice? I had to go home.

I looked up at Thomas and he was smiling at me, so happy and carefree. We'd pledged our love to each other. We were on our way to England, together. I loved him.

I loved him. I loved Thomas. I made the decision to be with him, forever. I left the island, and any chance of going home, behind. I chose to move forward. I said yes. Because I loved Thomas. Being with him was the life I wanted, the life I'd been given, the life I chose. Why else would the umbrella have brought me to the castle, to this exact place and time?

But I couldn't choose to abandon my family, not when I had the chance to go back. I couldn't choose to never see my mom and dad again, couldn't choose to never see Amelia and Pepper again.

I couldn't do that.

"Brolly, are you quite all right? You look as if you have seen a ghost."

His voice pulled me back to the present. My new present. I couldn't leave Thomas. I couldn't.

"Jane," he called, rowing us closer to the other boat, "look what Miss Parker has found floating in the water. The impossible umbrella!"

Thomas picked up the umbrella and waved it at Jane, who looked stricken. She jumped in her seat and shouted, "Brolly, you must be careful."

It was the first time she'd ever used my name.

I lunged for the umbrella and yanked the handle away from him, afraid it would open and I'd be left there without him, the worst of all scenarios.

"Brolly!" he shouted, startled.

"Brolly! No!" Jane screamed, just as the umbrella opened in my hands.

Thomas shouted my name as the breath punched out of me. A sudden, thunderous boom ripped through my chest and threw my body backwards. I didn't have time to recover when an explosive flash of light sizzled over my skin and through my veins, blinding me and burning through me. My body spun wildly and I couldn't react, couldn't think, couldn't do anything but cling to the umbrella handle and scream. Another flash and I was thrown to the ground in a heap.

Rain poured over me, soaking my hair and my dress.

"Thomas!"

"Brolly, are you okay?"

It wasn't Thomas. It was my mother. And I wasn't in a boat on a lake surrounding Chateau du Lac anymore, I was outside my house.

"Come inside, it's pouring." Mom was shouting to compensate for the rain.

It couldn't be.

No.

No, no, no, no, no.

A steady stream of raindrops slid down my cheeks in mock tear tracks as water seeped into my dress and my mind played one message over and over.

I'm back.
I'm back.
I'm back.
And he's gone.

TWENTY-NINE

My mind woke up before my body and the world was louder. The air conditioner whirred a rattling hum of cold air that raised goosebumps across my skin. A lawnmower chugged and sputtered across someone's lawn. Mrs. Rathbone's Pomeranians barked their disapproval next door. A TV downstairs blared a yogurt jingle. A car door slammed. The orchestra of sound hurt my brain, like tossed pebbles pounding against my skull. My eyes were closed but it was too bright, the lamp next to my bed shining down on me like a beacon. My bed smelled wrong, even though it was my bed, in my own time. Because the black umbrella had hurled me back through time without my permission.

The creak of my bedroom door forced my eyes open.

"Darling? How are you feeling?"

"Mom?" I launched out of bed and threw my arms around her, knocking her backwards. "Mom! I missed you. I missed you so much." I clung to her like I was Rose and she was the floating door.

"Darling, what's this? What's the matter?" I squeezed her tighter, unwilling to let go. She smelled like raspberry shampoo and sweet tea, like everything I'd missed. "Are you all right?"

I drew back to look at her, confused. "I was gone…I've been…I was gone."

"Gone where?" She brushed my hair back and squinted at my forehead. "You must have hit your head harder than I thought."

"I…what?" I looked down and saw green sweat shorts and a tank top from the rec center, not my dress from the castle.

"That fall must have been worse than I thought. Your bump hasn't gone down and you're getting a bruise. How do you feel?"

"What? No…I left…I was…" I reached up and felt a bump in my hairline above my left eye. "What day is it?"

"You missed school. I called Principal Ludlow and explained what happened. Do you have a headache?"

"School? No…today we were leaving…we left…" I paced the room. A rushing sound filled my ears like a deafening waterfall. I'd have to shout to hear my own thoughts.

My cell phone buzzed on the nightstand and I picked it up, the weight of it foreign in my hand. A text from Ben popped up wondering where I was and why I missed school. I looked at the date and gasped. It was the same day I opened the black umbrella on my front porch back in August. Here, no time had passed at all.

"No, this isn't right…I wasn't ready… I didn't…decide…I hadn't decided." I was talking to myself, the words coming out jumbled and half-spoken.

"Brolly, what's the matter?"

I fell down onto my bed and started to cry.

Mom sat down next to me and put her arms around my shoulders, pulling me into her. The tighter she held me, the harder I cried. Great, heaving sobs poured out of me as I shook with grief. Thomas was gone. I was back and…he was gone.

"Tighter," I said, needing her to hold me together so I wouldn't fly apart, "hold me tighter."

She squeezed as tight as she could, but it wasn't enough. It would never be enough. "Darling, what's happened? Are you in pain?"

"Yes," I said as my heart exploded into tiny, jagged shards inside my chest. I didn't decide. I hadn't decided. I didn't want to leave Thomas, would never have chosen to leave him.

"Shhh, try and calm down. I'll get you some water. Will you be okay by yourself for a moment?"

I nodded and watched her leave my room. As soon as she rounded the corner I ran to her room, tearing it apart looking for the umbrella. I had to get back to Thomas. I had to try. Mom found me on my knees in her closet throwing everything I could find out into the room.

"Brolly, what on earth are you doing? It took me forever to clean up the mess from this morning."

"Where's the umbrella?" I shouted, pulling her desk chair into the closet to get to the top shelf.

Mom grabbed the chair. "Stop this right now. And put all these clothes back."

"Where is it? I had it that morning, in the storm." She pulled the chair away from me and put it back underneath her desk. "Mom," I cried, "where is it? I need that umbrella." I was crazed, waving my hands in the air, tears streaming down my cheeks.

"What umbrella? What are you talking about?"

"The one I found in here. The one that sent me to him. Where is it? I have to get back to him, please, you have to give it to me."

Mom picked up an armful of jeans and walked into the closet. "You aren't making any sense."

"Please, Mom, I'm begging you. You have to give it to me. I'll come back, I promise, but I have to go to him. He doesn't know what happened to me. He won't understand. I have to go back." I sat down on the floor, exhaustion taking over, my head pounding. "Please. Please give it back."

Mom kneeled down next to me and pulled me into her arms. "I don't know about any umbrella, Brolly. If you had one with you this morning it must have blown away in the storm."

"No," I said, crumpling into her, "it didn't. I had it in my hands, it's what brought me back."

She smoothed my hair back from my face. "You've been sleeping fitfully all day. You must have had a bad dream." She kissed the top of my head and stood up, kicking a pile of clothes back into the closet, shirts and sweaters tossed into a heap, nothing where it was supposed to be. "Why don't I go make us a snack, hmm?"

I didn't want a snack.

I wanted the umbrella.

I wanted to go home.

THIRTY

After my outburst, Mom ushered me back to bed with instructions to rest, but I was too wired to sleep. I paced my room, going over and over it in my mind. Now I knew for certain the umbrella caused me to time travel. It was in my hands when I went to France, and it was in my hands when I came back. I had to find it.

I decided I would tell my mom the truth and accept whatever came next. If there was a way to get back to Thomas, I'd need her help. She was my mother. She loved me. I'd find a way to make her believe me.

I slipped down the stairs, the creaking wood so different under my feet than the cold stone floors of the castle. The wall of the staircase was filled with mismatched picture frames and quotes in calligraphy about embracing the life you're given and the love of family. It was so familiar, so second-nature, but I took it all in like it was the first time. Mom's shining face at her first book signing. Dad bent over like he was going to puke after riding the Barnstormer at Dollywood. Cale holding up a garden snake he found in the backyard with me screaming in the background. Mom framed and hung all her favorite candid photos. She said she'd rather see real life than a posed portrait.

I walked into the kitchen and pulled out a stool from under the counter. It was a familiar movement, something I'd done hundreds of times, but everything about my house felt foreign, like I'd forgotten the muscle memory of the every day. Mom was shelling peas from Dad's garden as I sat down, her elegant fingers cracking open the pods and pushing the peas into a ceramic bowl. "Are you feeling any better?"

I took a breath. My hands were shaking so I laced my fingers together on top of the counter. "I need to tell you something."

"What is it?" Her head was down as she shelled the peas. I couldn't read her face.

"That morning, the morning of the storm that knocked the power out?"

"You mean this morning?"

I breathed out hard through my nose, trying to calm myself. "Okay, this morning. I didn't fall on the porch and hit my head. I found an umbrella in your closet, before I left for school, and when I opened it, I went somewhere."

"No, remember? You were on your way out to your car and slipped on the wet porch stairs and bumped your head. I'm starting to think you may have rattled a few things loose in the process. Should I take you to see Dr. Collins?"

I wasn't sure where to start. *Here's the thing, Mom, I time traveled. By the way, I'm a time traveler. Hey, Mom, I time traveled to 19th century France and fell in love and now I'm back and my heart is breaking. Please give me the umbrella so I can go back to my two-hundred-year-old boyfriend.*

"I don't need to see Dr. Collins because I didn't fall. Something happened and it's hard to explain but I need you to believe me. That morning, when I was looking for my shirt before school, I found a brown shipping box in your closet. I pulled the tape off and there was an old, black umbrella inside. When I went out onto the porch, I opened the umbrella in the rain and Mom, I don't know how it happened but, I time traveled. I went to 19th century France. 1826 to be exact."

She stopped shelling the peas and looked at me, her expression unreadable.

"What are you saying?"

I leaned forward on the counter, my shoulders hunched into my chest. "I found an old, black umbrella in your closet when I was looking for my plaid button-down. The power went out, remember? When I opened it, something happened. There was like, an explosion, and I landed by a lake in France. I time traveled to 1826. I've been living in a castle there for the last few months."

"Brolly, there is no-"

"Mom," I said, leaning further across the counter, my butt totally off the stool, "I'm telling you the truth. I was there. I know it's hard to believe, it took me a long time to believe it myself. But it's true. I've been living in a castle with Lord West-"

"Brolly." Her tone was abrupt, but her eyes were squinted, like she wanted to believe me but it was impossible to do so. "You know I adore your sarcastic sense of humor, but time travel?"

"I am 100% serious about this. Ask me anything about what happened, I'll tell you. I'm not making this up."

She moved the bowl of peas aside and leaned down on the counter, mirroring my hunched shoulders. Our faces were close. She reached out and covered my hands with hers.

"Darling, this morning you raced outside to your car and slipped on the wet stairs and bumped your head. I carried you inside, not easily I might add, and dried you off. You had a headache but seemed to be fine. I called Principal Ludlow and told him you would miss school today."

"No. No, that's not what happened." I sat back onto the stool and pulled my hands away from her. "I'm telling the truth."

"Brolly, how could any of what you're saying be possible? An umbrella? Time travel?"

"I don't know." I started to cry. "I don't know how it's possible, I just know that it happened. It's something to do with the umbrella. We have to find it and I have to go back."

"Go back? Where, to the 1800s? Listen to yourself." Her eyes were kind, but her words skewered me like a thousand tiny arrows.

"I was there, Mom. You have to believe me."

"Darling," she said, reaching across the counter to put her hand on my cheek, "I think it must have been a dream. And it sounds like a wonderful dream, truly. A castle in France? We should all be so lucky to have such a wonderful dream."

There was no way to explain it to her, to get her to believe me. "It wasn't a dream, Mom, it was real. He's from Arrington! He's the Lord of Arrington!" I shouted it, hysterical, sure my mention of Arrington would make her realize I was telling the truth.

She didn't even flinch. "There, you see? It had to be a dream. Arrington isn't real, it's a fictional place I created. You've grown up reading those stories, Darling. It was just a dream."

"You're wrong," I said through hiccupping tears. "You're wrong."

"Brolly my darling, I love you, and I'm sorry this dream affected you so greatly, but it wasn't real." A dark sadness passed over her face as she straightened back up and began shelling the peas again. "I'm making chicken pot pie for dinner, your favorite."

Tears continued to stream down my face. Was she right? Was everything that happened just some dream? The castle and the lake and Jane and Thomas? I closed my eyes and pictured Thomas's face in the sunshine right before I found the black umbrella floating in the water. The way he said my name, how proud he was to take me home with him to England.

No, it wasn't a dream. It was real. Thomas was real. It was all real. I knew it in my bones.

I slid off the barstool and limped back upstairs, collapsing onto my bed and closing my eyes. *It was real*, I whispered to myself. *He was real and our love was real. He's real.*

"Darling," Mom said, knocking on my bedroom door and coming in at the same time. "Amelia called my phone. She said she's been calling and texting and you haven't answered. She's worried about you."

I was sitting on the floor flipping through the fourth book in The Arrington Series. I didn't know what I was looking for but there had to be something. There had to be a reference or a clue, something to prove I was telling the truth. "I turned my phone off."

"What are you doing with those books?"

"Looking for proof."

Mom sighed and knelt down next to me. "Are you still upset about the dream you had?" She picked up the second book in the series. "You won't find anything here. I made these stories up. They're fiction."

I pushed the hair out of my face and looked at her with watery eyes. "It wasn't a dream. I'm going to prove it to you."

She laid a hand on my shoulder, the soft kind of touch you give someone teetering on the edge of another emotional outburst. "Why don't you take a shower and I'll have Amelia come over. Maybe she'll help you feel better?"

Amelia, yes, I wanted to see Amelia. "Okay," I said, not looking at her. "Tell her to be here in half an hour."

I went into my bathroom, shut the door, and locked it. I

needed reassurance I'd be alone. On instinct, I pulled back the shower curtain and turned on the water, immediately stuck by how easy it was – turn a knob, hot water flowed out. I didn't need to boil water and transfer it to a freestanding bathtub in heavy buckets. Here, I could pee into a toilet and flush it away. I could slather conditioner through my hair. I could brush my teeth with a spin brush and whitening toothpaste. I didn't have to use stained rags when I was on my period.

It was too much, a reverse culture shock that sent a new wave of sadness crashing into me. I pulled off my clothes and sat down in the tub, letting the water flow over my head, beat on my body, rain down over me. For so long, I wanted nothing more than to be exactly here, and now I was a stranger in my own home. I'd left too much of me in the 19th century and now I was only half-me, half who I used to be and half who I should be.

I sat in the tub long enough for the water to turn cold. I pulled my knees up to my chest and noticed the long hair on my legs, the result of months without a razor. Proof I'd been gone! I considered screaming out for my mom and shoving my legs into her face saying, see? See this proof? But it didn't feel like enough. I needed something solid, something indisputable. I needed the umbrella. I reached forward to turn off the water and heard Amelia banging around in my room. I yanked on a robe as fast as I could and flew out of the bathroom.

"Amelia," I said, my eyes filling up with tears. I pulled her into a tight hug. "I missed you so much. So, so much."

She hugged me back. "Uhh, you know how much I love a dramatic reunion, but I saw you last night. What is going on with you? When I didn't hear from you this morning, I called Pepper to pick me up and we both got tardy slips."

"I'm sorry."

She waved me off like it was no big deal. Amelia had collected an impressive number of tardy slips throughout our high school career. "Are you okay? Your mom said you fell this morning?"

"She said that, yes." I slid down onto the floor at the foot of my bed. Amelia plopped down beside me and put her phone in my face.

"Look at this."

It took a second for my eyes to adjust to the image on the small screen. "It's…a wall?"

"Yes, the wall where the my peanut M&Ms used to be. Ludlow removed all the vending machines from the hallways, some kinda health initiative or something? You know how I get when I don't have access to my 2pm peanut M&Ms. I'm gonna have to tell my mom to buy them in bulk at Costco and smuggle them in. Oh, and you won't believe what I had to do to get Old Lady Rush to give me your assignment for Creative Writing. She made some brain-addled speech about Must Be Present To Claim but I prevailed. That woman needs to retire. I'll tell you who else needs to retire, Jeremy Barnes, that freak. He left a note in my locker asking me to go to Dunkin' D after school, like I would ever. Hey, are you okay? You look at little spaced."

When I was at the castle, I missed Amelia every single day, every single minute. Seeing her now, rattling off an entire day's worth of commentary in one long breath, solidified just how much I missed her. But I couldn't be what she needed right now. I couldn't talk about vending machines or Old Lady Rush or the long line of boys vying for her attention or anything else that should be second nature for me.

I wanted to tell her about Thomas, about his smile and his hair and the tender way he cared for me. I knew she would absolutely lose it over the blanket fort he built. But how could I tell her? How could I explain? She said it herself, she saw me last night when we went over to Ben's. Amelia was my best friend. I'd never kept a secret from her, ever. And I couldn't tell her the biggest thing that had ever happened to me.

"Brolly, you're scaring me."

I waited, hoping the silence would prompt a change of subject. Her pin-straight blonde hair was falling out of her hairband, and she was wearing a short, orange and yellow striped tank dress with beat-up white converse and no socks - so very Amelia. She stared at me, her round, blue eyes insistent, forcing me to respond.

"I'm just not feeling like myself, I guess. But I really am glad to see you. It's been so hard without you."

"Without me? For what?" She pulled a pink aluminum water bottle out of her bag and took a huge swig. "I wanted to wait and talk to you about this when you were feeling better so we could appropriately flail but did something happen with Ben? Everything seemed great between you two when Pepper and I left last night. I saw him today and he asked about you. He was genuinely concerned. Did he hurt you? I swear to God I will break his beautiful face."

Oh right, Ben, the boy I was supposed to be dating. Ben, who was flirty and cute and wanted me to be his girlfriend. Ben, who was here, in my time, and went to my high school.

"No," I said, turning to her, "no, of course not. Ben's great. I don't know how to explain what's going on with me. My mom said I fell in the rain and hit my head." I pointed out the bruised knot on my forehead. "Everything's just kind of jumbled up. I'm sorry I abandoned you."

The word hit me square in the chest. Because that's who I was now, an abandoned heart adrift in my own time, longing for someone I had no way back to.

"Is that what you're worried about? Babe, get ahold of yourself. I'm perfectly capable of dodging Central High's Neanderthals without you for one day. Speaking of, Aaron Kotras sat with me at lunch today and it was very cute. He bought me a brownie. Which, I texted to you and didn't hear back. Did you turn off your phone or something? This isn't like you."

"Maybe I'm different now," I said, my voice barely audible.

"Different from what? Why are you being so weird?"

"I need to lie down," I said, getting up from the floor and crawling into my bed.

"Yes, that seems like a good idea. I'm gonna tell your mom you should see a doctor about that knot on your head. It's like your eyes can't focus and your thoughts aren't making it all the way to your mouth."

That was Amelia, always understanding everything about me even before I did.

"I'm fine," I said. "I just need to rest."

"Okay, but turn your phone on. And text me when you wake up. If I don't hear from you in exactly three hours, I'm going into full freak out mode. Please don't make me go into full freak out mode."

"I won't. I'll text you."

Amelia blew me a kiss and opened the door.

"Amelia?"

"Yeah," she said, hoisting her heavy bag onto her shoulder.

"I love you. I probably don't say it enough, but I really do. I couldn't ask for a better best friend."

She smiled and put her hands on her hips. "I love you, too, you weirdo. Don't forget to text me."

I listened to her clomp down the stairs before I reached over to my nightstand to turn on my phone. Instead of scrolling through the many missed texts and calls, I called the only person in the world who might be able to help me in that exact moment – Pepper Comma Jones.

THIRTY-ONE

I'd thought about it in the shower, how I needed an ally if I was going to figure this thing out and evidently that ally was not my mother. Pepper's obsession with science fiction and time travel moved him to the top of the list.

"Brolly, most excellent to hear from you," he said. "I assume this call means you've recovered from your maladies?"

"Are you busy right now? Could we meet for coffee?"

He paused. "You don't drink coffee."

"I'll have tea," I said, thinking about Jane and her pots and pots of tea.

"You don't drink tea either."

"I do now," I said, digging through my closet for something to wear. Nothing in my regular rotation felt right. I found a once-worn black maxi-dress hidden in the back and pulled it out. "Can you meet?"

"Sure. The Grounds in fifteen?"

I held the long dress up in front of my full-length mirror. "I'll see you there."

I slipped the dress over my head, dug out some black flip-flops from under my bed, hurried downstairs and ran into Dad and Cale.

"Brolly Girl!" Dad said and wrapped me up in a huge hug.

"Dad," I whispered, sniffling into his shoulder and squeezing him so tight. "I missed you so much."

"Hey, what's with the tears? Your mom said you hit your head?"

"It's probably her cycle, Dad," Cale said. "That's what happens to women during menstruation."

"Oh yeah?" Dad raised his eyebrows at Cale. "What exactly do you know about menstruation?"

"Enough to be grossed out forever," Cale said, trudging up the stairs with his backpack thump-thumping behind him.

Dad turned back to me, his arms still wrapped around my shoulders. "Is everything all right?"

"Yeah, just had a rough...morning. I'm so happy to see you."

"Do you want to talk about it? We could sit on the porch swing?"

I paused, wanting to tell him but knowing I couldn't. Talks with Dad always worked for me. We'd sit on the front porch swing and talk through whatever problem I needed to work out. His advice always erred slightly trite, but it made me feel better every time.

"I'm actually on my way out. Can we talk later?"

"Sure. The offer stands if you need it."

"Thanks, Dad." I hugged him one more time and walked through the still open front door."Hey, Brolly Girl."

I turned around and Dad was smiling at me, the smile he reserved for times like these when he knew I needed to talk, even though I said I didn't.

"Yeah?"

"I love you forever."

When I was six, I watched a Netflix movie about a kid whose dad died in a train accident. I worried for a week straight that Dad was going to die in a train accident, following him around day and night to make sure he didn't come in contact with any trains. He tucked me into bed one night and said, "Listen, I can't promise you nothing bad will ever happen to me. That's not something we can know. But I can promise that I'll love you forever, no matter what." It was enough to quell my six-year-old fears. Since then, it had been our thing.

I smiled back at him. "Thanks, Dad. I love you forever."

I pulled into The Grounds at exactly 4:32 pm and Pepper's LeSabre was already in the parking lot. I found him inside at a small table against an exposed brick wall covered in canvas paintings from local artists. Pepper was sitting directly underneath a huge painting of a girl in a long, powder blue dress spinning in a night sky. I'd seen the painting before. Pepper, Amelia, and I sometimes hung out there after school, but this time it made me nervous. The girl in the painting looked like me, spinning though a sea of stars, eyes closed, limbs flung out like a starfish, unaware of what was happening or what was about to happen. I didn't want to be that girl. I wanted to be on solid ground with the people I loved. All the people I loved.

"Good afternoon, Mademoiselle," Pepper called to me in his characteristically odd way. It was exactly what Pepper would normally say but the familiar greeting brought fresh tears to my eyes.

"Hey," he said, reaching out to touch my arm as I slid into the brown leather booth, "did I say something wrong?"

"Yes. I mean, no. I don't know. Pepper, I need your help."

"I'm here for you. Whatever you need." His wide brown eyes were peaked with concern.

"Did you order coffee?" I said, wiping my tears away with the palms of my hands.

"Yes, and I ordered you an English breakfast tea with honey."

My mouth fell open. "How did you know that's what I would order?"

Pepper pushed his glasses up his nose. "Lucky guess?"

"Oh, Pepper," I cried.

He reached out again and laid a warm hand on my arm. "Brolly, did something happen? I don't think I've ever seen you cry before. You're making me nervous." It struck me how everyone in this time touched me so naturally, how familiar we all were with each other. I liked it. I'd missed it.

I wiped my face again and took a deep breath.

"Okay. First of all, I need you to just listen. I'm going to say some things that make absolutely no sense, and you will definitely think I've lost my grip on reality. But I need you to listen."

He straightened his posture and folded his hands together on top of the table, looking at my tear-stained face with determined scrutiny. "Okay."

"You remember the storm from this morning?"

"Yeah, it knocked out the power at my house."

"Mine, too. I was looking for a shirt I wanted to wear. I couldn't find it anywhere and I thought maybe my mom borrowed it. I went into her closet to look for it."

He didn't say anything, just listened intently. I hesitated, nervous about what came next.

"I found a box in her closet, like a shipping box."

"Okay."

"It was taped shut and I opened it. I have no idea why, but I opened it."

"Okay."

"There was an umbrella in it."

"Okay."

"Pepper, stop saying okay."

"O...sorry. I'm just trying to stay with you."

I gripped the table to steady myself. "It was weird because my parents have never owned any umbrellas. But like I said, I was looking for my shirt, so I grabbed it to go out and look in my car. I was stressed about running late and picking up Amelia so I rushed outside and…"

"And?"

"…and I opened the umbrella."

Pepper started to say something, probably *okay* but then stopped.

"It was like a bomb went off. I was thrown off my porch and into this, like, tailspin. I don't know how to describe it. It was like someone threw me into a washing machine set to wild. Honestly, I thought I was dying. Then it all just stopped, the turbulent spinning and scary blackness, it just stopped. I looked up and I wasn't in front of my house anymore. Pepper, I was in an entirely different place, an entirely different…" I looked around the coffee shop. There was only one person sitting near us and he was wearing giant noise-canceling headphones. "I was in an entirely different-"

"Here's your coffee, sir. And tea, for you." It was the barista, bringing our drinks. I waited while she set the drinks down, the words on the tip of my tongue. Pepper was staring at me like he knew what I was going to say. When the barista walked away, he waved his hand for me to keep going.

"I was in a different time."

"You time traveled." It wasn't a question.

"I…yes. I did. You believe me?"

"Yes," he said, pouring milk into his coffee. "Why wouldn't I?"

I couldn't help but laugh. "Because it's impossible? Because maybe I just dreamed the whole thing? Because of a million reasons?"

Pepper hunched over the table, pushing his coffee mug forward with his crossed arms. "Tell me every detail and don't leave anything out."

"Oh, my God," I said, "you don't know how happy I am that you believe me. I told my mom what happened, but she tried to convince me it was just a dream."

He squinted his eyes. "Where did you arrive?"

I took a sip of my tea, soaking in the fact that Pepper believed me. It was a pinprick of light at the end of a very long, very dark tunnel. But it was a light. "A castle on a lake. In France."

"When?"

"1826."

"Interesting."

My mouth opened and closed a few times before I was able to respond. "Interesting? That's what you have to say when I tell you I time traveled to the year 1826? Interesting? Why does none of this faze you?"

He shrugged. "Because I believe in the possibility of time travel. Because there are several clues that lead me to believe something supernatural happened to you."

"Clues?"

"For one thing, Amelia called me when she left your house today. She said you were overwhelmed when you saw her, like you hadn't seen her in a long time."

"I was gone weeks and weeks, months! I missed you guys so much."

"Exactly. And now that I see you, your hair is longer."

I reached up and touched my hair which now fell well past my shoulders.

"While I was gone...I met someone."

"Uh-oh."

"Yes. Uh-oh. He's an English Lord and he's, Pepper, he's - I love him." Tears welled up in my eyes again and I stared up at the painting of the girl in the stars. "I need to go back. I have to get back to him."

Pepper hadn't touched his coffee. He was still leaning forward, intently focused on my story. "Do you believe it was the umbrella that sparked your travel?"

"I think so, yes. Both times, when I went there and then when I came back, I was holding the umbrella."

"Did you bring it? I need to see it."

"No. My mom said it must have blown away in the storm. She said I fell and bumped my head. She said she carried me inside and dried me off, that I was out of it. But that's not what happened."

He rubbed his eyebrows together and his glasses slid down his nose. "You found it in her closet? It was taped up in a box?" I nodded. "Do you think she understands its power?"

"I don't know. She acted like she didn't know anything about it."

"I'd reason she does know about its power and is hiding it from you for some reason. Do you know why she would hide it?"

I wrapped my hands around the warm mug of tea, a sudden chill coursing through me. "But why would she do that? I told her what happened. I told her."

"Because she didn't seem upset about it being lost, even though she'd made an effort to keep it hidden in the first place. Surely something important enough to secure and hide would be worth looking for?"

I had nothing to say to that, instead staring down into my mug, the teabag floating to the surface. It was so obvious when he said it. Mom didn't seem concerned about the umbrella at all, which didn't add up. Why would she hide it and then not care that it was gone?

"Tell me what else happened," Pepper said, taking his glasses off and pinching the bridge of his nose with his eyes closed, "all the details surrounding the event."

"The only thing I know for sure is that I was holding the umbrella both times."

Pepper finally drank his coffee. He set the mug down and rubbed his chin with his left hand. "When you traveled the first time, what were you wearing?"

"Grey shorts and a Central High t-shirt. The one from that 5k we did."

"And were those the clothes you were wearing when you arrived in 1826?"

"Yes." A lump formed in my throat.

"And what were you wearing when you traveled the second time?"

I thought back to this morning when we left for England. "I was wearing a long cream-colored dress with complicated underwear and itchy stockings. I was dressed like I was from 1826."

Pepper straightened up and smiled. "It stands to reason the dress is what you were wearing when you arrived back at your house. Which means your mother would have seen you wearing it."

Goosebumps popped up on my arms. He was right, she would have seen me in the dress. "When I woke up in my room, I was wearing shorts and a tank top, not the dress."

Pepper's face went gravely serious. "You know what this means?"

It meant my mother was lying to me or at the very least, hiding something from me. It meant she might still have the umbrella. It meant there may still be a way back to Thomas. "I need to find the dress."

On my drive home, I couldn't stop thinking about Mom seeing me in the dress from the castle. If she did, she'd ask a zillion questions, would worry over every detail, would not rest until she knew all the whys and hows of where I got it and why I was wearing it. Her nonchalance attitude about the whole thing was troubling enough, but the idea she was intentionally hiding something made all the straight lines of my life go wavy. Mom was the kind of woman who told the cashier at Target when she had gas. She didn't keep secrets. It's what made her a great writer, her inability to hold anything back.

As soon as I got back, I ran up the stairs to her and dad's room to look for anything I could find - the umbrella, the dress, anything at all that would link me to the castle. Mom was suspiciously working at her desk and she never worked at her desk. She always worked in her favorite chair downstairs with her legs slung over the armrest or at the kitchen table or out on the back patio when the weather was nice, anywhere but her actual desk.

"Hello, Darling, are you feeling better? How was your visit with Amelia?"

I took her in, her posture and her smile and her eyes, looking for the deception. The lie. It was treacherous, being suspicious of my own mother. She'd only ever been all the good things a mom should be – nurturing and loving and strong and fun, a safe place.

"It was good. I was glad to see her."

Since I couldn't search the room that mattered most, I checked the downstairs hall closet, quietly opening boxes and board games, digging through a trash bag of clothes meant for Goodwill. I checked the guest bathroom, searching in between each folded towel and sheet set. I checked the guest room, opening dresser drawers and checking under the pillows on the bed. I searched coat pockets inside the closet, put away for the summer. I searched under the living room couch, the shelf in the laundry room, the large plastic tubs that lined the walls of the garage and held all the Christmas decorations.

The only thing I found was Cale's magic quarter.

Cale was in his room, headphones over his ears, silently

thrashing around. I grabbed him by the shoulders and he screamed.

"Dude! Don't ever sneak up on me when I'm practicing my sweet dance moves." I held up the quarter as payment for what I was about to ask. "You found it!"

"It was under the couch in the living room. And since I totally came through and found your quarter, I need you to let me check your room for something." I pulled open a dresser drawer.

Cale smacked the drawer closed. "No. Go away."

"It'll just take a minute." I opened his closet door.

He slammed it shut. "This is my personal area. Get out."

"Have you seen a black umbrella anywhere? Or maybe a long white dress that looks...old?"

"Get out. Now." He pointed to the door, his face scrunched into the meanest expression he could muster. I stared across the hall into my mom's room. It seemed the most obvious place for her to hide something and it definitely felt like she was hanging out in there, guarding whatever it was. But, if she was really hiding the umbrella, if she had my dress, I doubted she'd be so obvious about it. Of course, she'd had the umbrella in a cardboard box in her closet with nothing but flimsy tape to keep it closed. Perhaps my mother wasn't the master deceiver I was making her out to be.

I went to my room and picked up my phone from the bed. Amelia had been texting, preparing to go into full freak out mode. I typed out a reply.

Me: *I'm alive. Dressed even, but still a little woozy. Let's talk at school tomorrow.*

Amelia: *Lucky girl. You were seconds away from an Amelia Assault the likes of which this town has never seen. I hope you're prepared to spill all the Ben beans tomorrow because I have been waiting ever so patiently and a girl can only take so much.*

Me: *My beans will be yours for the picking.*

I held my phone against my heart, so happy to be able to talk to Amelia again. I knew I needed to focus on that, on the good. And there was a lot of good. Being back with my family and my friends was healing, stitching together a gaping wound that crept across my heart when I was in France. I was happy to be home, I was. But Thomas was now a part of me. I couldn't rest until I figured out how to get back to him.

THIRTY-TWO

I was in my room, headphones on, blaring classical music. I'd
been sifting through everything I could dig up from the
early 1800s, searching for the songs Thomas's string quartet
played for us. I should have asked the musicians what they were
playing but at the time, I never imagined I'd be here, lying on
The Hideous Blue Rug, scanning dead composers on Spotify.

The memory of Thomas ached like a bruise, tender when I
touched it. If my life were a movie, this would be the part where
the swoony montage played. Thomas's fingertips grazing my
waist. That first night in the rain when he reached for me, when
he saved me. The way he melted into the couch when he listened
to me read to him in the library, the setting sun on his face that
made his eyes shine like polished copper. Every moment with
Thomas was an impossibility. We never should have met, never
should have existed in the same space, the same time. But
we did.

I Google'd early 19th century string quartet composers and
found a few tracks from Beethoven. I toggled back to Spotify to
search Beethoven string quartet and pressed play on the first one
– String Quartet No.15 in a A minor, Op. 132. Soothing violin
strings streamed from my headphones, pouring into me like

slow honey. As the melody played, I pressed the mental bruise and let the castle memories wash over me.

I was twenty songs deep when a text popped up on my phone.

Pepper: *Any luck with the dress? Or the umbrella?*

Me: *No, neither. Mom's been guarding her room like a thick-necked bouncer.*

Pepper: *Maybe your house has a hidden trap door. Or a bookcase that's actually a secret door to a secret room.*

Me: *I've always wanted one of those.*

Pepper: *Same.*

The next song started to play, String Quartet No.5 in A, Op. 18 No. 5:4 Allegro.

Me: *You really believe me, don't you?*

Pepper: *Yes, I do. Also, I'm working on some ideas.*

Me: *Ideas?*

Pepper: *I'll keep you posted. For now, keep looking. You'll find something.*

Keep looking. You'll find something. I repeated Pepper's words out loud when a new text came in, this time from Ben.

Oh, God, I thought, *Ben.*

I hadn't taken one minute to think about how to handle Ben.

Ben: *Busy?*

I stared at it for the entire length of the song, an impressive six minutes and 14 seconds, give or take.

Me: *No. You?*

Ben: *Look out your window.*

I pulled myself up off The Hideous Blue Rug and looked out my bedroom window. There was Ben, waving at me from his truck parked on the street. My body turned to stone, like if I was completely still maybe he wouldn't be able to see me. Because for him, last night was sitting in his room, kissing and flirting and falling for each other. For me, last night was kissing Thomas in the kitchen and planning our life together in England. Whatever developing feelings I had for Ben had been extinguished. I'd never be able to say yes to him now.

I was in my pajamas, worn navy shorts and a pink t-shirt that said "ZZZZZ" in giant black letters across the front. I yanked my headphones off and made my way downstairs and out to the curb. Ben's arm was hanging out the window, his fingers tapping on the side of the door.

'Hey, you," he said as I walked toward the truck with my arms crossed over my chest, remembering too late I wasn't wearing a bra. I never wore a bra at the castle but somehow facing Ben without one left me too exposed. "Missed you today."

"Yeah, apparently I fell off my porch this morning and banged my head pretty good."

Ben got out of the truck and came over to me. He gently pushed my hair back from my forehead. "That looks painful. I'm guessing that's why you weren't answering your texts? I wanted to make sure you weren't avoiding answering my question."

"I was asleep most of the day. I'm sorry." For so much. I was sorry for so, so much.

"No need to be sorry, I'm just glad you're okay. I was sitting at home thinking about you and decided to come over and invite you on a late night, aimless wander."

It was exactly the sort of thing old me would want a guy like Ben to say at ten pm on a school night. Because Ben was exactly the kind of guy old me wanted to be with. And here he was, fulfilling every wish.

"Sounds cautionary."

"Oh, come on," he said, grabbing my hand and swinging it between us, "late night aimless wanders are the lifeblood to any interesting love story."

He wasn't making it easy on me, so earnest and sweet. And kind. And everything good. As an added bonus, he lived in my time and not in some ancient castle on the wrong side of history.

But he wasn't Thomas.

"I can't tonight. I've got a ton of homework."

He smirked. "It's the first day of school. You do not have a ton of homework."

"I just...I can't tonight."

He smiled and hung his head. "You're really gonna make me work for it, aren't you?"

"Ben, I-"

"Who's your friend?"

I whipped around and flat out glared at my mom who had somehow snuck up right behind me. I let go of Ben's hand and crossed my arms over my chest.

"Hi," Ben said with a little wave, "I'm Ben Hartfield."

Mom stuck her hand out. "Wonderful to meet you, I've heard so much about you. I'm Emily Parker."

"Nice to meet you," he said and shook her hand.

I was still staring at her, willing her to stop whatever charade this was.

"What are you two up to tonight?" she said, ignoring my glare.

Ben grinned. "I was inviting Brolly out for a drive. I hope that's okay, Mrs. Parker."

"I was just telling Ben goodnight."

She smiled at me. "It's a nice night for a drive. You should go." I could see my anger in the reflection of her eyes.

There was a weird moment where I was looking at my mom who was looking at Ben who was looking at me. "It's been a long day. I should go to bed," I said, eyes wide at my mom, willing her to leave.

She took the hint. "It was nice to meet you Ben," she said with a friendly smile. "You're welcome here anytime."

I watched her walk up to the porch and waited until she was inside before turning to Ben. "Sorry about that."

"I don't mind. But, hey, is everything okay? You don't seem like yourself."

I shook my head and forced a smile onto my face. "I'm fine."

He scratched through the hair above his ear. "No way I can talk you into time away from your pretend homework?"

"Sorry, not tonight."

"Okay. I guess I'll see you at school tomorrow."

I kept the smile plastered on my face. "Yeah, tomorrow."

Ben climbed back into his truck and waved as he drove away. I waved back and stood on the sidewalk until he was out of sight. Then I went inside to face my mom, who was picking up all the scattered shoes near the front door and putting them back into the basket.

"Ben seems nice," she said.

"Why did you come out there and practically shove me into his truck?"

She stood up and put her hands on her hips. "That's a little dramatic don't you think?"

"What I think is that you're refusing to believe what happened to me."

"What happened to you when?"

I leaned back hard against the front door. "Mom. I told you this morning. I time traveled. I've been gone for months."

She sighed and sat down on the stairs. "Darling. You have to get over this."

I looked down into the basket and remembered. The morning I left, I put Mom's green flip-flops on before I went out onto the porch. The green flip-flops that were now in France.

"Where are your flip-flops?"

She crossed her arms over her knees. "What flip-flops?"

I dug through the basket, tossing out Cale's baseball cleats and Dad's running shoes and three pairs of black flip-flops and a single brown sandal. "The green ones with the nick from that time you dropped a steak knife. Where are they?"

She shook her head. "Please clean up those shoes, I just finished putting them all back."

"I'll tell you exactly where they are. I put them on that morning, the morning I time traveled. They're at a castle in France in

1826. They blew off my feet when I landed in the storm, but later I found one floating in the lake. I kept it in the back of the wardrobe in the dressing room underneath all of the dresses I wore."

She stared at me, expressionless.

"Where are my grey shorts? My 5k t-shirt? I know you won't have an answer for that because I know they aren't here, either."

"Brolly."

"I'm telling the truth. Let me know when you're ready to do the same." I stomped past her up the stairs and slammed my bedroom door.

THIRTY-THREE

Pepper, Ben and I were at Big Mike's Pizza and Wings sharing an extra-large Cajun pepperoni pizza. Amelia had just started working there and was adamant we all come and sit in her section. It was karaoke night, a fact I wish I'd known before agreeing to show up. I was doing my best to act normal and not raise any more suspicions than I already had, but I was a walking time bomb, my emotions swinging wildly from extreme heartbreak to boiling rage. I'd skipped school again, claiming a headache from my alleged fall off the porch. Mom didn't argue, but she also kept a close eye on me the entire day so I never had a chance to turn the house inside out like I'd planned. I might as well have gone to school.

When I got to Big Mike's, Amelia dragged me straight into the bathroom and leaned against the door so no one could come in.

"Okay, now that your eyes are back in focus and you seem to have returned to planet earth, tell me. What. Happened."

I paled. Had Pepper told her? Did she know about Thomas?

"What happened with what?"

"Ha ha, very funny. If you don't tell me right this second

what happened with Ben after Pepper and I left movie night I will pterodactyl screech right in this bathroom."

I went with the truth, even though the memories were cloudy.

"We went up to his room and he kissed me and asked me to be his girlfriend."

Amelia didn't say anything, just stood there dumbfounded. Someone pushed on the bathroom door and she yelled, "Occupied!" and shoved up against it before turning back to me. "Babe, I'm gonna need more information, like a lot more. He kissed you? Like, he *kissed* you kissed you? How did it happen? What did he say? Did you say yes to being his girlfriend? I mean, of course you said yes, it's Ben. I cannot believe this. Did you-"

Amelia's rant was interrupted by someone else trying to open the bathroom door.

"We can talk about it later. People need to pee."

She grumpily moved aside from the door and a little girl rushed in, ran into a stall, and slammed the door. I made a quick exit and joined Ben and Pepper at the table. Ben pulled out the chair next to his with a big smile.

"Sorry I missed lunch today," he said to Pepper. "When I went to Coach Chang's office to talk to him about the swim team, he kept asking me questions about my old school. I guess he knew my old swim coach and saw me swim in some meets last year. I'm hoping that means I can get a walk-on spot on the team."

"So, what, you're some kind of swim celebrity?" Amelia asked, refilling Ben's water glass from a giant pitcher. A middle-aged woman in mom jeans was belting out "All By Myself" by Celine Dion on the tiny karaoke stage.

"Obviously," Ben said. "I gave Coach Chang my autograph and told him not to look me in the eye or my bodyguard would put the hurt on him."

"That's good," I said, participating. "Best to set clear boundaries right away or the fans could get out of hand."

Ben laughed and took a huge bite of pizza. "What about you?" he asked, covering his mouth with his fist while he chewed. "I was worried when you didn't show."

"I still wasn't feeling so hot this morning, although I wish I'd just powered through. My mom drove me crazy all day. She's on a deadline."

"Deadline?'

"Brolly's mom's an author. She wrote the Arrington series," Amelia said, motioning to another table that she'd be right over.

My stomach twisted at the casual mention of Arrington. In the background a woman with bright red hair and a bedazzled blazer started singing her best Reba McEntire rendition of "Fancy."

"Emily Parker writes with a precision and level of insight no other modern author has been able to capture," Pepper said. "It's almost as if she interviewed her characters in person before writing down their stories. She's an outstanding voice in 19th century fiction." He gave me a pointed look.

Amelia rolled her eyes. "God, Pepper, are you some kind of Emily Parker fanboy?"

"I make an effort to stay abreast of the latest in the literary world," Pepper said, affronted.

"And movies. And TV," Amelia said, ignoring the loud throat clearing from the table next to us with obviously empty glasses.

"I have a healthy capacity for entertainment, both in the written and visual form, yes."

"I guess I need to read these books," Ben said, pulling his phone out of his pocket.

"I don't know if you'd like them," I said. "They're sort of Jane Austen meets Real Housewives." And me. And Thomas. And Jane.

"My mom's obsessed with the housewives. Personally, I'm partial to Orange County."

I stared at him, annoyed by how perfect he was. Annoyed that he watched Bravo. Annoyed that he wanted to be with me. Annoyed that I should want to be with him.

"What are you doing?" I meant it literally, but I also wanted to know what he was doing in general. Why me. Why now. Why this way.

"I keep a list of books I want to read in my notes app. I'm adding your mom's books so I won't forget." He shoved his phone back into his pocket.

Amelia left to refill drinks for her other tables.

"Hey, did you know Jones and I are lab partners in chemistry?" Ben said, high-fiving Pepper across the table.

I pursed my lips and drew back. "You call him Jones?"

"Who calls who Jones?" Amelia said, back at our table way before she should have been.

I pointed a thumb at Ben and Amelia punched him lightly in the arm. "Why are you calling him Jones?"

"I'm sitting right here," Pepper said.

"This summer he introduced himself to me as Jones so that's what I call him."

"Whatever," I said, "At least if you're lab partners he can do all your homework."

"Oh, I get it," Ben said, "dumb jock can't do his own chemistry homework." His tone was menacing but his eyes were playful. He cocked his head to the side causing his swoopy blonde hair to swoop even further. I knew this was the part where my pulse should quicken and my cheeks should flush, which is what would happen to any other girl faced with the look Ben Hartfield was currently leveling at me.

"Maybe, but Pepper's a genius. Might as well let him flex his well-toned chem muscles. He did all my biology homework in tenth grade." I did my best to maintain friendly eye contact without sending the wrong message.

Pepper took that moment to inform us all he did not appreciate being the subject of discord. "I haven't provided Ben with the oral history of all of our exploits, but yes, I am always happy to assist those in scientific need."

Ben glanced over at me and playfully grabbed my knee. I smiled but crossed my legs away from his touch. I didn't know how to do this. How to fall back into the routine of being a Central High senior who gets pizza with her friends. I didn't know how to go to class and do my homework and date the jock and be normal.

Ben excused himself to the bathroom and Amelia went to the kitchen to retrieve an order. I texted Pepper from across the table.

Me: *H.E.L.P.*

Pepper: *Heroine Eats Lackluster Pizza?*

Me: *Very funny. I have to tell him.*

Pepper: *But what will you say?*

Me: *I was hoping you would help me with that part.*

I looked up to see Pepper shrug and shake his head no.

"Uhh, Brolly?" Amelia was back at our table carrying a giant pizza tray holding a steaming BBQ chicken pizza. Her eyebrows were so high they became one with her hairline. I followed her worried expression to the tiny karaoke stage – and Ben – holding a microphone, grinning so hard there was danger of his face cracking in two. He was looking right at me as he started to sing "I Want to Hold Your Hand" by The Beatles. He was literally singing about holding hands. To me. In Big Mike's Pizza and Wings.

He got all the way to the second verse before Amelia shouted, "Oh, my God, is he really doing this?"

"I believe he is definitely doing this," Pepper said over Ben's cracking voice.

All I could do was stare. When Ben got to the last chorus, he started to shimmy his shoulders back and forth and a table of middle-aged women near the front clapped their hands and squealed like Ben was a plate of macho nachos and today was their cheat day. Amelia, Pepper, and I continued to gape, not believing our eyes.

And Ben, he never broke. He smiled and shimmied his way through the entire song without a hint of embarrassment. On the last note, he held his hand out in my direction, the entirety of Big Mike's Pizza and Wings, including Amelia, cheering him on. I didn't know what I was supposed to do – act embarrassed? Go up and take his hand? I stayed in my seat and clapped as Ben took a bow and jogged back to our table, high fiving several people on the way.

"Wow, Ben, I had no idea you were such a showman," Amelia said, looking at me.

"I just thought it might cheer Brolly up," Ben said, taking a huge gulp of water. A chunk of ice dislodged from the bottom of his cup and smacked him in the nose. He laughed and set the cup down on the table, wiping his face with his hand. "Who's next?"

I pushed my chair back and pulled my bag onto my shoulder. "Not me. I gotta go."

"Come on, stay for a while," Amelia whined. "Or at least leave me a huge tip before you go."

"Yeah, stay. We could do a duet." Ben was smiling again. It was flirty and innocent and the very definition of disconcerting.

"I really should go." I pulled three $5 bills out of my wallet and tossed them onto the table and stood up.

Ben grabbed my hand and squeezed. "Didn't you like the song?"

It was an impossible question to answer. If I said I liked it, I was leading him on. If I said I didn't, I was an evil ice queen with no soul.

"Who wouldn't like a performance like that? It was great, Ben, really. I think that table full of grandmas wants to adopt you." I moved into the aisle. "I'll see y'all tomorrow, okay?"

Ben was already walking ahead of me, pushing open the door and waiting for me to walk through. He followed me out.

"I was surprised you decided to come. You seem like you're still not feeling well." Ben looked down as we walked, his hands pushed deep in his pockets.

"Amelia's power of persuasion."

He let out a soft chuckle. "I'll have to ask her for some tips."

I quirked an eyebrow at him. We were at my car, but before I could open the door, he was leaning against it, his arms crossed over his broad chest.

"It's obvious I'm working pretty hard over here, isn't it?"

"Ben."

"I just don't know what changed. We seemed to have a really great connection this summer and then the other night at my house and…after. Suddenly it's like you're, I don't know, not interested?"

Hearing him describe my behavior out loud made me sound like a real jerk. Because he was right. Before I opened the black umbrella, things between us were great. He was into me and I was into him and I was starting senior year with every category of my life exactly as it should be: best friends, awesome boyfriend, happy family, college on the horizon. But the black umbrella toppled everything to the ground.

The night air was thick and humid, weighing me down like a secret. I wished I could tell Ben the truth, wished I could make him understand that I wasn't suddenly disinterested, I was different. The worst part was, if Ben could accept the time traveling portion of the story, I knew he'd be nice about the rest. He was the kind of guy who'd be happy for me despite his own feelings.

"It's not that I'm not," I sighed and dropped my bag onto the pavement, "this is…you're…"

He put his hand up, halting my stumbling speech. "You can say anything to me." He pressed his lips together and uncrossed his arms to put his hands back in his front pockets, waiting.

"I think you're great. Like, really great. Weirdly great. Any girl would be lucky to-"

"Brolly, slow down. Just tell me how you feel."

I hated this. I hated being this person. "I'm just not ready… not able…to be your girlfriend. Anyone's girlfriend." He watched me, listening, his face unreadable. "I don't want to disappoint you."

He took my hands into his. "Like I said the other night, I like you. I like your intentionality and your aloofness that's really quiet observation. And it doesn't hurt that you're completely adorable. I know we haven't known each other that long but I feel like we could be good together. And if it doesn't work out, it doesn't." He let go of my hands and scrubbed over his face, thinking. "Who said it? Whitman? Better to have loved and lost than never to have loved at all."

"It was Tennyson."

"See? How could I resist you and your sexy brain?" I smiled, an honest, genuine smile. "If you just want to be friends, I will respect that. All I want is for you to be yourself and to be honest with me. That's it. And I promise to give you the same. But just know that I'm hoping for more."

I looked up at him, at his ocean blue eyes, so open and honest. Something I could no longer be. "I'd really like to be friends."

His shoulders sagged. "Friends. Ugh."

I hugged him then, not because he was my boyfriend, but because he was Ben and so nice and so willing to let me figure things out even when he had no idea how deep the rabbit hole went. When I pulled away, his smile didn't reach his eyes, his whole face shaded by disappointed.

I got into my car and waved good-bye. Ben waited until I was out of the parking lot before he turned and went back inside.

Amelia texted me as soon as I got home.

Amelia: *Did you break Ben? As soon as my shift is done I'm coming over.*

Two hours later, she barged into my room demanding answers.

"I need you to tell me this instant what is going on," she said, tossing her bag onto my bed and pacing around the room. "Let's run this down. You and Ben flirted like the world was coming to an end for the entire summer. Then you two were all barf-cute at his house. And you said he kissed you after Pepper and I left and that he asked you to be his girlfriend, although you didn't seem very excited about it come to think. Then he sings to you at Big Mike's and you barely even react? Then he walked you to your car and came back in looking like he'd just watched the opening montage from *Up*." She plopped down on the floor and pulled me down to sit next to her. "One of these things is not like the other."

My thoughts screamed through my head. *I understand you think it's a good idea for me to date the most gorgeous boy we've ever seen up close, and I know you think I'm nuts for not being excited that he likes me, but you see I can't date the hot lifeguard because I'm committed to an English Lord.*

"I don't know, he's..." I paused, trying to find the right words.

"Babe, I am going to die right here on The Hideous Blue Rug if you do not spill right this instant. Do not summarize. I want the director's cut."

"I told him I just want to be friends."

Amelia narrowed her eyes at me like she couldn't even believe what I was doing, shrugging apathetic at Captain Hottest Dude Ever. I narrowed my eyes back, hoping for a mind meld that would explain it to her without me having to use words. She laid down on the carpet and threw her arms over her head.

"Friends. The sexy lifeguard we thirsted after all summer is one hundred percent into you and you want to be friends."

"Ben's perfect," I said, "like, literally perfect in every way. He's kind and considerate and polite and caring and fun and-"

"Don't forget his status as a Greek god."

"That, too. At first it was fun, you know, hot lifeguard pursues unassuming girl."

Amelia sniffed. "I've seen that movie."

"Exactly my point."

"Let me get this straight. He's perfect, insanely hot, totally into you in a movie kind of way…yes, I can see how terrible that would be for you."

I let out a long sigh, trying to explain. "It's not terrible, he's not terrible. We just don't fit."

"You don't fit?" I could see her trying to listen to me and not shout in my face that I was being completely ridiculous. She didn't need to shout it. I already knew. "I mean, okay, good for you for being true to yourself and your feelings and girl power and all that, but it feels like you changed your mind super suddenly. You do remember the lethal dosages of lust we experienced this summer, right? You said your internal organs would melt if he ever even talked to you. And I agreed. I mean, this is the guy Pam Byers would sacrifice a freshman to be with, the guy we've since discovered is totally nice and great and you, you want to be friends."

I bit the inside of my cheek. "Friends."

She sat back up and stared at me. "Something's up with you."

She knew. Of course she knew.

"Nothing's up with me. I'm not automatically obligated to date Ben."

"No one's saying that. It's just…it's like you flipped a switch or something. You've been off for two days and I can't figure out why. And it's not even about Ben. You're not you."

"I'm me," I lied. "I'm totally me."

"Did you forget who you're talking to? I knew the day you got your first period before you did. In the 6th grade, I knew you had a crush on Jack Stamos before you even admitted it to yourself." She pointed her finger in my face. "I know you."

I wanted to tell her. I wanted to tell her more than anything. I wanted to tell her every detail about the life I left behind. It wasn't fully real because I hadn't shared it with her. But I couldn't do it.

"I'm fine," I said. "Really."

"Forget Ben. In fact, forget all of them, all the guys. I say we take a vow of male poverty."

"That's not the right use of poverty."

"The point is," she said, exasperated, "that boys are cute and fun to kiss but not if they do this to you." She motioned over my body, like it was broken.

"Ben didn't do this to me."

She eyed me quietly for so long I worried she was mad at me. Finally, she said, "It doesn't matter. Whatever it is, I'll still love you. And I'll be here, you know, whenever you're ready to tell me."

I laid my head on her shoulder. "You're really going to give up guys?"

"Why not? They're all completely useless."

I smiled "Except for Pepper."

"Yes, God bless Pepper."

THIRTY-FOUR

I spent Saturday locked in my room, skimming through my mother's Arrington books, looking for the tiniest morsel to corroborate my story, any shred of a clue. The books were painfully familiar, both because I'd read them before and because the dialogue and setting were so much like the life I'd left behind. But there wasn't anything concrete, nothing I could use to prove I was telling the truth. I never actually went to Arrington and it wasn't like Thomas showed me photos of Arrington on his phone. Every detail from the books could have come from a vivid retelling of a history book.

I took every opportunity I could to search my parents' room. If Mom was really hiding the umbrella and the dress, she was doing an amazing job. I'd searched the entire house, done everything but tear the shingles off the roof to look underneath. I avoided the thought of what I'd do if I did find any damning evidence. It would prove my story but then what? How could my mom possibly know about Arrington? Would it mean she knew about Thomas and Jane, too? She'd had the umbrella, had it hidden in a box in her closet. It had to mean she knew it's magic, knew what happened if you opened it. I couldn't think of a rational reason why she'd hide that fact.

Google searches were a dead end. I found one mention of an Arrington from the 18th and 19th centuries on a site about English estates, but no mention of Thomas or the Westbourne family. No photo. Nothing tangible. I searched for Chateau du Lac but it was another dead end. I searched for Thomas, Elizabeth, even Jane and Phillipe, but there was nothing. It was as if none of them existed, a thought I couldn't fully process.

Sunday afternoon I got a text from Pepper.

Pepper: *I have an idea. I'm not promising it's a good idea, but I'm wondering if you'd be willing to try something?*

Me: *I'll try anything*

Pepper: *We'd need to do it on your front porch, probably without your parents knowing. Is that possible?*

Me: *They're going out to dinner with some friends. Should be gone by 7:00.*

Pepper: *I'll see you then.*

Pepper showed up at five after seven carrying a huge armful of umbrellas. He laid them all out in neat row on the porch.

"I think we need to eliminate a few possibilities," he said. "I've been doing some research and I think there are two, maybe three theories we could work from. One, the umbrella was the time travel catalyst. Two, the storm, possibly a charge from a lightning strike, was the time travel catalyst. Three, it was a perfect storm of both, pun intended."

"I think it was the umbrella. It wasn't storming when I left France."

"I considered that, but there is a theory that suggests you need a certain set of circumstances to travel from one particular point. Maybe this point," he said, pointing to the front door, "requires a storm. Maybe it doesn't. That's why we need to do some eliminating."

I put my hands on my hips and scanned the umbrellas. "Okay, so what are we doing with these?"

"Experimenting," Pepper said. "We try opening them from the same spot where you traveled the first time. See what happens."

My jaw clenched. Was I ready to do it right then? Ready to jump back in time without really knowing what would happen? I looked at Pepper's umbrellas again – a small, purse-sized black umbrella with a plastic handle, a long navy blue one with a wooden handle that curved up into a U-shape, a giant green and white golf umbrella and a kid-sized clear dome umbrella. None of them looked anything like my umbrella.

"If you're right, and I open one of these, it might take me somewhere totally different," I said. There was only one place I wanted to go. I had no intention of accidentally ending up in the Dark Ages or Ancient Rome or like, the 1950s.

"That's why it's an experiment." Pepper picked up the golf umbrella. "I am willing to take the risk and open the first one."

"Pepper, no."

"Just to see what happens," he said.

I pulled him away from the door. "I can't let you do that. What if it goes wrong?"

"Brolly, I am perfectly capable of making-"

"I know you are. I know. But it has to be me."

He shook his head but handed me the golf umbrella. He didn't want me to be right, but he knew I was right.

I stood in front of the door, in the same place where I was standing when I traveled the first time. Pepper and I looked at each other, a silent permission and a potential goodbye. If this worked, if I found Thomas, I would come back. I would be right back. I planted my feet firmly on the wood planks of the porch, took a giant breath and opened the umbrella.

Nothing happened.

Pepper watched, wide-eyed, as I went down the line, opening each umbrella. A grave expression passed over his face when I opened the last one. He wanted it to work almost as much as I did, and I loved him for it.

"I'm sorry," he said, as I closed the last umbrella and tossed it next to the others.

"Like you said, we're eliminating possibilities. Now we know I definitely need my umbrella to get back to Thomas."

"Still, I wanted this to work for you. I mean, I wanted it to work for science, but mostly for you."

"Me, too, Pepper. Me, too."

Late Sunday night I was tossing and turning in my bed, staring down another week of unanswered questions. Harder still, I had no pieces of Thomas to cling to. I didn't have a text history. I didn't have a saved voicemail to listen to, no photos to hang on the wall or scroll through on my phone. I didn't have a sweatshirt of his that still smelled like him. Thomas was a vapor. A thought. A memory. So, I did the only thing I could think to do to calm the racing thoughts in my brain.

"It's after midnight. What are you doing down here?" Dad said, flipping on the kitchen light. "And in the dark?"

I was eating toast and drinking tea by candlelight. I squinted into the harsh, bright lights over the kitchen table when Dad flipped the switch. Making the toast had been comical, the bread pre-sliced, nothing to do but push a button to get a perfect, even toast on both sides. I didn't have to burn my hand on the toast basket or hold the bread over an open flame. The tea came in pre-made bags, not loose leaves like we used at the castle. Mom had an electric kettle that boiled water on command.

"I could say the same to you."

Dad pulled out a chair and slumped down into it. He was wearing plaid pajama pants and a white t-shirt. "You made tea?"

"I did."

He scratched through the stubble on his cheeks. "You don't drink tea. Unless this is some big secret you've never revealed to your 'ole dad – that you only drink tea in the middle of the night."

I laughed because it was kind of true. "Do you want some?"

"Sure, why not."

I got up to get another teacup and saucer from the china cabinet in the dining room, where Mom kept the real china. Mom and Dad normally drank tea in coffee mugs, but I liked the delicacy of Mom's special china, like what we used at the castle. I poured a cup for Dad and we sat in silence for a while, drinking our tea, the teacups making that tinkling scratching sound when they hit the saucer.

"What are you doing down here so late?" I asked.

"Couldn't sleep. Thought I'd come down here and look for a snack."

I raised my toast in salute and took a bite. The bread was thinner than the castle bread and the strawberry jam obviously from a jar and not homemade.

He was quiet for another minute before he said, "You know, if there's something you need to talk about, I'm a good listener."

I met his eyes but didn't say anything.

"It's pretty obvious you're going through something. I won't push if you don't want to talk about it, but I wish you would. It's not good to keep things bottled up."

"Did Mom tell you?" I'd been waiting for this. I assumed she'd told him.

"She mentioned you had an upsetting dream, said you're still pretty wound up about it."

I huffed out a sarcastic laugh. I couldn't believe she was lying to Dad, too. Apparently, my mother was a completely different person than I thought.

"I'm fine," I said. I didn't want to rehash it again, didn't want him to give me the same sad look Mom had been giving me.

I got the sad look anyway. "Seems like you're still pretty upset. Do you want to tell me about it?"

"I think I'm just stressed about school. Senior year, you know. Lotta pressure." It worked. He smiled at me, relieved that I wasn't hung up on some dream I was convinced was real.

He stretched his arms over his head. "Thank you for the tea. I'm going to turn in. You coming?"

"I'll be up in a minute."

He walked around the table and kissed the top of my head. "Don't stay up all night."

"I won't. Goodnight, Dad."

Alone again, I noticed the cup full of pens and pencils in the middle of the table. Mom had put it there a few years before for Cale and me to use for homework and it never really left. I lifted a black marker out of the cup and pulled the cap off. I drew a thick, dark W on the back of my right hand, right next to my thumb.

It had been four days since I'd seen Thomas. Four days since I'd heard his voice or felt his touch. Four days since I teased him about his castle full of Ws. How many more days would I have to endure?

THIRTY-FIVE

urned out it was weeks, not days. With no sign of the umbrella, no dress, no hint of recognition from my mom, I trudged through each day doing my best to be present, to walk through the halls at school and eat lunch and take notes and paste a smile onto my face. I even went over to Ben's for another movie night, this time as friends. He made stovetop popcorn and Amelia brought a huge bag of peanut M&Ms. I sat on one end of the sectional couch in Ben's basement and Ben sat on the opposite end with Pepper and Amelia between us. The three of them chatted about school and Amelia and Pepper argued over what movie to watch. I ate handfuls of popcorn and avoided Ben's sad glances.

Amelia's patience wore thin. One morning before school she grabbed my right hand and held it up to my face. "What's with the W?"

I'd been re-drawing it on every couple of days when the ink wore off. It was my one connection to Thomas, my physical reminder of him. "Just a doodle."

She rolled her eyes. "A doodle? Seriously, what is with you? I haven't asked this question because it's too impossible to be real but, did something happen with Ben? Was he mean to you or pushy or a bad dude or something? Because you've been weird since that night he kissed you."

"Ben is in no way a bad dude."

"Obviously. I'm just trying to figure out what happened. You've been moody and mopey for weeks."

The look on her face dissolved whatever was left of my self-imposed secrecy. I couldn't keep it from her, didn't even know why I was trying to. She was my best friend. She'd understand. "Let's talk? After school?"

She sagged with relief and nodded. "I don't want to jump the gun, but this feels like a big conversation. Should we make strawberry cupcakes?"

"Yes," I said, a weight lifting off my shoulders, "that would be perfect."

After school we drove together to Amelia's house. I asked her if we needed to stop for ingredients and she smirked. Amelia always had the ingredients for strawberry cupcakes.

We walked into her house, Amelia flipping on every single light even though it was the middle of the afternoon. Amelia's mom believed things should be as bright as possible. Every room in their house had overhead lights and lamps and Christmas lights and novelty string lights galore. Once when I stayed over, I timed Amelia turning off all the lights before bed. It took her fifteen minutes.

In the kitchen we gathered mixing bowls and strawberries and butter and vanilla. It was a practiced dance, one we'd done dozens of times before. Amelia always made the cupcakes and I made the cream cheese frosting.

Amelia sliced some strawberries and dumped them into her mom's bright red food processor. Then she cracked the eggs into a bowl. The recipe called for a mixer to beat the eggs, but Amelia insisted on doing it by hand.

"It's my secret weapon," she'd say, whipping the egg with a fork, her hand a blur across the bowl.

My portion of the baking was simple, which I liked. I mixed

the cream cheese, butter, vanilla and sugar together and let it chill in the refrigerator, which was my idea of baking. Amelia didn't call it baking unless thirteen bowls were involved along with some chopping and mixing and whipping by hand.

"So," she said, inspecting her work and moving on to sift the flour, cornstarch, baking powder and salt into yet another bowl, "you wanna talk about the W?" She scooped the butter into her mom's red mixer and turned it on high, raising her voice over the whirring of the machine.

"The W," I said, moving her used bowls to the sink and putting the blended frosting into the refrigerator. I watched her add the remaining ingredients to the mixer with precision, never taking her eyes off the batter. She knew exactly when it was done, said you couldn't be off by a second.

I knew I wanted to tell her, was going to tell her, but the words were stuck in my throat.

"Let's wait until the cupcakes are in the oven."

"Okay," she said, eyeing the batter as it churned in the mixer. She glanced at me for a tenth of a second before declaring the batter a velvety perfection. Together we finished the final steps and put the cupcakes in the oven.

"Let's sit down," I said, pulling a chair out from under the kitchen table.

She plopped down onto a chair next to me, her eyes wide, her chin in her hand, waiting.

"I know I've been difficult to deal with lately and I'm sorry. I didn't know how to talk about it. But I'm ready now if you're ready to hear it."

"Please. God. Yes. I've been waiting."

I reached down and ran my thumb over the inked W on my hand. "The W stands for Westbourne, Thomas Westbourne. He's the reason I'm not with Ben. He's the reason for everything."

I watched her take in the information, try to make sense of it. "We don't know anyone named Thomas Westbourne."

"What I'm about to tell you is going to be hard to hear. You're not going to believe me. All I can ask is that you listen to everything I have to say."

She waited, listening, ready for more. So, I told her. The whole sordid tale. About the storm and the umbrella and the castle on the lake and the wardrobes full of dresses and Jane and Thomas. I told her everything about Thomas. About his stoic nature and shy laugh. How he'd never been in his own kitchen before he met me. How he accidentally rammed his boat into me when I was swimming naked in the lake. How much we both changed in our time together. How he loved me. How I loved him. And Amelia Vine, my best friend, she never wavered. Sure, she screamed several dozen times and fell down on the floor more times and slapped various parts of my arms and legs in a complete aghast state, but she never wavered.

The cupcakes were out of the oven, iced and partially eaten when she was finally able to digest what I'd been saying.

"You time traveled."

"Yes."

"I mean, I know that's what you've been saying for the last two hours but...you actually time traveled. Like, you're saying you have a magic umbrella and you went back in time and fell in love with a Lord. That's what you're saying to me."

I laughed because of course she would boil the biggest news of my life down to the plot line of some angst-ridden teen romance novel.

"Yes."

"Okay."

"Okay?"

"You have a tell when you're lying. You crack the knuckles on your middle fingers. You haven't cracked your knuckles since you got here."

Now that I'd said it, I had no idea why I waited so long. "I'm sorry I've been keeping it from you."

She cocked her head to the side, assessing me. "I think I understand. Even though it's me and you should know you can trust me with anything, I get it. It's not every day someone travels through time with a magic umbrella."

"That we know of."

She laughed, a high tinkling sound that smoothed over the rough edges of the last few weeks. "Right? Now I'm going to be suspicious of literally everyone I meet. Wait! We have to tell Pepper! Can we tell Pepper? He will explode into a million fanboy particles. You know how he feels about time travel."

I grimaced. "Don't be mad, but he's the first person I told. I figured he'd be the easiest to tell, you know? That he would believe me."

"Seriously good call. I mean, I cannot *believe* you didn't tell me first, but if you had to tell someone, Pepper was the right one even though you broke every single law of best friendship."

I reached out for her to take my hand. "Can you forgive me? Not for that, but for my behavior these last few weeks? I know I've been a terrible friend."

"No forgiveness needed," she said, squeezing my hand back and smiling. "It's a clause in the by-laws: If Best Friend Time Travels and Meets Handsome Lord All Dramatic Crying Shall Be Forgiven. Although, there's one thing you haven't told me that I need to know right this second. Did Thomas the Lord walk toward you at sunrise through a field of mist like Matthew McFayden and say you'd bewitched him body and soul? Because if he did, I will die right here, right now."

"No, but he did secretly bring a string quartet to the castle to play for us during dinner because I told him I missed listening to music."

She rolled her head back on her shoulders. "Oh, God, no wonder you've been moping around like Eeyore's sad little sister. Thomas the Lord sounds like a real life-ruiner."

I smiled at the nickname and about how right she was. "In the best way."

THIRTY-SIX

Once Amelia knew the truth, her sole focus in life became getting me out of the house and happy again. She had every confidence I would find the umbrella and reunite with Lord W, but until then, I was expected to act like a real 21st century girl. Amelia's determined enthusiasm was like having a brand-new puppy – overly-hyper and wiggly and kind of a mess but also irresistible. Which is how she talked me into getting a job at Big Mike's. I didn't mind. It was a better use of my time than wallowing over how much I missed Thomas. Cale loved that I worked at Big Mike's. Eleven-year-old boys possess no limit for leftover pizza and wings brought home in Styrofoam containers.

Working at Big Mike's was also a great way to avoid my mother. When we were both at home, I did my best to be in whatever room she wasn't in. She didn't take any action to spend time with me either, so my guilt level was at zero. If I wasn't at school or at Big Mike's, I was hanging out at Amelia's or Pepper's or Ben's or just driving around aimlessly. With my new job, I had plenty of gas money.

The uniform at Big Mike's was a Nashville Predators jersey or Tennessee Titans jersey with a whistle on a black and white checkered lanyard. I had no idea why since Big Mike's wasn't a sports bar, more a middle-aged hangout with all-you-can-eat wings and build-your-own pizza. Ben loved that I had to wear a whistle, reminding me of all the teasing Amelia and I inflicted on him over the summer when he would sit in his lifeguard stand and twirl his whistle around his finger. He and Pepper usually came in on Tuesday nights for 2-for-1 pizza and karaoke. Ben even reprised his brief stint with karaoke stardom. There was a specific group of women who, I believed, came in on Tuesday nights just in case Ben showed up to sing. The best part, he was a terrible singer. The women were only interested in the eye candy, obvious from their cat calls and toothy smiles. Ben took it in stride, aware of the effect he had on people while being completely unaware.

Ben became an integral part of our friend group, fitting neatly into the space Amelia, Pepper, and I had created. Amelia was convinced Ben wasn't over me but if that was true, he never made it obvious. We got to a comfortable place, able to talk about our classes or joke about Pepper and Amelia's constant arguments about pop culture.

When I wasn't at school or working or sneaking around my house searching for the umbrella, Amelia and I made dinners at her house, trying to recreate some of the things I loved from the castle. Cook made a roasted chicken that was so juicy, so crispy, so flavorful, it ruined me for all other chicken. I tried to make it, guessing at Cook's technique and searching cookbooks and recipe websites for various ways to roast a chicken, but mine were never as good as Cook's. Probably because I used an oven and she used an open flame, something I wasn't equipped to try. We also attempted lobster bisque, sending Amelia's mom into a fit when she came home to us lowering a live lobster into a pan of boiling water. Who knew you could buy lobster meat pre-cooked?

One particularly slow Wednesday my manager at Big Mike's let me leave early. I sagged against the table I was wiping down, so ready to escape to my room, pull the covers over my head and turn off the world. As much as Amelia's Get-Brolly-Happy plan was working, I hadn't fully shed the heavy stone of sadness constantly weighing me down. I hadn't found the umbrella, hadn't found the dress. Every day that ticked by, even the good ones, was another day separated from Thomas.

I clocked out of my shift and walked to my car. The September air was thick and warm, like walking through someone's breath. I opened the car windows to let the air flow over and through me. September at the castle was cooler, clearer, the air easier to breathe. September in Tennessee suffocated me, the air too hot and too close. I wished for the wide-open sky of the castle, the tall cypress trees, the shimmering blue of the lake.

When I got home, I slipped in the front door as quietly as I could, hoping to avoid Mom. I was making my way up the stairs, pulling my whistle from around my neck, when I heard my parents talking in the kitchen.

"I know you're right, but it seems unfair to keep it from her."

My foot hung in the air, waiting to step down onto the next stair.

"It's for the best," Mom said. "If she knows, it will kill her."

I slipped back down the stairs, my heart pounding harder with each word I overheard.

"That's not the point. This has gone on too long. She deserves to know." I inched toward the kitchen. "Did I tell you I found her the other night sitting in the dark, drinking tea with a single candle lit on the table?"

Mom sighed loudly. "I know you're right. I'm just afraid of what might happen. What if we're wrong?"

"She deserves to know."

"What do I deserve to know?" I asked, standing in the doorway to the kitchen.

Mom dropped a glass into the sink and it shattered loudly against the stainless steel. Dad was leaning against the counter next to her. No one said anything. No one took a breath. My heart pounded so hard my chest was vibrating.

"Brolly," Dad said, "I thought you were at work."

"What do I deserve to know?"

"Why don't you sit down."

"No. I will not sit down. Is this about Arrington?"

Everything inside me pulled tight, a rubber band about to snap.

Mom hadn't said a word since I walked into the kitchen, but her face was ashen.

"I know you have my dress, the one Thomas gave me. I know you know what happened to me. I don't know why you're hiding it but that's over. You have to tell me the truth. Right now."

Dad put his hand on Mom's shoulder. "Brolly, why don't you go up to your room and your mom and I-"

"No. Tell me right now what's going on."

"Brolly!" Dad yelled, making me jump. He'd never taken such a harsh tone with me before. "Go to your room. Your mother and I will be there in a minute."

I looked back and forth between them. They didn't look like people harboring a secret. They looked scared.

I walked slowly up the stairs, unsure how to feel. It wasn't clear whether they were going to tell me what they knew or not. And I couldn't handle another misdirect. I took off my uniform and pulled on cropped grey leggings and a black v-neck t-shirt and pulled my hair into a topknot. I was pacing the floor when my parents came into my bedroom.

Mom was holding the dress.

My dress.

From 1826.

I ran over and grabbed it from her, held it up to my face and breathed it in. It still smelled like the castle, like the rosemary oil I used in my hair, the rough soap I used in the copper tub, like Thomas. A sob burst out of me and I fell to the floor. The whole time I'd been back, struggling, questioning my own memories, she had my dress. She knew. Holding the dress in my hands broke my heart open like the shattered glass in the kitchen sink, the shards of my emotions scattering in every direction.

My parents sat down next to me on the floor. Mom rubbed my back as I sobbed.

"You know how much pain I've been in. For weeks," I cried. My breaths came out in stuttered gulps. "Why did you tell me it was all a dream when you knew it wasn't? Why did you lie?"

Suddenly I was angry. Enraged.

"You knew," I screamed. "This whole time you knew and you let me suffer." I was hysterical. My entire body shook with rage and pain and disbelief. "How could you do that to me?"

Mom was silently crying and Dad's cheeks were red.

"You lied to me. You're my mom and you lied. And Dad? You knew?" I kept screaming, my voice finding new decibels of pain.

"Brolly, there's a lot we need to tell you and in order to do that, you need to calm down."

"Calm down? *Calm down*?" I jumped up from the floor and resumed pacing back and forth across my room, hugging my dress to my chest. "I just got confirmation I time traveled 200 years into the past and both my parents knew about it and lied to me. I don't think this is the time to calm down."

"Okay, I can see how that would be a lot to take in."

"A lot to...a lot to take in? Do you have any idea what I've been going through? I thought I was losing my mind. I thought I made it all up in my head even though I knew in my heart it was real."

"Darling," Mom finally said, her voice small and wounded, "we never meant to hurt you."

"Go easy on your mom, kid, she's been through a lot, too."

"Oh, really? I doubt it could even come close to what I'm experiencing at this exact moment."

Dad's eyes bored into mine. "You're not the first one to use that umbrella."

That shut me up. I stopped pacing, stopped shouting, and took in their faces, the terror in their eyes, my mom's tears, and sat back down on the floor.

"Brolly, your mother and I," he took her hand, "we weren't... born here."

"What does that have to do with anything? Have you been listening to anything I'm saying?"

He ignored me. "Your mother was born in Sussex, just outside of London. And I was born in London." I stared at them both, Dad's words swirling around in my brain. "And more importantly, you need to know when we were born. My birthday is June 12th, 1785. And your mom's is December 14th, 1788."

The air evaporated from the room. "What do you...what?"

"Darling, I'm so sorry about all of this," Mom said through her tears.

I was rooted in place, my eyes bouncing between Mom and Dad.

"Your mother and I knew each other in London. I was from a rather well-to-do family and your mother was a maid in my family's London home. She was 19 and I was 22." He looked over at her. "I thought she was the most interesting woman I'd ever met."

"But we could never be, you see, because he was a gentleman, and I was a maid."

I nodded, remembering Elizabeth's cutting remarks to Thomas about me. It was never an option for her to get to know me. I wasn't appropriate simply because of who I was. Or wasn't.

"But I was so drawn to her," Dad said, "her smile and the way she looked at me. We would meet in secret and talk for hours. And I found out she was so much more than just a maid with a pretty face."

"We fell in love."

"Madly in love. But we could never marry." They were no longer looking at me. "I decided to risk it all and tell my mother and father about her. I was going to marry her no matter what they said."

"You would have lost your fortune," Mom said, gazing at Dad.

"I didn't care."

"But I...I became pregnant. With you." She turned back toward me. "Not only would he never be allowed to marry a servant, he especially would never be allowed to marry an unwed pregnant servant, even though he was the father."

I couldn't keep up. Every word coming out of their mouths was too ridiculous. And exactly right.

"We confided in your mother's sister. She was working as a maid at Arrington Estate."

My breath caught in my throat and the hairs on the back of my neck stood up, every memory of Jane rushing through me like a cold wind. The way she seemed so familiar from the start. The way she cared for me. How she knew so much about what happened to me. "But that can't be."

"What is it, darling?"

"Your sister, the one from Arrington, was her name Jane?"

Mom practically lunged at me. "What did you say?"

Her hands were on my face as I shook my head from side to side. "Because I met her. Jane. She was at the castle. She works for Thomas."

"That's...impossible." Mom's lips trembled, her face went white.

"She seemed so familiar, and she took such great care of me. She reminded me of you, Mom."

"You met Jane?" Dad asked. "How is she? You met her? You met Jane? Did she know who you were?" Mom moved her hands away from my face and put them on her own.

We all three stopped talking, digesting the grand impossible coincidence. The room spun on a tilt. It was difficult to form a coherent thought, difficult to speak. I thought about Jane, about her careful way with me, her enthusiasm for my relationship with Thomas. I thought about our conversation in the dressing room as we packed the trunks for England, how she knew. How she understood.

"I think she did know who I was, yes. She never fully said, always talking in riddles. And not until this moment did I believe it. But, somehow, yes, I believe she's the same Jane. I believe she knew I was from the future."

"She was with me when I got the umbrella," Mom said, almost laughing.

"Jane?" I croaked, unable to absorb one more incredible detail. "Jane knew about the umbrella?"

"When I found out I was pregnant with you, I was so scared. I went to Arrington to see Jane and figure out what to do. We were walking in the trees behind the castle and wandered pretty deep into the forest, further than either of us had ever been. We came upon an old woman gathering kindling. She saw that I was crying and asked me what was wrong."

"She was a witch," Dad said.

"We don't know that she was a witch."

"Then how else would she have had the umbrella?"

"What happened?" I interrupted.

"She had such a kind face and I was so distraught, I told her the truth. She said she could help me find a safe place for my baby."

"She gave you the umbrella?" I asked.

"Yes. I sent word to your father to join me at Arrington as quickly as possible. We knew we couldn't stay in London," Mom said, wiping tears from her eyes. "We decided to take the risk. The woman told us if we opened the umbrella, it would take us somewhere we could be safe, where we could be a family. The three of us were together when your dad and I left. I was devastated to leave Jane and terrified of what would happen."

"But you did it," I said, seeing her in a whole new light, her bravery, and her love.

"Yes," they both said, looking at each other. Dad leaned over and kissed mom full on the mouth. It was a tender moment and I felt like an intruder.

"What happened? When you opened the umbrella?"

Dad wiped a tear from Mom's cheek, never taking his eyes off her. "We arrived here, in America, a little over eighteen years ago."

"In the 21st century."

"Yes," he smiled the spell broken. "That was a difficult time, trying to find a place to go, where to fit in. We didn't understand the currency or modern transportation or any of the modern customs. It was quite terrifying."

"James," Mom said, "do you remember when we saw the cars driving by?"

He laughed. "Brolly, you have to understand, we'd never seen anything like a car in our lives and suddenly there were dozens and dozens of them speeding past our faces. We thought we'd died or maybe arrived on another planet."

"We landed in a field," Mom said, "just off Hwy. 31, where the Publix is now. We walked to the road, completely disoriented. A police officer picked us up."

I couldn't believe anything they were saying. "What did you tell him?"

"That we were lost, which wouldn't be hard to believe by the looks on our faces. He took us to a shelter for runaways."

Dad smiled at me. "They took us in and helped us. We owe them our lives. And yours, too."

None of us heard Cale walk into the room. "Hey, Mom, we're out of Doritos." He looked at the three of us all crying and holding onto each other. "Uhh, who died?"

"No one, darling, we're just talking. There's a bag of Doritos on the top shelf of the pantry."

"Chicks and grown-ups, man," Cale said, backing slowly out of the room. "Super weird."

I waited for him to be out of earshot before continuing, my mind exploding with questions. "But you don't have English accents? I mean, I've always thought you both have unusual accents, but you don't speak like Thomas or Jane."

"After we arrived, we worked very hard to fit in, to adapt. It took us a long time but, we tried to hide who we were as best we could. We were scared of what might happen if someone discovered our secret."

"A kind woman named Georgia ran the shelter," Dad said. "She taught us everything, even taught me how to cook. She helped us blend in."

"Did she know about the umbrella?"

"We hid the umbrella from her. She knew, obviously, that we weren't American and hadn't arrived by traditional means. But she loved us, loved you," Mom said, rubbing my calf, "so she helped us."

"Where's the umbrella now?"

They gave each other a grave look. "Brolly, you can't-"

"I need to see Thomas. He doesn't know what happened to me."

"Tell me about Thomas?" Dad asked, his eyebrows furrowed together.

"He's the Lord of Arrington, Lord Thomas Westbourne."

"Westbourne," Mom said, "you never said his name was Westbourne. Brolly, we knew his family."

Dad nodded. "The Westbournes were high society. John Westbourne owned half of London."

My shoulders sagged as a new wave of despair washed over me like an ocean tide, up and back, relentless. Hearing my parents talk about Thomas's family should have made things better, but it didn't. This new confirmation only deepened the wound of missing him, longing for a love I couldn't get to.

"The umbrella took me to a castle he owns in France. His

parents both died and he was staying at the castle for a while. He's...Dad, he's my person. I love him. And he doesn't know what happened to me. I have to go back."

"You're so lucky to have returned home," Mom said. "How did you manage to do that?"

"We were getting ready to leave France, we were going to Arrington. I found the umbrella floating in the water. The whole time I was there, I searched and searched for it, and then the day we were leaving, there it was. I pulled it out of the water and it opened in my hands. Then I was back."

Mom and Dad glanced at each other.

"When you vanished that morning, in the storm, I thought I'd lost you forever. I fell on the ground screaming your name. And then, a moment later, you were back, wearing that dress," Mom said, pointing to the dress I still clung to, my lifeline to another dimension.

"But I was gone for so long."

She smoothed my hair behind my ear. "Here, it was only seconds."

"That's good. If you give me the umbrella, I can go back to Thomas and explain. He may not even know I left."

Mom and Dad were quiet, a silent conversation happening between their eyes. Mom took a breath. "Brolly, when the woman in the forest gave me the umbrella, it came with a kind of warning. She recited it twice and I'll never forget it." She looked at Dad before repeating the words.

A journey forged through time and space
The traveler's heart alone must face
It's equal part one shall pursue
If soul's desire is love's virtue
Care not for travel, care not for place
But only once, else all's erased

She said it one more time, slowly, all three of us absorbing the words.

"What does it mean?" I asked.

"I think it means it's too dangerous to use again. You can't open the umbrella."

I looked down at the dress, the lace ribbons and tiny pearl buttons, the delicate fabric. "Shouldn't that be for me to decide?"

Mom's eyes were sad and a little bit desperate. Dad's expression was resolute, a decision already made.

He shook his head. "This is all so much, so quickly. I think we should take some time to think about it."

I sat up as straight as I could and looked them both in the eye. "I'm not going to change my mind."

THIRTY-SEVEN

The next morning, I was lighter, freer, like taking the harness off after riding an intense roller coaster. I didn't have the umbrella, but it was only a matter of time. I texted Pepper and Amelia to meet me in the school parking lot, I had news. Pepper texted back a *Doctor Who* gif and Amelia texted back one hundred exclamation points. I pulled on my favorite pair of black jeans and a black and white striped top, folded my castle dress and put it in my bag.

I dropped off Cale and made it to the Central High parking lot to see Pepper and Amelia waiting next to his LeSabre. It was a 2007 burgundy monstrosity his grandmother willed to him. But it was huge and fit everyone so Pepper always drove when we all went somewhere together. I hopped out of my car with a big smile on my face.

"Hello, Miss Urgent Text," Amelia said, hands on her hips.

I opened my bag and pulled out the dress. Amelia shrieked and Pepper's eyes and mouth went equally wide. I heard him whisper, "yes."

"Where was it?" Pepper asked, his mind already spinning with possibilities.

Amelia hip-checked him. "Seriously? Even for you that is a

ridiculous reaction to seeing the dress. Like, this is major time-traveling news."

"You should have seen him when I told him what happened to me. Barely an eye twitch."

Pepper gave Amelia a withering look. "I presume you had a different reaction when you heard the news?"

"Are you kidding? I nearly ripped my skin off. I screamed my throat raw from shock. I had a *reaction*," she said, waving her arms in the air.

Pepper rolled his eyes and turned back to me with his eyebrows raised, ready for the details.

"My parents gave it to me." I talked fast, so I could get it all out before they asked a million questions. "When they told me how they used the umbrella themselves. When they came here from England. From the 1800s."

"Wait," Amelia said, "that means your parents are, like, two hundred years old? Man, they look amazing."

Pepper side-eyed Amelia. "I think it means it was the 1800s when they left England." He turned back to me. "Brolly, this is incredible news. A family tie to the magic makes complete sense. I've had my suspicions given your mom's proclivity for writing about the 19th century, but I didn't want to presume. Did they explain how the umbrella works? Do you have it?"

Amelia reached out to touch the dress. "I have to see you in this."

"I don't know everything yet, but I asked them to give me the umbrella so I can go back."

"Go back," Amelia said, taking a step closer to me. "You can't leave."

"It's okay, you won't even know I'm gone. The last time I left, it was like a moment had passed. My mom said I was only gone for a few seconds."

Pepper and Amelia shared a look. "What if you can't come back?" Amelia said.

Pepper grimaced. "The properties of the umbrella are

unknown. It's possible you won't be able to travel back to the same place and time. You should really think about this."

The first bell rang and we walked toward the door. "You know how much I care about you both but, I have to try. I want you both to be there when I go."

"Yes," Pepper said without hesitation. Amelia was not so easily convinced.

"When is this happening?" she asked, her forehead creased into a worried sadness.

"As soon as I convince my parents to give me the umbrella."

Three days later I was sitting on a barstool in the kitchen, eating Lucky Charms by the handful, when Mom and Dad came in, a unified front. My iciness toward my mom had thawed as soon as I learned the truth. We'd both apologized, each understanding why the other behaved the way she did. I paused with my arm half-way in the box. "What's up?"

"We've decided you're mature enough to make the decision about the umbrella yourself. You know our concerns, Brolly. We're scared to death to lose you but, it's your decision to make."

I pulled my hand out of the Lucky Charms box, a unicorn marshmallow stuck to my thumbnail. "Wow, I did not expect that to be your answer."

"You're almost eighteen," Mom said. "I was nineteen when we arrived in America. And honestly," she looked at Dad, a wave of sadness passing over her face, "we've never forgiven ourselves for not making an effort to return home."

"But the cryptic poem."

"Who knows what the poem means. We could have tried. And we didn't. We don't want to take that chance away from you."

I looked at my dad in disbelief. "Dad? You agree?"

"Do you love him?"

My heart flipped inside my chest. "Yes."

"Then you will know what you should do. It's hard for us to let you go but, we believe it's the best decision."

Mom started crying.

"Mom, don't cry. I'll come right back! If it all goes right, you won't even notice I'm gone."

"I love you," she said, throwing her arms around me. I hugged her back, my hand knocking the Lucky Charms box, cereal spilling across the counter.

"I love you, too, Mom. And I love you, Dad. I won't take this lightly."

No one noticed Cale walk into the kitchen.

"Geez, everyone's crying again? And you, too, Dad? What is with this wacko family?"

"Come here little brother," I said, jumping off the stool and hugging him as tightly as he would allow.

"Wow, gross. Get a hold of yourselves, Parkers. I just came in here to get a ride to school but on second thought, maybe I'll walk."

"I'll take you," I said. I picked up my bag and pulled on my black boots.

"Not unless you dry up the waterworks. I don't want my friends thinking I'm related to Moaning Myrtle."

"No," I laughed, "wouldn't want that."

We all gathered on the front porch; Mom, Dad, Amelia, Pepper and me. Mom arranged for Cale to be gone to a friend's house for a sleepover.

"I'm not ready to tell him," she'd said.

I couldn't sleep the night before, the promise of seeing Thomas so close. I imagined what he'd say and what I would say, how I would explain what happened. What I would do if he didn't, or couldn't, believe me. I knew everyone was concerned about the risks – that I wouldn't return to Thomas or that I wouldn't be able to get back home – but I wasn't. I was confident I'd find him and confident I'd get back. Maybe that meant I was a fool for love, but I'd rather be a fool than a coward. I had to try.

Mom handed me a box with the umbrella inside. No one wanted to risk handling it except for me. I was wearing my castle dress paired with black chucks. I hoped the shoes would help my story in case Thomas had a hard time believing me.

"We love you, darling, and we hope this works. But if it doesn't, if we never see you again-"

"You will," I said, and hugged them. "It's going to work and I'm going to be right back."

Amelia hugged me so tight her arms seemed to wrap around me twice. "This dress is blowing my mind," she said, backing up to look at it again.

"Right? I knew you'd love it. I had a million more at the castle."

"Bring one back for me."

I'd considered this, what I could bring back. Specifically, if I could bring Thomas back. I planned to tell him the whole truth, all of it, and then ask him to come back with me. Maybe Jane, too.

"Brolly," Pepper said with a shallow bow, "thank you so much for letting me participate in this epic moment."

"It makes me so happy that it makes you so happy."

I hugged my crying parents one more time and stood on the top stair, the same stair I stood on the first time I traveled, and steadied myself. I set the box down, took out the umbrella and held it in front of me. My hands shook, part fear part nervous energy.

"I'll be right back," I said. Even though I was confident, even though I had my umbrella back, there was a tiny part of me that worried it wouldn't work. That I'd end up in pre-historic Africa or the south pole or some future world none of us had considered. I looked around the porch at the people I loved and really felt the risk I was taking in leaving them.

"I love all of you," I said and opened the umbrella.

Nothing happened.

No flashes of light. No spinning. No floating. I was still standing on my front porch, my parents and my friends watching me.

"Was that it?" Amelia asked. "Are you back? Did you see Lord W?" She leaned up on her toes to look all around me.

"No, I…didn't…" I closed the umbrella and opened it again. Nothing.

"It's not working," I said, turning to my parents. "I need to go back. Thomas doesn't know…he'll think I left without saying goodbye. And Jane, Mom, Jane! I have to go back!"

"Wasn't it storming the first time you did it?" Amelia asked.

"It wasn't raining when I came back from the castle," I said. "I was in a boat with Thomas, rowing away from the shore. The sun was shining. It was a beautiful morning, just like now." I could hear myself getting hysterical. "It wasn't raining."

Pepper shook his head. "I suspected this might happen. I

can't be certain, never having traveled myself, but perhaps the conditions need to be similar when departing from a pre-existing location?"

He'd said that before when we opened his umbrellas on the porch. But I didn't want to believe it.

"One of you try it," I said, panicking and shoving the umbrella at my parents. "One of you go and tell Thomas that I'm here and I still love him and I'm sorry."

"Darling, we talked about this. There's no guarantee we would land in the same spot, or even the same time. And what if we couldn't get back?"

"Brolly, she's right," Pepper said. "The linear movements of time travel are completely unknown. Targeting a specific destination, a specific time, is difficult to harness."

"No," I said, moving back to the step, "No."

I opened the umbrella again.

And I remained exactly where I stood.

THIRTY-EIGHT

Understanding seeped into my skin like a toxin, burning through my thin curtain of hope. I would never see Thomas again.

Every other painful experience I'd been through since that fateful day in August contained some small amount of hope. I always believed I would somehow get home from the castle. And since I'd been back in my own time, I knew I would try and return to Thomas one way or another. When the umbrella didn't work, every spark of hope I'd had snuffed out, pitching me into a new level of darkness.

I asked Mom to write down the poem from the old woman and I read it over and over, memorizing each line, each word, each syllable. But it didn't explain why the umbrella didn't work. I opened the umbrella again and again, one night running outside into a thunderstorm. Rain poured down over me as lightning lit up the night sky. I screamed into the storm and opened the umbrella.

But nothing happened.

Pepper got to work researching the poem online to see if there was any history he could find. I set up a Google alert for any mention of magic umbrella, black umbrella, time traveling umbrella hoping for even a hint of information. Mostly I got notices for sales on umbrellas at Wal-Mart.

There was one bright spot. During his poem research, Pepper found a tiny, grainy photo of a painting of Thomas on an obscure, historical website. In the painting, he looked like he did the first time he came to my room the morning after he found me, so stiff and dignified. So handsome. Underneath the photo it read:

Lord Thomas John Westbourne of Arrington
1807 – Unknown

"That's him. That's Thomas," I said, pulling the laptop as close to my face as I could. "Why does it say unknown?"

"Faulty record keeping? Could be he became a recluse. Didn't you say he was hiding out at the castle in France?"

"No, he wouldn't do that. He had a whole life, he…he wouldn't do that."

Pepper printed out a copy of the photo for me. I kept it inside my phone case.

I went through what Amelia called The Dark Period. My parents hovered, worried, eventually leaving me alone to cry in my room. Cale had no idea what to do, unable to blame my mood on "the cycle" and too afraid of my crying jags to pull any pranks. I continued my habit of late-night toast and tea, sitting alone in the kitchen with only the light of a candle, headphones blaring my classical playlist. Mom and Dad didn't mention it. No one knew how to handle me, how to handle my grief.

It had been a month since the umbrella didn't work, and I didn't know how many days since I'd seen Thomas. I stopped counting when the number got higher than my hopes would allow. I was doing my best to be a functioning human, answering Amelia and Pepper's questions of concern, saying, "I'm fine. It's fine. I'll be fine." Ben doted, anxious about my new level of sadness, the dark circles under my eyes. He didn't question it. His way of saying "are you okay" was doing nice things for me. Buying me a cookie at lunch. Leaving me ridiculously large tips at Big Mike's. Singing cheesy karaoke songs in an attempt to make me smile. I'd done all I could to hide my sadness from him, but I could tell he knew enough.

Time passed faster than I expected it to. It was late-October and I'd been picking up Amelia every morning (she was grounded from driving again due to a selfie-while-driving mishap). We arrived at the senior parking lot at the same time as Pepper.

"Good morning, Miss Parker, Miss Vine, how are you both this beautiful morning?"

"Mixed," I said pulling the strap of my bag over my head and across my chest.

"Excellent answer. Aren't we all an adolescent trail mix of pubescence and adulthood, becoming who we are and clinging to who we used to be?"

I shot him a look and he silently apologized, not realizing what he'd said until it was too late. He and Amelia had been good sports, listening to my endless stories about Thomas and Chateau du Lac, hugging me when I needed it, leaving me alone when I needed to cry. Together we'd dissected every moment, Pepper focusing more on the mechanics of time travel and Amelia focusing more on Thomas's dark hair and the way he kissed me in the back of the garden. I knew they were trying. I loved them for trying.

Ben jogged over to us with his backpack slung over his shoulder. "Hey, guys," he said, "check out this flyer." He handed Pepper a bright orange sheet of paper I instantly recognized.

Pepper smirked. "Ah yes, Halloween in the Timbers, Central's premier gathering of miscreants and drunkards. How delightful."

"Sounds like fun, right?" Ben grinned at all of us. None of his hopeful shine had worn off in the first few months of school. He was still smiley, radiant Ben. We couldn't help but love him for it.

"I don't know if fun is the right word," I said, "but yes, we usually go." We walked through the side doors of the school, the glass covered in bright orange flyers.

"Awesome, so we can all go, yeah?" We went every year but seeing Ben's joy in asking made us all nod in agreement. "Cool, great, I'll see you guys at lunch," Ben called before disappearing into the crowd.

After school, Pepper cornered me in the parking lot. "I hate to ask this, but it's something I've been thinking about. Have you considered opening the umbrella again?"

I let out a long sigh. "I have opened it. A lot."

"Oh." He tried not to look disappointed, tried to look scientific and emotion-less, but his face fell when he heard what I couldn't say out loud. The magic was gone. I was never going back.

"What if…" I looked at Pepper and then looked away, "what if I was wrong? What if it never happened? What if I'm losing my mind over an elaborate dream?"

Pepper put his hands on my shoulders, forcing me to face him. "Is that what you think?"

"No."

"Then don't give up. I believe in you. Amelia believes in you."

"I know you're right, it's just that…sometimes I think I might be losing my grip on reality, like I'll never be able to-"

"Hey, friends," Amelia said, startling both of us. Her ponytail was askew and she had on shiny, bright pink lip gloss. "What are you two talking about? You look like you're plotting a bank heist."

Pepper sniffed. "If I were going to plot something, it certainly wouldn't be a bank heist."

"Too good for you? You're more of an art thief kinda guy?"

"No. I'd rather spend my time learning how to break the laws of time and space."

"Too late," she beamed, "Brolly's already done it." Amelia

opened the passenger door of my car and threw her bag in. "Come on, Brolly. I told my mom I'd be home by five."

"Where are you ladies off to?"

"Thrift store," Amelia said. "I need a costume for the Halloween party. I set the bar pretty high last year as Wonder Woman, so this year has to be amazing."

"What are you going as," I asked Pepper.

He grinned a wide mischievous grin. "You'll see."

Amelia and I got into my car and I pulled out of the lot. Ten minutes later we were at Granny's.

"I need some inspiration," Amelia said, climbing out of the car. "So far I have zero ideas." She pushed open the rickety door to Second Chances: Thrifting For A Cause. The store was run by a white-haired woman named Granny who wore thick glasses and a patch over one eye. No one knew her by any other name than Granny and the store always smelled like dust and Febreeze. We waved hello to her as we passed by the front counter.

"I've been looking online and the only costumes I can afford come with thigh highs and a push-up bra. Call me naïve, but I've never seen a female police officer wearing thigh highs and a police shirt that's two sizes too small for her heaving bosom."

"Me neither," I said, laughing. I was trying to do that more, laugh, but it came out all wrong, like sarcastically laughing at a dad joke. There was no life in it.

Amelia and I scanned the racks and held up various options for each other.

"I mean, who wore this?" Amelia held up a mid-thigh length, teal blazer with white, plastic buttons shaped like flowers. "It could only have ended up here from someone who actually wore it."

"It's perfect."

"No. Way. I don't care if it's for a costume, I'm not putting teal polyester on my body. I'd rather wear my own clothes and go as a troubled teen."

I smiled a half-smile. "What would you wear?"

Amelia thought about it, looking down at her scuffed Adidas, ripped jeans and hot pink tank top under an open white button-down. "Probably this?"

She kept scanning the rack while I drifted over to the men's section. I pulled out a long, brown trench coat that sparked an idea for my own costume.

"Who's that for?" Amelia said as I walked over, holding up the coat.

"It's an idea under construction."

She held up a cream and peach sweater with a sparkly thread woven into the front in the shape of a snowflake. "How are things going lately, with Ben?"

"That's hideous and we're friends."

She put the sweater back. "It's just so sad the way he's still trying to woo you. You think he'd give it up already. You should just tell him you have a boyfriend overseas or something. What about this?" She held up an orange wrap dress covered in black polka-dots.

"How would I explain when I got this overseas boyfriend? That I never see and never will see again? And that's perfect. Totally Dolly-Parton-chic."

"I'm just saying. He thinks there's hope. I hate seeing his sad puppy dog eyes whenever he thinks you're not looking at him."

We went back to scanning the racks, swiping hangers across the steel wardrobe pole, the grating sound on the metal sending a shiver down my spine.

Amelia stopped swiping and turned to look at me. I knew what was coming by the look on her face and I was not in the mood. "Are you okay?"

"Obviously not." The words shot out of me, angry and hot, before I had a chance to reign them in. The mood between us shifted, all my careful pretenses melting away like wax over an open flame.

She glared at me. "You've got to stop this."

"Stop what?"

She put a green silk shirt back on the rack so she could talk with her hands. "Do you really want to turn into a sad old woman who hides in her house pining for a guy two hundred years in the past?"

"I don't do that," I said, my tone sharp. "I'm still mourning, yes, but I'm not crying all day anymore. I'm smiling. I'm participating. Everything is fine."

She grabbed my right hand and held it up, a fresh black W branded on my skin.

"What? Now I'm being judged for writing on my hand?"

She let go and shook her head no. "Like it or not, I know you. And I know you're putting on a brave face even though you're heartbroken."

"Yeah, so."

"I don't want to say this. I can't even imagine how you must feel knowing you can't see Thomas again but, Brolly, you're dissolving right in front of me."

I rolled my eyes. "I'm not dissolving."

"Today at lunch I told you that Pepper and I are dating and that he's an inferno sex beast of hotness. You didn't even blink, you just said 'cool.'"

"That's not the right use of inferno."

"You're missing the point."

"And what's the point," I snapped. I knew what she was trying to do. I didn't want to hear it.

She put her hands on her hips. "I refuse to let you give up. You're still alive and you're still here, with us. You need to come back to the land of the living."

My blood boiled. How dare she assume it was so easy, to just let go, to admit to myself I'd never see Thomas again, to pretend like it never happened. "Thanks for the speech but you don't get it. Thomas wasn't just some summer crush or high school boyfriend you're so fond of liking for a week and then dumping. I was, I am, in love with him. And I have no way to get to him.

I'm not going through a break-up, it's like...it's like he died. Or maybe I died. And he doesn't know where I am or what happened to me. And there's nothing I can do about it. I didn't just lose him, he lost me, too."

"Listen," she said, unwilling to back down, "I know you love him. Obviously. You guys connected on some epic level the rest of us mere mortals cannot comprehend."

I twisted the trench coat around my arms and looked away from her, far enough that she wasn't in my peripheral vision. "Your sarcasm is noted."

"Brolly," she sighed, "I love you. I hate to see you slipping away like this."

"I'm not slipping away, I'm heartbroken. Can't you see that?"

"Yes, I do see it. It's killing me to see you hurting so much. But-"

"There is no but. It just is."

Granny shuffled over, no doubt alarmed by our raised voices. "Do you ladies need any help today?"

Amelia forced a smile. "Thanks, Granny. We're fine."

Granny waved and shuffled back to the front of the store. A terrible silence stretched out between me and my best friend. Amelia was a talker, liked to solve things with words. Her silence spoke louder than any argument she could make.

"Can we go?" I asked.

"I'm not done talking."

"Are you ever?"

She sighed loudly through her nose. "I'm going to let that slide because I know you're hurting, but there's no need to be mean. Yes, you shared something incredible and life-altering and amazing with Thomas. Lots of people never find that their whole lives and you did! It's incredible!"

"Not helping."

"But that can't be it. What you experienced, it's not the only greatness you will ever have."

I looked over at her. Her blue eyes were wide and wet. Her

hands were in the air, paused, trying to work out exactly how to fix her broken friend. "Am I that bad?"

"Yes."

"Wow, thanks."

"That's not what I mean."

"Then what do you mean? Because so far this conversation isn't exactly making me feel less-worse."

She inhaled and blew out her breath, her cheeks puffed out like she'd just had her wisdom teeth removed. "All I'm saying is, maybe this isn't the end. Maybe meeting Thomas was the start of a whole epic something you don't even know about. Maybe this whole time traveling business was a lead-in to something greater. Something more. Your life doesn't have to end here."

I pressed the palms of my hands to my eyes, the trench coat bunched up in my arms. The rational side of me knew she was right, but the emotional side wasn't there yet. I had no idea how to get there. "It's hard to imagine ever arriving to a place where it doesn't hurt so much. Time allegedly heals all wounds, right? What about a wound inflicted by time itself? How am I supposed to heal from that?"

She reached over and put her hand on my arm. "Look at me."

"No," I said, my eyes still covered.

"Look at me," she said, tugging on my wrists.

I lowered my hands and looked at her, tears threatening to fall from my eyes.

"Brolly J. Parker, you are enough. You, all by yourself. A relationship doesn't define you, not even one with a Lord in a castle. I know you love Thomas, but you also need to love you. You did your best to get back to him and it didn't work. It's time to accept that and move on."

We were both quiet for a long time as silent tears trailed down my cheeks.

"What if I can't?"

She pulled the trench coat from my arms, laid it over the metal rack and took my hands in hers. "You can. You were a whole person before you met Lord W and you're a whole person now. You were so brave to try and get back to him. Now, you need to be brave again. You need to remember the Brolly we all know and love. We want her back."

"And who was she?"

"A girl who wouldn't let a heartbreak define her. A girl who would accept the circumstances however bad they may be. A total badass."

A fraction of a smile found its way to my face. "I've never been a badass."

She smiled back at me, "Maybe it's time."

THIRTY-NINE

Halloween in The Timbers was an inescapable Central High tradition. The Timbers was the biggest, richest neighborhood in our suburb. Every single house went to the utmost extreme to out-decorate and out-treat every other house. Hordes of kids within a fifteen-mile radius came every year to trick-or-treat, including us. It was tradition.

Amelia came over early to get ready. She decided to go as a roller derby girl complete with lime green and black spandex shorts, a lime green tank top, black elbow and knee pads she borrowed from Cale and a chin-length hot pink wig under a skull-and-crossbones helmet. And actual roller skates.

"You're going to kill yourself on those skates."

"Who cares, I look incredible. Your costume is," she curled her lips in confusion, "nice."

"I'm a time traveler," I said, grinning. It was fun to say it out loud without worry someone would overhear me. I'd taken Amelia's words at Granny's to heart. Because she was right. I had to emerge from my cocoon of sadness. I had to live. It didn't mean I missed Thomas any less, didn't mean my love for him had faded. I had to find the balance between living a life without him and wanting nothing more than to live a life with him.

So, I was going out for Halloween with my friends. And I was going to have a great time.

"They're here," Dad shouted from the bottom of the stairs.

Amelia rolled too fast out of my bathroom and into the hall. She sat down on the top step and scooted down the stairs on her butt.

I looked in the mirror and adjusted my tie, buttoned my suit jacket. The black rimmed glasses were the final touch and I was putting them on as I walked down the staircase to meet Pepper and Ben.

When I saw Pepper, we stared at each other, mouths open wide in hilarious shock. I walked down the last few steps and stood directly in front of him, pointing. He was dressed exactly like me – brown pin-striped suit, brown tie, long brown trench coat, black chucks and black-framed glasses.

"Hello, Doctor," Pepper said, bowing and laughing.

"And you, Doctor," I said, unable to stop giggling. "I cannot believe you're The Doctor."

"I can't believe *you're* The Doctor."

"Who's the Doctor?" Ben asked. Pepper and I turned to look at Ben, who was wearing a full-on Thor costume with an authentic helmet, breastplate and flowing red cape. I burst out laughing, remembering how I'd thought I could never date him because he was the Thor to my Natalie Portman.

"Ben, you seriously look 100% incredible," Amelia said.

"Thank you," Ben said, raising a giant hammer over his head in a genuine Thor pose.

"Cool! *Doctor Who!*" Cale shouted, coming into the foyer from the kitchen dressed as a Ninja Turtle. "And Thor, yes!"

"Leonardo, I presume," Pepper said.

"Doctor," Cale said, holding up his ninja swords and posing.

"Who's the Doctor?" Ben asked, still holding his hammer in the air.

"Is no one going to comment on my costume?" Amelia said, pouting.

"You look exemplary on this night of nights," Pepper said, shuttling Amelia out the door.

"Thank you, finally!"

Pepper helped Amelia and her roller skates down the porch stairs and over to his LeSabre.

Amelia shouted, "shotgun," and got into the front seat. I climbed into the back seat with Ben, his Thor hammer between us on the maroon velvet seat.

He looked over at me, assessing my costume. "You look really great, although I'm not sure I get it?"

It was quiet in the front seat, Amelia and Pepper both straining to hear what was happening in the backseat. Since Granny's, Amelia had been gently pushing me back to Ben. I think she thought being with Ben might help me get over Thomas.

"I'm the tenth doctor," I said, "from the show *Doctor Who.*"

"I don't know who that is, but you look very cool," Ben said. As much as I resisted the idea, I could see Amelia's point. Ben was everything you could ever want in a guy.

Pepper spent the drive over explaining to Ben the television phenomenon that was *Doctor Who,* while all four of us pretended to listen to Pepper's eclectic pop playlist he created for the occasion – Jones Jams Vol. 8.

"So, you and Pepper are both dressed like this doctor guy?"

"He's a Time Lord," Pepper said.

"A time traveler," I said, catching Pepper's eye in the rearview mirror and grinning. I loved saying it and planned to say it as much as possible all night.

"Don't even, Ben," Amelia said. "Pepper's been trying to get me to watch that show for forever and I just do not get it. There's like, weird aliens and cat people and a giant piece of skin that talks."

"Skin that talks?" Ben said, squirming.

"Here we are, The Timbers," Pepper announced, "neighborhood of the affluent and opulent. Gird your loins ye socially gauche and unrefined."

Pepper's LeSabre chugged up the main road toward the back of The Timbers. He drove at a snail's pace to avoid trick-or-treaters lining the sidewalks and spilling into the road. Every year, Pam Byers hosted an "After Treats" party at her house, which wasn't something you got used to seeing. House wasn't a fair descriptor, more like southern mansion on steroids. The gate at the bottom of the driveway had "Byers Manor" etched in wrought iron and the long, winding drive led up to the biggest residential structure I'd ever seen. When I was eight, we lived in an apartment for six months while our Waterson Heights house was being built. That entire apartment building was smaller than Pam's house. I couldn't begin to estimate the square footage, but I'd say it had all of them, all the feet. Plus a basement.

Pepper parked the LeSabre at the bottom of the long driveway and Amelia stumbled trying to get out of the car and onto the sidewalk. I held her hand so she could focus on not falling and the four of us made our way up the driveway. We ran into David Ray right in front of an 8-foot-tall, animated dancing ghost in the front yard and a two-story black spider crawling up the front of the house cast in a strobe light.

David Ray was one of Amelia's former almost-boyfriends and resident of The Timbers. She hung out with him several times last spring and went on one official date. He took her to Chez Marche in Nashville where they ordered ratatouille tartine and shared a chocolate soufflé. She said he was funny and charming and sweet. At the end of the night, he walked her to the front door and they continued talking for another hour while standing on her front porch. She was sure he was going to kiss her and definitely wanted him to kiss her. As he said goodnight, instead of leaning in, David raised his hand for a high-five and said, "Thanks, dude." Amelia, shell-shocked, high-fived him and he went home. She called me immediately. "Babe, I just got high-five-dude'd." They never went out again.

In true David form, he'd been enjoying some pre-party beverages.

"Heeeeeeeey party people. What'r you guys's s'posed to be like…CIA agents dudes or something?"

Pepper bristled. "Brolly and I are paying homage to David Tennent's brilliant turn as the tenth Doctor from *Doctor Who*."

"Doctor whaaaaat? Amelia's bangin' though hi Amelia," David slurred.

"Bye, David," Amelia said, pulling me forward. "What was I thinking with him?"

"You said he was nice."

Pam's parents were usually in attendance for the After Treats Bash, but they were the ones who bought the alcohol, so it didn't technically count as a chaperoned event. A hired DJ set up lights and a huge dance floor on the massive back deck complete with smoke machines and swirling lights. There were tables set up on both the deck and the patio loaded down with catered food. A bonfire roared down by the huge pond behind the house. We barely made it to the back deck before people were shoving cups of beer into our hands. It was 8:45pm and the deck was already packed with sweaty, costumed dancers filled with liquid courage.

"Beer?" Ben asked, offering me a cup.

"No, thanks. I'm more of a wine girl."

Amelia grabbed my arm to keep from falling down. "Since when do you drink wine?"

"Since my trip to France," I said, raising my eyebrows.

We were interrupted by a couple of guys Pepper knew, all very, very impressed with his *Doctor Who* costume. I received my own round of praise and took it accordingly. I was glad some people got it, but really, I wore it for myself. I told as many people as I could that I was a time traveler, a thrill running down my spine each time I said it.

We made our way to one of the food tables and Amelia

immediately began scooping heaps of guacamole onto thin tortilla chips.

"I'm the master," she said, talking with her mouth full. "Haven't broken a chip yet."

Pepper laughed. "With this gift you shall go far in life."

"It's all about the scoop. You have to be delicate but deliberate."

Ben picked up a chip and assessed its width before digging into the guacamole. The chip immediately broke into three pieces making us all laugh.

When I first got back home, I resisted any feelings of belonging, shut down any potential happiness. But looking around at my circle of friends, I could see that this was what was real, had always been what was real. Amelia and Pepper and my family and even Ben – they were my life. Thomas was…I didn't know… maybe an elaborate dream. Even as I thought it, I knew I didn't believe it. But I had no way to get to him. I wasted so much precious time crying in my room in the castle, time I could have spent with Thomas. I didn't want to waste any more time wishing away days I could be spending with people I loved. I had to rejoin my life. I wanted to.

I grabbed a chip, dipped it into the guacamole and raised it, unbroken, into the air. "To best friends."

Amelia smiled and raised her own chip, nudging Ben and Pepper to do the same.

"To best friends," they said.

FORTY

Mom and Dad were sitting on the couch watching TV when I got home. I squeezed my way in between them and propped my feet up on the coffee table.

"What's with the trench coat?" Mom said.

"I'm a Time Lord from *Doctor Who*."

Dad laughed and shot finger guns at me. "Nice. I'm guessing you walked around all night telling people you were a time traveler?"

"You know it."

"That's my girl. I was just going to make some popcorn. Do you want some?"

"Sure."

A commercial for a mattress store blared on the TV. "You should have seen how many trick-or-treaters we had tonight," Mom said. "I bought two of those huge bags of candy from Costco and we ran out before eight o'clock."

"Where's Cale?"

"Upstairs. Sorting. He came home with a pillowcase full."

I looked at the TV as the mattress store jingle ended. "Seriously, why are there so many mattress stores around here? How often do you even buy a mattress? There's like three within walking distance from our house."

"It's true," she laughed. "We are overrun with mattress stores." It was nice to be normal. To sit on the couch and rant about mattress stores. I peeled off my coat and suit jacket and tossed them onto the chair next to the couch.

"We have, what, five mattress stores in our area? Imagine how many there are in all of Nashville! No one needs that many mattresses."

A commercial for New Channel 5 came on.

Local Spring Hill woman alarmed earlier this evening when two strangers seemed to suddenly appear inside her apartment in what looks to be a Halloween prank gone wrong.

An image flashed on the screen of the two strangers. But they weren't strangers to me.

Police apprehended the costumed pair and are investigating. We'll have this story and more tomorrow morning on News Channel 5 at 5.

"Mom," I said, my voice quiet but my blood rushing to my head, "please rewind that."

"To what, the mattress commercial?"

"No, the news clip."

She rewound it as Dad sat down next to us on the couch with an overflowing bowl of popcorn.

"Pause it," I shouted, jumping up and knocking the bowl to the floor.

"Brolly! You spilled all the popcorn."

I grabbed the remote from Mom and rushed over to the TV. I rewound it to what I was looking for and stared at the photo on the screen, sure my eyes were deceiving me. Because it was him. It was Thomas. And standing next to him was Jane.

"It's them," I said, but before I got the words out of my mouth my mom was standing next to me.

"Jane?" she said, her chin trembling. "Is that my sister, Jane? On the television?" Mom reached out and touched Jane's face on the screen.

Dad came and stood next to me, his mouth moving but no sound coming out. We all three stared at the screen, at the paused image of Thomas and Jane being led out of an apartment in handcuffs. Jane was wearing her black dress and apron, her hair falling out of her bun. Thomas had on his tall black boots and cream-colored pants with his starched white shirt and navy waistcoat. It was them. They were here.

I rewound to the beginning of the 15 second news clip. We watched it three more times.

"It's Thomas," I screamed. "He's here!"

Dad was already dialing News Channel 5.

"Yes, hi, my name is James Parker. I'm calling about your story on the Spring Hill woman who found some people in her apartment? Yes, do you know where the police are holding them? Yes, I'll hold."

Mom and I waited, staring, crowding around Dad, unable to process what was happening. Thomas was here. He was here!

"Yes, thank you so much," Dad said and hung up. "They're holding them at the Spring Hill police station."

Without a word, we all three left the house and got into Dad's car. Luckily Dad drove because I was unable to think, let alone drive. Thomas was here. In my world. My time.

"How did they do it?" Mom asked.

"I don't know," Dad said. "We have the umbrella. Are you sure it's them?"

"It's them," I said, my voice quivering.

We only lived a few miles from the police station and made it there in less than ten minutes. Dad had barely put the car into park before Mom and I were out and running for the door. In our haste to leave the house she'd forgotten to put on shoes. I was still in half of my Time Lord costume, suits pants and a white t-shirt. A police officer was sitting at the front desk staring angrily at his computer monitor.

"We're here for the people," I shouted, breathless.

"Excuse me, the who?"

Dad rushed in behind me. He was wearing slippers and what he called his home pants. He'd never, ever left the house in his home pants. "We are here to inquire about the two individuals who were involved in a mix-up this afternoon? At someone's apartment? We heard the story on the news."

"Oh yeah, the two cosplayers who refuse to break character. Shady, those two. Do they belong to you?"

"Yes," we all three said with a little too much enthusiasm. The man behind the desk was not amused.

"May we see them?" Dad asked.

The man picked up a black phone on his desk and mumbled something into it. A moment later another police officer strolled through a locked door. "You three here for the costumed jokers?"

"Yes, we are," Dad said. If he weren't there, Mom and I would have been lost, both of us twisted into a mute mixture of fear, disbelief, and monumental joy.

The police officer motioned for us to follow her back through the locked door and my heart, already racing, sped up so fast I felt faint. We walked down a narrow hallway back to an area with two holding cells. In one of them, miraculously, sat Thomas and Jane. My Thomas. In the same room as me. They were sitting next to each other on a bench, heads down. Thomas's arm was around Jane and they both looked terrified.

"Thomas," I screamed, startling the police officer.

Thomas's head jerked up and his eyes went wide. He ran over to me and reached out through the bars of the cell. "Brolly? Oh, Brolly, my darling, I found you. I found you."

I reached through the bars to hug him. It was clumsy and awkward and the bars were cold and none of it mattered because he was here. Thomas was here. I reached up and kissed his face through the bars while he pulled me closer. I was touching him, could see him with my own eyes, but I still didn't believe it.

"Jane!" Mom shouted.

Jane was already next to Thomas, reaching out for my mom who grabbed her hands and kissed them. "Emily! James!"

"All right, everybody, calm down," the officer shouted over us. "I take it you know these two," she said to my dad.

"Yes, and we'd like to take them home if that's possible."

"You're in luck. Mrs. Barton chose not to press charges. Just make sure these two don't go sneaking into anymore apartments, okay?"

Dad reached out to shake the officer's hand. "Yes, absolutely. We will make sure of that, thank you. Are they free to go?"

Thomas and I were still clinging to each other. He leaned into my ear whispering *I love you* and *I found you* over and over.

"Yes, but you'll have to let go of them first."

Mom, and I peeled ourselves away from the bars and Thomas and Jane stepped aside so the officer could open the cell door. As soon as she did, we all gathered into one giant group hug, my arms around Thomas and his arms around me and Jane clinging to us both and Mom and Dad, too. The officer cleared her throat.

"As much as I love a touching reunion, it's time for everyone to clear out."

Dad walked to the front desk to sign some paperwork while the rest of us walked outside to the car.

"How did you do it? How did you get here?" I asked, my arms wrapped in a vice grip around Thomas. He was holding me just as tight and kissing the top of my head.

"Let's get them home," Mom said, "and we can hear the whole story."

"Emily, look," Dad said, walking out of the police station. He was holding a black umbrella.

FORTY-ONE

My parents were crying and Jane was crying but Thomas and I were clear-eyed, smiling so bright sunbeams were shooting out the front windows of my house and spilling into the street. Because he was here. In my living room. With me. I could see him and touch him and hear his voice. Overwhelmed was a fraction of what I felt.

The car ride home had scared Thomas and Jane half to death. It took some convincing to get them inside and buckled in.

"Not again," Jane had cried, backing away.

Thomas had squeezed my hand. "We were placed inside a similar carriage when the officer brought us to this place. It was," he shivered, "quite an experience."

"It's a car. It's sort of like a carriage but without the horses." They'd eyed both me and the car with equal suspicion. "It's totally safe, I promise. And it will get us to my house much faster than walking."

"We do not mind walking," Jane had squeaked, shaking her head at the idea of getting into another car. "We should walk."

Mom put her hand on Jane's shoulder. "It takes some getting used to, but it will be all right. Trust me."

Reluctantly, they'd climbed into the back seat. I got in between them and helped them buckle their seatbelts.

"What is this for?" Jane asked.

I knew it was best not to mention crashing, so I said, "It's to help you fit into the seat."

Thomas jumped when the engine started. Jane screamed in terror when Dad put the car into reverse to back out of the parking space. I grabbed their hands and pulled them close to me.

"It's okay. We're safe," I said. They had both stared out the window with giant eyes, speechless. Dad drove slowly, trying to quell the fears of our new passengers. A car behind him honked loudly and zoomed past, the driver throwing a middle finger out their window. Fifteen minutes later, Dad pulled into the driveway and turned off the car. Thomas and Jane relaxed beside me.

Cale was sitting in the living room watching TV and eating the spilled popcorn when we walked in. Mom gasped, putting the pieces together that we'd forgotten him in our mad dash to the police station.

"Oh, hey guys," he said, totally unconcerned.

"Cale," Dad said, "isn't it past your bedtime?"

"Oh, sure," he huffed, "forget I'm even here and then banish me to my room. I see how it is. Cool costume," he said as he passed Thomas and tromped up the stairs.

"Why don't we sit down?" Mom said, ushering us all into the living room.

Everyone wanted to sit next to everyone else and there wasn't enough room on the couch, so we all slid to the floor in a huddle.

"It was Jane," Thomas started, taking my hand. "After you disappeared, she told me everything she knew. She said she believed you were her sister's daughter."

"And that was right," Mom said, clinging to Jane.

"I didn't know," I said to Jane, "I didn't."

She reached across the small circle to kiss my cheeks and hug me again. "We are all together now, all of us."

"But how did you get here?" Dad asked. "How is there another umbrella?" The second black umbrella was on the floor at his feet.

"It was the poem from the old woman in the forest," Jane said, looking at Mom. "Do you remember it?" Mom nodded, tears in her eyes.

"Jane told me about the old woman," Thomas said. "We traveled back to the castle and searched through every book in the library that might hold the key to the riddles from the poem. We studied it until we concluded there must be a second umbrella."

"But how," I said. I'd repeated the poem to myself hundreds of times but the only thing I figured out was how I came back to the exact moment I left, everything from the castle erased.

"It is in the third line and fourth line," he said. "*It's equal part one shall pursue / if soul's desire is love's virtue.*"

"How did you know it meant there was another umbrella?"

"We hoped," he said, looking deeply into my eyes, "but we did not know. I was prepared to do anything I had to do to find you."

"We traveled back to Arrington," Jane said, "to look for the witch in the forest."

"She wasn't a witch," Mom said, "she was just a nice old woman."

Jane rolled her eyes, the same way she rolled them at me at the castle, and continued on with the story. "Brolly, until you arrived, I never knew if your parents were alive or dead. I never knew if the magic of the umbrella truly worked. All I knew was one moment, Emily and James were standing in front of me and the next moment, they were gone. When you arrived at the castle, I suspected the magic was real. And then when you disappeared…"

"We set out in search for the old woman," Thomas said, "in the forest behind Arrington."

I leaned my head against his shoulder and Jane picked up the story. "It took these many weeks to find her. Each day we would set out at sunrise and roam the forest throughout the day."

"You," I interrupted, looking at Thomas, "roamed the forest every day?"

"My one purpose was to find you," Thomas said. "There was nothing else that could possibly matter to me."

"And you found her?" Mom asked.

"Yes. It was many weeks of searching, but we indeed found the very same woman from your first encounter. She resides in a small, strange dwelling, several miles into the forest. She is very old now. She would not see us at first."

"Mean as a snake, that one," Jane said.

Mom smiled. "I remember her being lovely."

"It took some determination on our parts," Thomas continued. "She would not open her door nor respond to our many requests for an audience. I stood at her door for three days and explained my theory about the umbrella, about the love I lost. When she finally opened her door, I once again explained my plight. She was not so easily swayed, would not admit to the magic of the first umbrella."

Jane scoffed. "Said she never heard such a tale in her many numbered years. Can you believe that, Emily? Tried to act like it never happened. M'lord convinced her."

"I told her my interpretation of the poem, how I believed there to be a second umbrella I could use to find my love." Thomas's eyes were shining. "I told her my heart was pure, my love was virtuous. That is what turned her spirits to kindness. I told her of you, Brolly."

"And she put a spell on a new umbrella?"

"I do not know the manner in which the umbrella came to be nor how that mad old woman bewitched it," Thomas said. "I only know that we succeeded. I found you."

"Our umbrella doesn't work anymore. I tried," I met Thomas's eyes, "I tried to get back to you. I tried so hard."

"It is no matter, my darling," he said, wrapping his arms around me and pulling me to him, "I found you."

We stared at each other, reconnecting. There was something different about him. He looked more awake, more alive.

"Brolly," Mom said, "we should let Thomas and Jane rest."

"Right, yes. I remember how much the journey takes out of you."

We all unfolded ourselves and stood up. Dad picked up the umbrella carefully and held it out, squeezing it tightly with both of his hands. "I'm going to put this away. Don't want anyone accidentally traveling tonight."

Mom took Jane up to the guest room where Jane passed out before her head hit the pillow. Thomas and I sat on the couch in the living room, sinking down into the soft, grey cushions, limbs tangled, trying to catch up on everything we missed.

"I can't believe you managed to get another umbrella. I mean, what if it didn't work?" My arms were wrapped around his chest and his arms were around me, all worry about propriety gone. "What if the magic had taken you to an entirely different time?"

He brushed a hand through my hair. "After you vanished, I was stricken most terribly. One moment you were in the boat and the next moment you were gone. I scarcely knew what to think. The pain of losing you was so acute, I believed my heart would burst within me."

He pulled my face up to his, pressing his lips to mine. There was a new heat behind it. His hands drifted to my waist as he pulled me into his lap. It was different than before, reckless, with none of the carefulness from our time at the castle. Thomas moaned into the kiss, his fingers digging into my hips, my body melting into his. I sank my hands into his thick, dark hair as we kissed and kissed. Suddenly, he pushed me away, his chest heaving with stuttered breaths.

"Brolly, we...your family is...and I'm..."

I moved to get off his lap, but he held me there. I happily

stayed. Since the police station we'd been drawn to each other like magnets, always touching, never able to be completely apart. His new looseness, his touches and the closeness of his body to mine, was dizzying.

"Do pardon me for getting so carried away. It seems that I... your lips and your," his breath caught, "that was extraordinary. I might be freaking out."

I laughed right out loud and buried my face in the crook of his neck. He pulled me even closer and kissed my forehead.

"I love you," he whispered, "so very much."

I leaned up to look at him. "It's so surreal to me that you're here. I didn't think it was possible. But even though I thought I would never see you again, I never stopped loving you. Not for a minute."

We kissed again, slower this time. Because we had nowhere to be but with each other.

"Tell me more of the story," I said, laying my head against his shoulder.

"We were not entirely certain how the magic worked. The old woman gave us no instructions, just handed me the umbrella and shut her door rather forcefully. I remembered how violently you arrived on the shore and worried for Jane. I tied myself to her using some rope. She held onto me as I opened the umbrella. The reaction was quite severe."

"Yes," I said, thinking about how my body swirled and twisted. The feeling my bones would crack and shatter. Then the weightlessness.

"I landed with a great thud onto the floor of an unfamiliar room, no longer tied to Jane. She landed next to me. We were quite disoriented and a bit perplexed by our surroundings."

"The news said you were in someone's apartment?"

He traced a pattern on my arm with his fingers. "There was a woman, quite frantic and hysterical. She was quite adamant we leave her house, but I could not find a proper door."

I laughed at how they must have looked, probably bowing

and curtsying and apologizing for the intrusion while this woman lost her mind at two strangers appearing in her living room.

"What's this?" he asked, circling the black W on the back of my hand.

"It's a W, for you. It made me feel closer to you."

He tried to say something, but a huge yawn cut him off.

"You must be exhausted."

"Yes, but I do not need sleep. I do not wish to leave you," he said, yawning again.

"No," I said, pulling his hand up to my lips and kissing his fingers. "Never again."

We fell asleep together on the couch, wrapped in each other's arms.

FORTY-TWO

woke up a few hours later and all the living room lights were still on. I slipped out of Thomas's embrace, pulled off his boots and laid a blanket over him. When I turned off the lamp next to the couch, he stirred.

"Brolly."

I kissed his forehead, his cheeks, his lips. "Shhh, I'm right here. Go back to sleep."

I went into the kitchen to make some tea and found Mom already there, pouring herself a cup.

"Couldn't sleep," we both said at the same time.

I walked around the island to hug her. "Mom, I can't believe he's here."

"He's quite something. I can see why you're so taken with him."

"And Jane!"

She shook her head. "I never imagined I would see her again. And now she's here, in our house. I'm happier than I ever thought possible."

We pulled ourselves up to sit on the countertop and drink our tea. Orange and pink rays of sunrise climbed up the slats of the kitchen window blinds, warming our shoulders.

"There's something else you should know," Mom said. "Your middle initial? It's for Jane. You were named for my sister Jane."

I slipped my arm around her waist and lay my head on her shoulder. "I love that."

"I'm sorry, darling, for everything." I pulled back to look at her, confused. "When I didn't tell you what I knew, when I pretended not to believe you, I believed I was protecting you."

"Mom."

"No, please listen. When you disappeared with the umbrella, I was terrified you were gone forever. It ripped my heart in two. And then a moment later you were back, wearing a dress so familiar to me. I knew what had happened and I thought... I believed it would be easier for you if you were convinced it was only a dream. Had I known what I know now, I never would have..."

"It's okay, Mom. I think I understand."

"Can you forgive me? I never meant to hurt you."

I hugged her again and kissed her cheek. "There's nothing to forgive."

She chuckled softly. "You were pretty mad at me."

"I should probably be the one to apologize for being an insolent teenager. And I do apologize, but time traveling to the past really takes it out of a girl."

"I know the feeling," she said, shaking her head at the memory. "That's not something you can forget."

We sipped our tea while the house slept.

"Something I've wanted to ask you. The Arrington Series – is it real?"

"Not real, but based on my real life, yes. I made up the characters and the situations. Writing about it made me feel less alone, like I was still connected to my home."

"Do you miss it? Living in England?"

She laughed and hopped off the counter to refill her teacup. "The England I left didn't have electricity. Or wifi."

We both turned at a noise in the doorway. It was Thomas,

rumpled and sleepy-eyed and fantastically gorgeous. My body hummed at the sight of him.

"Good morning, ladies," he said, bowing. I noticed he'd put his boots back on. It was ridiculous and so out-of-place and utterly great. "If you will pardon my saying so, but I seem to be in a bit of a predicament."

I hopped off the counter. "What do you need?"

"A bath, actually. Normally my footman Girard would…"

"I should sic Jane on you," I laughed. "Come on, I'll show you where the bathroom is."

I led him upstairs, watching him marvel at every single thing he saw. I kept having to pull him along when he got distracted by family photos hanging on the wall. "These small paintings are so rich in color, so lifelike."

"They aren't paintings, they're photographs."

He considered this, looking closely at a photo of me and Cale holding sparklers on the Fourth of July. "I can see I have much to learn in your world."

In the bathroom, he startled when I showed him how to turn on the sink. "Water flows from this nozzle inside your house?"

"Yeah," I said, "and it's hot, too." I held his hand under the water once it was warm.

"A marvel," he said, eyes shining.

"Indoor plumbing was something I definitely missed at the castle."

I showed him how to work the shower, showed him the soap and the shampoo, laid out towels for him and a spare toothbrush, showed him the tube of toothpaste. He looked like a kid surrounded by freshly opened Christmas presents, so eager to try everything at once. His cheeks flushed red when I explained how the toilet worked, but I could tell he was grateful.

"Yes, we were shown a similar device from the officer where you found us. Quite an experience."

"Trust me, you'll love it once you get used to it. If you want to give me your clothes, I can wash them for you. I'll bring you some of my dad's clothes you can wear in the meantime."

"Oh…I…" His face turned even more red.

"I mean, once you take them off, leave them right outside the door. Don't worry. I'm not planning to steal your virtue. Yet," I said with a wink.

He was still grinning when I shut the door.

An hour later, his dark hair still damp, Thomas came into my room wearing grey sweatpants and a worn navy-blue t-shirt, looking nothing at all like a castle Lord. Looking every bit like the proverbial boy next door, only hotter. All those times at the castle I'd tried to imagine him in my time, tried to picture him as someone I'd know at school. But I never imagined this. The t-shirt stretched across his broad chest and the sleeves strained over his arms. The sweatpants hung on his hips and he was barefoot. I bit the inside of my cheek.

"Forgive me for bathing so long. The bath was wonderful, standing under the hot water…astonishing, truly. And the paste for my teeth seemed to come to life inside my mouth like a winter's storm. All of it, truly, was so wonderful, thank you. Although I should imagine I look quite ridiculous," he said, gesturing to himself.

I couldn't find the words to tell him how he looked. He was the same person I fell in love with on an island in France, but now, he was more. He was everything good, every joy and every happiness. He was everything I wanted. He was mine. My heart pulsed inside my throat. "You look perfect."

I took his hand and led him over to my bed to sit down. With zero hesitation, I climbed into his lap.

"Brolly," he said, his voice cracking, "we cannot." He slipped his arms around me, his bare arms I'd never seen before, never touched. I smoothed my hands across his skin, warmth coursing through me. I wanted to touch him everywhere.

"That is," he closed his eyes, "quite indulgent, the feeling of your skin against mine."

He mimicked my movements, sliding his hands over my arms, my shoulders, my neck.

I moved my hands up to his damp neck. "This is my time, my world. There's no one here to tell you what's expected of you or what's considered polite by some unobtainable society standard. In this room, it's just you and me. Thomas and Brolly."

"My love," he whispered, cradling my face with his hands.

"That morning when we were leaving for England and I found the umbrella, I was so scared. I'd been looking for it for so long, but then when I found it, I wasn't ready to leave. I didn't want to leave you. When it opened in my hands, it brought me back here, to the exact moment I disappeared. It was like I never left, like my time with you never happened at all." He kissed me softly, a light brush of his lips. I tightened my arms around his neck and moved my lips to his ear. "I missed you every day, every moment. I thought there was no way to get back to you and now…Thomas, you're here. And I want you."

"Brolly, my love, there is so much that I want," he said, kissing my neck. "I do not know how or where to begin." He kissed my ear, my jaw. "These many days without you I longed to…to use my lips and my hands to convey what my words cannot."

He pulled me closer. His lips were warm and urgent as he kissed my mouth. His arms, bare and firm under my hands. I was lost in it, lost in him, my body responding to every touch and taste.

"Brolly!" Cale yelled, pounding on my bedroom door. "Mom says to come down for breakfast."

Thomas and I jumped apart like Phillipe had just barged in with Elizabeth hot on his heels. I fell off the bed and landed on the floor in a thud. Thomas leaned over the side of the bed with a concerned look on his face. "Are you quite all right?"

I burst out laughing, the situation too bizarre to be real. We'd spent so much time alone at the castle, which had dozens and dozens of rooms where we could have made out for hours if we'd wanted to, but waited until we were here, with Cale banging down the door and Mom cooking breakfast twenty feet away, like real 21st century teenagers.

FORTY-THREE

own in the kitchen, Mom and Jane were making breakfast together, Jane yelling every few seconds over the electricity or the microwave or the freezer.

"Look at this, Emily. There are tiny squares of ice right inside this box filled with frozen air!" Mom closed the freezer door and showed her the in-door ice dispenser, eliciting another scream from Jane. "This kitchen is nothing short of magic. What might this silver box be?" She was pointing to the dishwasher.

"This," Mom said, pulling open the door, "is a dishwasher. You load your dirty dishes inside and add some soap. Then you push these buttons, close the door, and it washes all of the dishes for you."

Jane leaned against the counter and covered her mouth with her hands, shaking her head.

We all gathered around our dining room table with its six chairs, just enough. Mom went totally overboard making breakfast. The table was loaded down with sausage patties and scrambled eggs and bacon and homemade biscuits and cinnamon rolls and two different kinds of pop-tarts and a giant bowl of fruit. There were also several boxes of cereal. Cale was elated.

"Where shall I sit?" Thomas asked, posture straight in his borrowed clothes.

"Next to me. And you can sit wherever you want, there's no assigned seating in this house."

"My goodness," Jane said, her eyes watery, "I always ate in the kitchen with the other servants."

Mom pulled out a chair for her sister. "You're not a servant here."

Everyone sat down and passed bowls and dishes and boxes of cereal around the table, each person taking what they wanted. "We don't do it 'a la russe' here at Chateau du Parker," I joked.

We all took turns explaining our new house guests to Cale, who took it in stride.

"Is this why everyone's been crying so much?"

"Yeah," I laughed, "sorry."

"I just found out my family is filled with time travelers. I think I'll be okay." He eyed Thomas with brotherly suspicion. "I guess you're the dude my sister's been wailing about this whole time?"

I could see Thomas didn't understand, but he smiled and bowed his head willing to play along. "It is a pleasure to finally meet you, Cale. I looked forward to spending time with you in the coming days."

"Okay, okay, calm down," Cale said. "We can just hang out, no need to get so creepy about it."

I squeezed Thomas's hand and whispered, "You're doing great."

Thomas grinned and took in everyone around the table. "Madam Parker, this is wonderful," he said, taking a bite of my mother's homemade biscuit smothered in butter and strawberry jam. "I do not believe I have ever experienced a meal so warm and full of love."

"Thomas," Mom said, "please call me Emily."

"Oh, it would not be," I poked him in the ribs and he laughed. "Do pardon me. I suppose more than a few customs have been altered in the last...I apologize but I do not know. What is the year here?"

I grinned, ready to blow his mind. "It's 2023. You traveled nearly two hundred years into the future."

A tiny wave of fear washed over his face. I knew the feeling.

Cale cut in. "So, what's up, are you staying here or going back to England or that castle place in France? Not that you asked, but I'd recommend you stay here. After breakfast I can introduce you to my Xbox."

Thomas glanced at Jane and then over to me, a nervous look in his eyes. He set his fork down and put his hands in his lap.

"Pardon me for not understanding the correct way to do this as I do wish to be as clear as possible." He looked over at Dad. "Master Parker, I love your daughter. I understand the circumstances of our meeting were quite peculiar, but it is my intention to take care of her for as long as she will have me. In my time, that would mean marriage. If the custom is different now, I will conform to whatever you deem appropriate so long as Brolly is by my side."

"You want to stay," I said as tears filled my eyes. Everyone at the table was quiet, waiting.

"If you will have me."

"Yes, Thomas," I threw my arms around him, "yes."

Thomas held me, whispering words of love into my ear. I'd assumed he would stay, didn't even consider it an option for him to leave, but hearing him declare it out loud thrilled me. He was here, with me. Nothing was going to separate us.

"What about your life," I said, "all your money? What about Arrington?"

He brushed my hair behind my ear. "You asked me once what I wanted to do with my life, who I wanted to be. Arrington was never mine. I should very much like to learn about your world and discover what part I may play in it."

I cupped his cheeks with my hands and kissed him, hard. It

took Dad clearing his throat for us to remember we had an audience.

"I'm trying to eat here," Cale said, making a gagging sound.

"It would be an honor to have you," Dad said. "We're so glad you made it here, and with Jane, too."

Mom was looking at Jane, her eyes wide. "What about you? Will you stay?"

"Would that be quite all right?"

Mom grabbed Jane out of her chair and hugged her, crying.

Cale rolled his eyes and took a huge bite of a cinnamon roll. "Great, everyone's crying again."

Thomas and I spent the morning exploring the house, me showing him every modern amenity. His favorite thing was all the photographs Mom had scattered all over the house. He especially loved any photo from a story I'd told him at the castle, like one of me and Cale and Dad peering out from one of our blanket forts when I was 9 and Cale was 3. "Photography is a marvel. You are able to capture such emotion, such beauty. It is like a memory coming to life."

"Watch this," I said and snapped a photo of him with my phone. I handed him the phone so he could see the photo.

"This looks like me and it does not look like me." He held my phone in his hand, looking at it back to front. "Show me?"

I opened the front camera and showed him how to angle it so we were both in the frame. "Touch the white circle."

He pressed it and captured us together, smiling. He gasped,

unable to believe such a thing could exist. We stared at the photo together. It was true, he did look different, nothing like the stiff Lord who took me on that first walk in the garden. Now he was radiant, a constant smile.

We sat on the front porch swing, Thomas exclaiming every time a car drove by. A car ran the stop sign up the block and another car honked, causing Thomas to nearly jump out of the swing.

"I remember your declaration that your world was much louder than mine. How right you were. The noise here is a constant presence."

I crossed my legs onto the swing and angled my body toward him.

"When I arrived at the castle, that night in the storm, what did you think of me? Who did you think I was?"

He looked up at the porch ceiling, his left foot lazily pushing the swing back and forth. "I do not think I could say. You were an impossibility. I was quite perplexed by every part of you."

"Did you ever suspect I was from the future?"

He laughed. "How could I conjure such a thought? Another world, possibly, but this future, this time, was unimaginable to me. Being here is like being inside a dream."

I looped my arm through his and leaned against him. "A dream come true?"

"Miss Parker," he said, covering my hand with his, "you are a dream so marvelous I shall never wish to dream again."

FORTY-FOUR

That afternoon, we all gathered in the living room to discuss what to do about the umbrellas.

"We should destroy them," Mom said, "there's too much risk. This time it turned out okay, but we could have lost Brolly forever. I don't want to take any more chances."

"But what about me?" Cale whined. "You all got to do it. It's only fair I get a chance to do it, too."

"Not a good idea, buddy," Dad said.

"But you let Brolly go!"

"We most certainly did not. If we'd known, we never would have let her use the umbrella."

"But if I hadn't," I said, "I never would have met Thomas. We never would have found Jane. I agree that there's a big potential for disaster, but there's also the potential for magic."

Mom turned to Jane. "What do you think?"

Jane worried over the question, squeezing and rubbing her hands together. "If not for that umbrella," she said, pointing to the floor where both umbrellas lay, "I should never have met my beautiful niece. But if not for that umbrella," she said, pointing to the second one, "I should never have been reunited with my family."

"True," Dad said, "but the umbrellas are also the reason we were separated in the first place."

"A choice we made, not the umbrella," Mom said.

"Thomas," Dad said, "what do you think?"

Thomas straightened up, assuming Lord W status. "We should keep the umbrellas, but perhaps in an environment where they cannot be happened upon. We could have access to them if needed, but otherwise they should be out of reach of anyone with less than desirable intentions."

We took a vote and unanimously, minus Cale, agreed. Locking them away (in something a little more secure than a brown shipping box) was the best course of action. We didn't plan to use them again, but no one was ready to erase all possibility.

"Good, it's settled," Dad said. "I think this family's had enough magic for one lifetime."

"Or several lifetimes, as it were," Thomas joked. He was my Thomas, the Thomas I knew from the kitchen in the castle. And he was joking with my dad in my living room. Somehow, I'd managed to get the best of both worlds. I got to be with Thomas and never had to use a chamber pot again as long as I lived.

I noticed him sneaking glances at me and caught his eye.

"Forgive me, Brolly," Thomas whispered next to me on the couch, "for I have not yet grown accustomed to the way you dress in your time." I was barefoot and wearing cut-off denim shorts and a grey, v-neck t-shirt. "There is so much..." he raked his eyes over me, sending a shiver across my entire body, "...skin."

"Wait until we go swimming in the summer," I said, wiggling my eyebrows.

He groaned and hid his face between my shoulder and the couch. I leaned down and kissed his head, whispering into his ear. "It's okay to like it, you know."

He raised his head and looked into my eyes, a crackling heat flaring between us. "Admiring your beauty has never been a hardship for me."

There was a loud knock at the door and I jumped up to answer it. I had invited Amelia and Pepper over to meet Thomas and Jane without telling them that's what they were in for. I opened the front door and Amelia was hopping from one foot to the other. "What's going on? Why did we have to rush over here?"

She walked inside and screamed the second she saw Thomas. She threw her arms around him, nearly tackling him to the ground. "You HAVE to be Lord W there is no WAY you're not Lord W are you HIM?"

"Meet Amelia," I said, laughing. I invited Pepper in and closed the door. Amelia still had her arms around the waist of a nervous Thomas the Lord when I introduced them.

"Amelia, Pepper, this is Thomas Westbourne, my..." I hesitated, not knowing if I should call him my boyfriend? Future something? Person who traveled through time to be with me? "I guess he's my boyfriend?"

"How did you GET here? How did this HAPPEN? Do you have ANY idea how DEVASTATED Brolly was when she thought you were GONE FOREVER? This is AMAZING! I am DYING!" Amelia continued to shout in capital letters while Pepper pulled Thomas away from her and sat him down to immediately grill him on the mechanics of his traveling experience.

Amelia grabbed me in a spinning hug, shouting in my ear about how happy she was and then whispering in my ear about how hot Lord W was. We walked over to join Pepper and Thomas and they were already down the road in the story.

"There is a second bewitched umbrella? Incredible," Pepper said. "Do you know more about the ancient magic behind it? Was there a specific process involved to activate the umbrella?"

Thomas looked at me in desperation. "Oh no," I said, hands in the air, "you're on your own with these two."

"All right," Dad said, getting everyone's attention. He wheeled a small safe into the living room on a dolly.

"Where did that come from?" I asked. In all my desperate searching around the house I'd never seen it before. Mom gave me a knowing look, answering my question. It's where they'd hidden my dress and the umbrella. But where had the safe been? I doubted she'd ever tell me.

"Are we ready to do this?" Dad said.

"Do what?" Amelia asked.

"We're going to lock the umbrellas away in this safe. We've all agreed it's for the best."

"Lock them away," Pepper shrieked, looking around the room for the umbrellas he was so eager to study. "But there's so much we can learn from them. Surely there's another way?"

"It's decided," Mom said. "We're all together and none of us want to be separated ever again."

"But...there's...if I could just..."

Amelia looped her arm through Pepper's and tried to calm him. "It's okay, Wonder Boy, we'll find another time travel device for you to study."

Dad set the dolly down in the middle of the room and opened the safe to reveal the two umbrellas, side by side. The room went quiet, all of us staring at these normal looking objects that had wreaked so much havoc in our lives. So much had happened because of them, our lives changed forever.

"I just want to say," I said, breaking the silence, "that I'm grateful I found the umbrella. It's been hard at times," everyone laughed quietly, "okay, really horrible at times, but I'm still grateful. I know we need to lock them away, but I'm glad I found the umbrella. I'm glad everything happened the way it did."

Thomas took my hand. "I shall be forever grateful as well."

"Hear, hear," Jane said, a huge smile on her face.

We stood, all of us, in a circle around the umbrellas, some of us saying goodbye, some of us, Pepper and Cale, wishing we could keep the story going. Dad shut the door of the safe, locked it and Jane let out a whoop.

I put my arms around Thomas and looked up at him. "I guess you're stuck with me forever."

"A miracle," he said and picked me up into his arms.

Amelia, Pepper and I cooked up a plan to take Thomas to a movie. We invited everyone, but no one else wanted to go. Jane said she wasn't yet ready to experience all the modern world had to offer. She was still getting used to the kitchen. Thomas, on the other hand, gulped down anything new, ready to see and experience everything my time had to offer.

I found some of Dad's jeans for Thomas to wear with a white t-shirt and a navy hoodie. Thomas worried over the distressed parts of the jeans and I reassured him they were supposed to look that way. Of all the things he'd seen so far that day, jeans with holes in them worried him the most.

Pepper drove the LeSabre and Thomas squeezed my hand in the backseat, attempting a brave face. He'd initially balked when we said we had to go by car to the movie.

"Will this one go very fast?" he'd asked, eyebrows raised.

"Yeah right," Amelia said, "I don't think Pepper's LeSabre can get over fifty."

"Fifty?" Thomas asked, a worried frown on his face.

I told him not to worry about it and hurried him out the door. Pepper queued up Jones Jams Vol. 8 and cranked the volume.

"Music," I said.

Thomas winced. "Quite different from the string quartet. A bit louder, too."

It was amazing, how open he was to the avalanche of new. Nothing made sense to him, but he approached it all with an open curiosity, wanting so much to see and touch and learn and discover. He was handling his time traveling experience much better than I did. It made me love him even more.

When we got to the theater, Thomas gawked at the movie posters, the digital marquee, the ticket kiosk where I paid for our tickets with a card instead of money, the massive concession counter. We stepped into line for popcorn and peanut M&Ms and cokes.

"I'm sure there's a lot about the modern world that's amazing to you," Amelia said to Thomas, "but peanut M&Ms will rank right up at the top."

"Amelia," Pepper huffed, "candy is hardly one of the wonders of the modern world."

"Brolly introduced me to Lucky Charms this morning, a sweet and crunchy delight."

I squeezed his arm. "Admit it, you hated the Lucky Charms."

He grimaced. "Perhaps it is an acquired taste?"

Amelia grabbed his shoulder. "Trust me, Lord W, you will love peanut M&Ms right from the jump."

"I trust you," Thomas said. "Brolly spoke of you often, both you and Pepper. I feel that we are friends already."

"We've heard nothing but Thomas, Thomas, Thomas since Brolly's been back," Amelia said. "It's amazing to finally be able to talk to you. Hey, we should take a photo to commemorate this special occasion."

The four of us scrunched together and Amelia snapped a photo.

"I supposed I shall need to acquire one of these contraptions," Thomas said, motioning to Amelia's phone, "so that I may also take a, what did you call it, a self?"

"Selfie," Amelia said. "And don't worry. Brolly and I will totally hook you up."

"Excellent. I shall look forward to being hooked up."

Amelia and I burst out laughing and Pepper rolled his eyes and pushed his glasses up his nose. "Don't worry Thomas, I'll make sure these girls don't lead you astray."

"Excuse me," Amelia said, "I would never. Thomas is too adorable for words and I will protect him like the little time traveling bunny that he is."

Pepper was about to argue when we heard a voice in line behind us. "Hey, guys."

We turned around to see Ben standing in line with Jeremy Barnes, one of the guys on the swim team and one of Amelia's many admirers.

"Ben, hey," Pepper said, "great to see you."

"Hey Amelia," Jeremy said, breathing a little too hard.

I could read Pepper and Amelia's minds, both of their thoughts matching my own. Would Ben be mad we hadn't invited him? The four of us had been inseparable since the summer and on a normal day, we never would have gone to the movies without Ben. Thomas showing up had thrown everything off balance.

Ben looked at me, at my hand linked with Thomas's, recognition crossing his face. "This must be him," he said, a friendly smile on his face.

I'd never told him about Thomas, but maybe it hadn't been so hard to figure out. "Yes," I said, "he's...yes."

We exchanged a look that felt a little bit like an exhale. It shouldn't have been hard for me to believe Ben would handle this so well. Perfect Ben, nice Ben, good Ben. Somehow, he understood.

"Hi," he said, extending his hand to Thomas, "I'm Ben. I'm friends with these guys."

"Ben," Thomas said, recognition crossing his face as they shook hands. "I am Lor-," he paused and looked at me. I nodded, silently assuring him. "I am Thomas Westbourne. It is a great pleasure to meet you, Ben."

"What movie are you guys seeing?" Jeremy asked.

And just like that, everything fell into place. We were all seeing the same movie and sat together, all of us in one row, all the people I loved.

Thomas found the popcorn curious, loved the peanut M&Ms much to Amelia's delight, and choked on his first sip of coke. "It burns," he said, struggling to swallow and making us all laugh. I loved that I was with him for every new experience, every amazing discovery. When the theater screen lit up with the first movie trailer, Thomas squeezed my hand, the biggest, happiest smile on his face. And I knew I was exactly where I needed to be.

We watched an action movie full of car chases and ridiculous dialogue and heroes hanging from helicopters, doing things no human could ever do. I kept sneaking glances at Thomas, wishing I could hear what was happening inside his head. I tried to prep him as best I could, explaining about special effects and movie magic. I could tell he had no idea what to think about anything I was saying. He watched the screen with adorable, open-mouthed wonder, drinking it all in, even though he couldn't possibly understand anything that was happening.

Half-way through the movie, Thomas leaned close and whispered in my ear. "Your world really is quite magnificent. I have never been more confounded and yet I cannot seem to stop smiling."

"It's our world now, you know," I said, pulling him close to me. "You and me."

"Yes," he said, beaming, "our world."

Later that night Thomas and I were snuggled deep into the cushions of the grey couch. Everyone else had gone to bed but we weren't ready to say goodnight. I had my arms wrapped around him with my head on his chest as he rubbed lazy circles into my back. In all the time we were apart, this is what I wanted, what I longed for, hoped for.

"How are you doing, after today," I said. "I know it was a lot to throw at you all at once."

"Would you understand what I meant if I said I am still not quite certain where I am or what it is that is transpiring around me?"

I laughed because, yes, I completely understood. "It took me forever to accept it when I showed up at the castle. I couldn't believe I was in the 1800s, even though I so obviously was."

"Yes, you were quite out of your element, shouting at me in your bed clothes."

"You liked it," I joked.

Thomas pulled me up to face him, something like heartbreak on his face. "I want you to know that this, being here with you..." He paused, focusing on me. His eyes welled up with tears. "I should never in a thousand lifetimes have imagined such a gift. When you arrived on my shore, I was terrified of you, of what you might be. If only I could have known then what I know now."

The way he said things, it made my heart swell inside my chest. "What do you know now?"

He smiled, a bright happy smile that raised his cheeks and

squeezed his eyes shut, one lone tear escaping and rolling down his face. I kissed it away.

"I know now that it is possible to love another so completely, so thoroughly, so unreservedly, a person would be willing to abandon the whole of their life to keep it."

I didn't know if he meant himself or me, but it didn't matter. We'd both risked everything to be together.

If I'd met Thomas the traditional way, walking the halls of Central High or serving him pizza at Big Mike's or bumping into him at Pam Byers's house, I would have liked him. He would have liked me. We would have gotten together. We would have fallen in love. Because it wasn't about a castle or an umbrella or traveling through time. Thomas was my other half, the person I wanted to be with, always. We belonged together.

"Have I said thank you today?" I asked him.

"What would you need to thank me for?"

"For reaching out your hand to me in the storm. For giving me a chance when everything about your world told you not to. For coming to find me when I was lost."

He put his hand on my neck and pulled me to him, kissing my forehead. "Do you not see, my love, it is I who was lost, and you who found me."

ACKNOWLEDGMENTS

THANK YOU
(is not enough and could never be enough)

Tim Parker, illustrator and designer to the stars, thank you for the book cover of my dreams.

Elise Stawarz, thank you for wading through my earliest, most terrible drafts and still believing. It's one of the many (many) reasons you're the #1 best. And thank you for nicknaming Lord W. I couldn't do any of this without you and would never want to.

Sarah Van Goethem, thank you for holding my hand all these years, for being an inspiration, an incredible writer, and mostly for never, ever giving up on this book.

The NNF –Beth Lee, Nina Woodard, Jordyn Harris, Jill Tomalty, Kristin Byrne and Elise Stawarz, thank you for being legit hilarious and amazing and the best friends forever. And for believing in me, always.

Brittany Kelley, thank you for the gorgeous interior. You're the treble to my bass.

Kristin Maher, thank you for reading (and reading) and pushing me to publish the book already!

Brandi Manes, thank you for skipping church to finish reading and for being The Best.

Kirsten Van Goethem, Heather Griffin, Stacie Vining, Chuck Hargett, Thom Oliphant, Starla DeKruyf, Leanne Schwartz, Lori Jones, Katie Mohre, Leigh Ann Beard, Heather Davis, Luke Woodard, Jillian Scalf, Kat Davis, Nivah Eckert, Michelle Buckingham, Kelley Kirker, Bridget Heuton, Sarah Lai, Heidi Groff, Becka Blackburn, Amanda Snyder, and Michelle Tabb, thank you for reading early drafts, believing in this book, and encouraging me to keep going.

You, Kind Reader, thank you for excusing my historical inaccuracies and comma splices.

Betty Harris, Kelley Harris, Drew Harris, Kellie Harris, Addison Harris, Dawn Illingworth, Vern Illingworth, Leslie Hogle, Shawn Hogle, Rachel Hogle, Josh Hogle, Angie Poston, Micah Poston, Elle Poston and Silas Poston, thank you for being the greatest non-time traveling family there is.

Harry and Franklin, my entire heart. Thank you for being my absolute favorites. Keep trying to be funnier than me. Maybe someday you'll get there.

Ryan, my only fish. Thank you for loving me.

ABOUT THE AUTHOR

JoAnna Illingworth became obsessed with the romantic side of time travel the first time she watched Richard Collier risk everything to meet Elise McKenna in *Somewhere In Time*. Thankfully, her debut novel has a much happier ending. She lives in Nashville's suburbia with her very funny husband, even funnier two boys and very, very bad dog.

twitter.com/glamorousjo

instagram.com/glamorousjo

tiktok.com/glamjo

Made in the USA
Monee, IL
22 March 2025

14399489R00184